ANNOUNCING TROUBLE

ANNOUNCING TROUBLE

AMY FELLNER DOMINY

Entangled Publishing, LLC
2614 South Timberline Road
Suite 105, PMB 159
Fort Collins, CO 80525
rights@entangledpublishing.com

Crush is an imprint of Entangled Publishing, LLC.

Edited by Stacy Abrams and Judi Lauren
Cover design by Bree Archer
Cover photography by
Look Studio and LightField Studios/Shutterstock
ca2hill/GettyImages

Manufactured in the United States of America

First Edition August 2019

To Terry Lynn Johnson for always reading, listening, commiserating, understanding, encouraging, supporting and inspiring me.

Chapter One

For a cold day in hell, it's unseasonably warm.

I squint against the sun, but unfortunately that doesn't change the view of what's ahead—or the fact that I'm heading there of my own free will. A baseball field. The one place I swore I'd never step foot again.

Mai stops me with a hand on my arm. "How do I look?" A breeze ruffles the spiky edges of her chin-length bob.

"Nervous," I say.

"This is a bad idea, isn't it?"

"Yes," I tell her. For about the tenth time. "I've never seen you this crazy over a boy before."

"I know, and I don't like it." She's wearing her usual—a button-down shirt over leggings and sneakers—but she's added red lipstick. She never wears makeup. Mai is one of those naturally beautiful girls who doesn't try and doesn't care.

Until Anthony Adams turned his million-watt smile on her six days ago.

"We can still leave," I say, making it sound like the best idea ever. Because it is.

"I can't," she groans. "My girl parts have staged a coup and taken control." She glances to the field where our baseball team, the Cholla High Wildcats, is now jogging out for the start of the first inning. She grabs my hand and holds it against her chest. "Feel how fast my heart's beating?"

"He's a jock, Mai. You don't even like sports."

"I know." She looks at me helplessly. I guess I shouldn't be surprised. Mai is the kind of person who's intense about everything. It makes sense that when she finally decided to fall in lust, she'd fall hard.

But Anthony is the complete opposite of Mai's dream guy. I know. I've seen her checklist. I get the whole bad-boy vibe with the longish hair, the tees that hug his muscles—even the heavy chain he wears around his wrist is kind of hot if you like that look.

Which Mai never has.

But Anthony is also a player—in every sense of the word. This year I have to pass his locker, and a few of his teammates', to reach mine. I've seen the constant rotation of girls. Maybe it's innocent, maybe he's a great guy, but I grew up around baseball and I've seen enough that, I'm sorry, but they're guilty until proven innocent.

Especially when it comes to my best friend.

But even though I've warned Mai, here we are. This is so far from her comfort zone, I'm hoping that watching a game will be enough to crush her crush. But still...*baseball*. There's a clear crack as someone's bat finds the ball and then a cheer from the crowd on the bleachers.

I shudder under the warm Phoenix sun. I vowed it would be a cold day in hell before I ever watched baseball again. But Mai is my best friend. You do not send your bestie into enemy territory without backup.

I grab her arm. "Let's get this over with."

Hell, here I come.

We're in the fifth inning. Anthony Adams is, as I predicted, uninterested in the brainy girl mooning at him from behind home plate. The bleachers are surprisingly crowded, which is why we're so close to the action. My seat is partially blocked by the elevated broadcast booth, which I didn't mind at first, but now I'm getting annoyed. I can hear everything the announcers are saying, and these guys are awful. I'm sure the only people listening are parents and grandparents, but even so, they deserve better.

"That's a hit from Clemens." It's the one with the higher voice. He must be right by the door because I hear him the loudest. "Too bad it was caught by the right fielder."

I knock my knuckles against my forehead. "It's not a hit if it gets caught."

"Shhh," Mai says. "Don't distract me with actual information about the game."

"I thought you liked learning new things."

"Not about this."

"Mai Senn." I add her last name because I know she hates it. It sounds like you're saying "My Sin." Her first name is actually Maya. It has something to do with a Greek goddess, springtime, and the month of May—which is when her parents adopted her. But everyone calls her Mai.

I'm thinking about how to get her out of here when she squeezes my arm. "Did you see that? Anthony almost caught the ball with his mitt-thing."

"It's a baseball glove."

Mai has to be the only one here who knows less than the announcers. To be fair, the guy doing play-by-play knows his stuff. But the guy who's supposed to add color with his commentary—hence the title "color commentary"—could have his brains completely removed with a teaspoon. "He's terrible," I complain.

"Who?" Anthony is adjusting himself at third base, and Mai is riveted.

"He's wearing a cup," I say. "It's not real."

"Do not kill my buzz."

I swallow a laugh. Mai is kind of adorable when irrational. Who knew.

Then I hear the announcer again, his words setting me on edge. "That should have been called a balk. That pitcher didn't come set."

I shoot to my feet. "I can not listen to this for one more second." I take two steps down and tug the door open. Both guys turn at the noise. I ignore the blond who's doing the play-by-play and point a finger at the blithering idiot closest to me. "You. Stop. You are terrible."

"What?" He gapes at me.

"My ears are bleeding. I can't take it anymore."

He yanks down the microphone piece attached to his headset. "You can't come in here!" He looks to his partner for support.

I recognize Blondie. Even if you hate sports, it's hard to avoid knowing who the star athletes are at our school. Not to mention he's one of the other players whose locker I walk by every morning. His name is Garrett Reeves and he's hurt this year, which is probably why he's in the booth. I'd heard broken arm, but other than a scar on the inside of his elbow, he looks ridiculously fit. If he's supposed to carry me bodily from the booth, he could do it.

He adjusts a knob on the equipment, then swivels his stool toward me but makes no move to get up. "And you are?"

"Annoyed," I answer. "You can't have a balk without a runner on base. This guy obviously has no idea what the infield fly rule is, and that foul ball he was raving about? It was a hit by pitch."

A slow smile works across Garrett's face. "And you could do better?"

I scoff. "In my sleep."

"Big talker. Should we see if she can back it up, Nathan?"

"What? No way," Nathan blusters. "She needs to get out of here. Now."

Garrett is still grinning. I roll my eyes. Dark blond hair and denim blue eyes. Completely gorgeous. He's such a cliché. "Shouldn't you be doing your job?" I ask. "Number 54 just walked. We got a sub coming to the plate. You want to tell the listeners?"

Eyebrows a few shades darker than his hair shoot up. He studies me another second with a look of approval and something else that makes his eyes spark and the back of my neck warm. Then he tips his head at Nathan. "She's right about the balk. And you were wrong last inning when the pitcher struck the hitter's hands."

Well. Blondie knows his baseball.

"Come on, Nathan," he adds in an easy voice. "She obviously knows her stuff. Let's see what she can do when we're live."

Nathan yanks off the headphones. "If I leave, I'm not coming back. You're on your own. For the competition, too."

There's a silent exchange I don't understand. It lasts long enough for the player at the plate to foul off the next pitch. Then Garrett shrugs. "Do what you gotta do."

Nathan tosses the headphones on the counter and manages to jab his elbow into my arm on his way out.

"Ow! Jerk face!"

"Sorry about that," Garrett says. "You okay?"

"Fine," I mutter, rubbing the sting out of my arm.

He gestures to the now vacant stool. The backstop rattles at the impact of another foul ball, and he glances down at the field. "Let's get you on air."

On air.

I take a steadying breath. I'm thrilled that the bad smelling cologne was Nathan's and not the guy I'm left with for the next two innings. *But the next two innings?* My heart drops like a breaking ball and I realize I've just committed myself to calling the rest of this game.

I blame it on this sport. It makes me lose my mind.

"You sitting?" he asks. "Or was all of that a show?" He crosses his arms over his chest. I wonder if that's a practiced move to make his biceps flex. Which they do.

I shake off my nerves. I'm not one to back down—and no way am I backing down from a ballplayer. His smirk is too much like all the self-centered players I grew up around.

Too much like my father's.

I sit and lift my gaze to his. "Plug me in, Blondie."

Chapter Two

Garrett stares a second in surprise—not sure if it's my tone or the nickname—but I like that I've thrown him a curve. Then he starts fiddling with a panel the size of a long computer keyboard, and I take a second to look around. The broadcast booth is bare bones and no bigger than a walk-in closet. It reminds me of a house someone forgot to finish, with plywood walls, a cement floor, and a brown laminate countertop that looks glued on. Expensive-looking equipment is spread out on the counter, cords running like veins from one thing to another. I'm not a techy person, so I really hope I'm not expected to touch any of it.

Garrett adjusts his headset and says, "Sorry, folks. A little change going on in the booth today. Nathan had to step out, and just up from the minor leagues we have..." He pauses for me to answer.

"Josie."

"Josie," he repeats into his mic. He gestures to the headphones that I hope aren't crawling with Nathan germs as I settle them over my ears and shift the arm of the microphone.

"All right, folks," he says. "We've got Evan Harris up at the plate. Tucker Lewis is on first with a walk, and Cooper Davies is stretching a lead at third base. You with me, Josie?" He gives me another cocky smirk. The boys must practice that in Little League. I ignore him, repositioning my stool so I can sit on the edge and lean my elbows on the counter.

Field awareness. It's one of the first things my dad taught me. I was still in diapers when I'd stand beside him at the fence of a ball field. I'd stick one sneaker through the metal links the same way he did.

See what's there, but see what's coming next.

My father lied about everything else, but never baseball.

Now, I quickly scan the situation. The booth is elevated to give us a view of the field and the scoreboard through a huge cutout window. There's no glass, so I'm not sure how they cover it for the five days every year that it rains here, but it does give us great sightlines.

I'm not an expert at sports broadcasting, but I do know it's Garrett's job to update the audience on everything happening on the field. As the color commentary person, I'm supposed to add in stats about the players and opinions on how they've been doing. It doesn't help that this is my first game in four years at Cholla. On the other hand, it's not as if I can't talk baseball.

"The catcher is setting up outside," I say. "Looking for Evan Harris to chase one." Sure enough, he swings at a ball that's at least a foot off the plate.

"Harris's swing catches nothing but air. The count is Oh and One," Garrett adds.

Two more balls follow along with another strike. "The Tigers' pitcher is throwing really well," I say. "He's got a sharp curveball with great depth to pair with his sinking two-seam fastball."

Garrett nods. "You have a good eye."

"Better than Evan Harris. He just swung at what would have been three balls."

Garrett winces as Harris does a walk of shame to the dugout. "The Wildcats leave two runners on base. We head to the seventh, down four to three."

He turns two knobs on what I think is the soundboard. "We're on mute." He swivels toward me. "Not bad." He measures me with his eyes, taking in my messy brown ponytail, *Jane Eyre* T-shirt, and my comfy but clunky sandals. He's wondering where I fit. Five years ago, I would have said right here.

I watch the teams change place on the field. It doesn't feel real that I'm here. In a stadium. At a game. I blink as if the field might disappear, but it's there along with the sound of the ball smacking gloves as the players warm up their arms. It even smells like baseball. I used to devour the scents of grass, sun, chalk, and sweat like they were cotton candy. Now, I feel slightly nauseous. Everything is tainted by memory.

I study the equipment, looking for a distraction. "How does this work?" I ask.

"It's pretty basic. Laptop. Mixer board with channels for our two headsets. The video camera and the crowd mic." He points to a microphone strapped to the window with bungee cord.

"So you've got audio and video?"

"Yep." He gestures to the laptop, and I can see the video feed of the stationary camera, along with audio levels.

"Everything's plugged in to the school's wifi, and the broadcast is available through a link on the school's website. The video is grainy, but most families tune in for the commentary."

"And Nathan was the best color guy you could find?"

He fiddles with one of the knobs. "It's a new program. Started this season, home games only. This is our fifth broadcast."

The pitcher is done warming up, and a player for the Tigers steps into the batter's box. Garrett unmutes us, and we're back on.

I'm immediately in the flow, a little surprised at how quickly all the nuances of the game come back. Without realizing it, I find myself leaning forward, a sharpened sense of sight…a sharpened sense of everything as I tune in to Garrett and to the ebb and flow of a game that apparently still runs through my blood.

For most of my life, I loved baseball as much as I loved my dad.

Now, I hate it as much as I hate my dad.

And just like that, I'm anxious to get out of here.

The Wildcats pull out a win in the bottom of the seventh, and the crowd is still cheering when Garrett says, "That's all from the booth. I'm Garrett Reeves and my partner today was Josie…"

Again, he looks to me for a name. I don't give it to him because I don't want it to be official. I want to forget I was here. I pull off the headset as he turns off the mics.

"How come I've never seen you out here?" he asks, pulling off his own headset.

"Because I've never been."

"I've seen you in school, though." But he doesn't sound like he's sure, even though I pass by his locker most days. I'm not the type of girl a guy like Garrett Reeves would notice. I've seen the girls hanging out with him and the other players—all the *P* girls. Pretty. Popular. Perfect.

I stand and shove in the stool to clear my path to the door.

"Wait." He stands, too. I'm five eight, but he's still four or five inches taller than I am. He slides his hands in his pockets, smiling with the confidence of someone used to issuing orders and having them followed. "What's your story, Josie-with-no-last-name?"

"No story. Just a baseball angel of mercy."

"You were good."

"I know." It seems like a good line for an exit, so I take it, turning for the door and ignoring his "*Wait!*" as I let it close behind me.

I give my eyes a second to adjust to the bright sunlight. Mai is still in the same spot on the bleachers, standing now, with the other fans. The fence around the dugout begins to rattle and shake. The team appears, one at a time, loaded down with bat bags and water jugs. Mai grips the fence as she watches. Her eyes look a little glazed over. Oh hell.

"Hold up a minute." It's Garrett, framed by the open door to the booth. "If that was meant to be a tryout, you've got the job."

"Not what that was." I reach Mai and shove her backpack into her arms as I grab mine.

"You can't leave me without a partner. I got rid of Nathan for you."

I roll my eyes. "You got rid of Nathan because he doesn't know baseball."

"Josie. I need you." He widens those baby blues and curves his mouth into a flirty smile. A smile that I bet gets him a whole lot of *yes*.

"No," I say. Before he can answer, I grab Mai's arm and tug her toward the exit.

She follows, a dreamy smile on her red lips. "That was amazing."

"No, that was a mistake. You were supposed to get over your crush."

"But this could be my grand passion."

"You don't believe in grand passions."

"I'm reconsidering." Her brown eyes have gone melty. "You should, too."

I stop at the edge of the parking lot. Heat from the asphalt rises in a wave that makes me dizzy. Or maybe it's a delayed reaction. All that baseball and testosterone. Memories that cling to me like sweat. Itchy and uncomfortable.

"We are not changing our minds," I tell Mai. "Crush on him from afar if you have to, but no more baseball."

Not even my best friend is going to drag me back to another game.

Chapter Three

"Mom?" I call. "You home?" I set my pack on the table. The kitchen is usually bright with sunlight when I get home, but it's in shadow now. She won't care that I'm back late. But *why* I'm late...

I decided on the drive home not to mention the game. I never lie to my mom, but I can't bring myself to say the word "baseball" in this house. It's not *that* cold of a day in hell.

"Hi, honey."

I jump, my hand flying to my chest. "You scared me."

She's carrying a small tub filled with tubes of hydrating serum. "I was in the back bedroom, counting."

"Inventory? I thought you were going to do that this morning."

Mom runs AromaTher, a one-woman company she created to sell beauty products with essential oils. Her focus is skin care, but along with moisturizers and toners, she carries a full line of essential oils for everything from insomnia to indigestion.

In another few months, it's going to be *our* company.

"I was." She clears her throat. "I got a little distracted."

Now that I'm paying attention, her eye makeup is smudged and her hair is loose. She always complains about how hot her hair is on her neck when she's working. She must have gotten more than a little distracted if she didn't take the time to clip it up. "Everything okay?" I ask.

"Fine." If anything, her skin turns even pinker. One of the reasons Mom does so well with AromaTher is that she's beautiful. But it's the girl-next-door kind of beautiful that ordinary people think they could have with just the right products. Her shoulder-length hair is thick and glossy, dark brown like her eyes, and her smile is apple-pie sweet. I've got the same coloring, but I'm more of the Amazon-next-door. Mom says she envies my athletic build. I tell her any time she wants to trade her size six shoes for my size nine, I'm in.

"I'm almost done," she says. "I've got juniper berry, geranium, and palmarosa left."

"I'll help you finish."

She starts toward the office, and I follow. I'm not sure what palmarosa is, but it's good for skin tone. It doesn't smell bad, either. That's the AromaTher promise: *Scents that make Sense*. That was my line, and it's now on the bottom of Mom's business cards. Once I turn eighteen in May and become an official partner, I'll have business cards of my own. I'm trying to come up with a new line for me.

Josie Walters. I want to make a healthy profit.

Yeah, probably not. I love the business and the fact that I'll be a co-CEO at the age of eighteen. But to me, essential oils are a product, not a passion. Mom can heal the world. Me, I'm going to expand our client base and build the company.

I stop short at the door of the bedroom we've turned into our office-slash-warehouse.

"I know," Mom says. "It's a mess."

It's always a mess. This is more of a disaster.

She frowns at the tubs that are on the carpet instead of the shelves. "I got partway through and..." Her voice trails off, half finished like the inventory.

I draw in a breath, and that's when I smell it. Smell her. I lean closer and sniff her neck. "Oh my God, it's ylang-ylang."

She bats me away with a hand. "Don't be silly." But her cheeks have gone from pink to cherry red.

I know very well what the essential oil of ylang-ylang means. "Were you having a nooner?"

"It's much too late for a nooner." Then she smiles.

"Mom. Eww." James must be back. James is Mom's gentleman friend (she won't let me call him a boyfriend), and even though I love him, I don't want to see evidence of *that*. "Did he just get home?"

"This morning."

James sells computer equipment, so he travels a lot, but they've been dating for almost a year, so I know the signs. I sniff again. Yep, there's driftwood and cinnamon bark. Mom is into essential oils for everything. Including sex. After the divorce was final and she started to date, I always knew there was a new guy because Mom would put together a special mix of fragrances to use in the diffuser for when they were doing *it*.

My mom, unlike me, has sex. Two years ago, she insisted we have *The Talk*. She asked if I was interested, and I told her no way would I ever do *that* with any of the guys I know. I couldn't see letting any of them get that close to me.

That's when she told me she might be a mother, but that didn't mean she was sexually dead. I stopped her before she could say something from an eighties movie like "women have needs."

It's not as bad as at Mai's house, where her scientist parents announce it the way they might announce lunch. *"Daddy and I are going to have sex now."* When Mai's brother, Ethan, was back from Harvard, they had a family meeting. Both kids asked if they could please come up with a euphemism. So her mom started saying things like, "*Dad and I are going to wrestle in bed,*" or "*We're going to have a bouncy nap.*"

So that didn't work.

Mom keeps it low-key, which is cool, but I swear it's starting to feel like she's only using him for *it*. He sneaks in and out when I'm not home, and he doesn't come over just to watch TV and eat burned grilled cheese sandwiches with us. He wants more. I've heard him say so. I'm not sure why she won't let it move beyond…bouncy naps.

"You know, it would be fine if he hung out here," I offer. "I like James. I've told you that a million times."

"I know." She kneels in front of the shelves and starts replacing the tubs.

I get down beside her and do the same. "So then what's the deal?"

"No deal. He has a life. So do I."

"You could have a life together. You deserve to be with a guy who puts you first for a change."

She pauses, holding a tub of turmeric. "I'm not in any hurry. I like that it's just you and me."

I smile because I like it, too, even though I know I'm not supposed to. "My friends think it's weird. They can't wait to get out of their houses and live in the dorms."

"You can still do that if you want."

My stomach clenches at the thought because no, I don't want. "Why should I share a tiny room with someone who might have terrible taste in music and eat peanut butter out of the jar with a finger?" I add, "Besides, my classes are mostly online, so I'll be here all day—running the business with you. It doesn't make sense to waste time and money on a dorm room and a commute."

"What about the social part?" she asks.

"Mai will be gone, but I can still see Jasmine and Avi on the weekends."

Our eyes meet, and even though everything I've said is 100 percent true, her gaze says she knows none of it is the real reason.

I shrug and speak through a suddenly tight throat. "I want this to be home for a little while longer."

"It is your home, Josie. For as long as you want."

She slides the last tub in place with a sigh, and I know we both feel the weight of those years, those moves. I didn't mind at the time. Didn't think I minded. It was part of the deal—while my father was chasing the game, we had to move to where the opportunities were. I knew it wouldn't be like that forever. But I still woke up some mornings not sure where I was. And even though I got good at walking into strange schools, it never got easier.

It wasn't until he was gone that the nightmares started. I'd wake in the middle of the night in a panic—afraid he was leaving. That he would leave me behind. I'd fly out of bed, heart pounding, before I remembered that we were in Phoenix now. That he'd already left me behind. Shame and disgust would follow me back to bed. Even after everything, I was still trying to follow him. I haven't woken up like that in a long time, and I never want to again.

"We're in a good place now," Mom says.

"The best," I agree.

"And I have some great news," she adds as we both stand. "I made an appointment with the business attorney. We'll sign the partnership forms and make it official on your eighteenth birthday." She squeezes my shoulder. "Melissa and Josie Walters, Partners."

"Or maybe Josie and Melissa Walters. That sounds even better."

She laughs. "Already power hungry. I like it." Her smile

reflects my happiness. "But we do need to be ready."

I brush a streak of dust off her sleeve. "Why does this feel like a segue into the website?"

"Because it is." She looks at me with a hint more exasperation than the last time she brought it up. "You still haven't started it, have you?"

"You're awfully bossy for a partner."

"We're not partners until May fourth. I'm still in charge for another eight weeks."

"I'm going to start it this week. I promise. It'll be done by the time we're official."

Her eyes soften. "We've come a long way from that first summer, haven't we?"

"You didn't think we could do it."

"I couldn't have without you."

I nod, my heart full. Dad had left, but Mom didn't want to uproot me, so we stayed in Florida for my final year of middle school. Money was tight. Dad promised the checks would come, but he promised a lot of things. Mom had started AromaTher a few years before, building it slowly. But now it's our main source of income. I had to help Mom expand things, tagging along to parties and working farmers markets. It started as a necessity, became a distraction, and then an anchor.

Now here we are in Phoenix where Mom grew up. This room might look like a mess, but the business is established now. Grounded. Like I am. Mai thinks AromaTher is my way of settling for stability. But after the way I grew up, stability isn't a bad thing.

It's everything.

Chapter Four

The hallways are packed before first lunch. It feels like we're being carried along by a stampede of wild animals, all of them braying at the top of their lungs. Mai is shoved by a skinny girl in a shirt that reads, "I hate people." When Mai turns to her with a "Hey!" she gets a middle finger in response.

"That's who I'll be talking to." Mai raises her voice in frustration—and to be heard over the crowd. "Do you see what I'm up against?"

"It doesn't matter what you say," I tell her. "She won't listen."

We take a left and start the trek from Building A to B and my calculus class and Mai's AP Stats. It's warmer in this hall—even the inspiring quotes stenciled on the maroon walls look wilted.

"It's my job to make her listen. I've been given a sacred task to guide these people into the future."

"You're taking this valedictorian thing too seriously."

"It is serious. I want to leave these deviants with advice they can use."

"Go easy on the body spray?"

She pauses to glare at me. "That's not the direction I was hoping for."

I laugh. "I thought you already had the speech written?"

"I did. I'm rethinking."

"Why?" I ask. "It was good. Work hard. Choose your path wisely." I veer left and Mai veers right to avoid colliding with three kids who are pooling spare change. It reminds me that today is Wednesday—churro day at the food cart. "What else do you need to say?"

"My mom read it," Mai says. "She thinks my vision for the future is bleak."

"That's your mom." I flip a hand dismissively.

Uncertainty flashes across her face, and I realize she's not dismissing this at all. "What if she's right? What if—"

Mai gives a sharp cry and lurches forward.

I grab her arm, steadying her as someone stumbles into me from behind. For a minute it's a drunken dance as we regain our balance. A wave of students is heading our way, creating a bottleneck. Then I see who's made the wave. The tall, broad-shouldered variety of boy. They're like coyotes. They rove in packs.

Cholla High is not a bastion of intellect. We're a public school in a not-so-rich area and though we've got a respectable number of brains, they don't produce trophies. Our school is known for two things: baseball and football. They bring us glory, which is why the players who compete are treated like heroes. I try to steer clear, but it's impossible to miss them. I'm not sure they actually attend class, but they do use the same halls.

Mai pops up on her tiptoes, and I know she's searching for Anthony. "There he is." She presses a hand over her heart. "I had my thighs wrapped around that neck."

I sigh, blaming myself. If I hadn't been working extra

hours at the bookstore over spring break, Mai would have been safely floating on a raft in her backyard pool with me. Instead, bored on her own, she went to the public pool. Anthony was there, along with a group of his buddies, and a game of chicken started. Anthony needed someone to ride his neck and knock other girls off other well-muscled shoulders. He picked Mai. She described it to me in hushed tones—as if it was a moment when time stood still. *Their eyes met. Their DNA called to each other.* Personally, I think he saw a beautiful girl light enough to carry around easily. And as it turned out, Mai is a ferocious chicken competitor. No surprise there.

"You've got to admit," she says now, "it will be the best 'why-we-got-together' story in history."

A twinge of worry filters into my voice as I say, "You know this thing with Anthony isn't real, right?"

"I know." A small, secretive smile tugs at her lips. "But it feels better than real. It feels…fun."

Mai is driven—she always has been. She's into science, like her parents, and when she says she wants to save the world, she means it. One day, she's going to be on the team that discovers a cure for cancer or Alzheimer's. I always thought she thrived on that sense of purpose. But *thrived* is maybe not the same thing as a laugh-riot. I feel guilty for raining on her Anthony parade. I'm even ready to send good vibes his way, but then I see Blondie and my heart ticks up. He's in the middle of the crowd, his arm raised for a high five with another nameless hulk, grinning like he owns the world. Or at least this hall.

Suddenly, his gaze hooks on mine. His eyes widen. "Josie Walters!" he calls. "I've been looking for you."

How does he know my last name?

"Where have you been hiding all day?"

I grip the strap of my pack. "In classrooms. You might

visit one before graduation."

His grin widens. "I thought I'd dreamed that acid wit."

"Garrett Reeves is dreaming about you?" Mai asks.

Heads turn my way. The girls following along like human magnets are wondering who I am, and more importantly, why Garrett knows who I am. I roll my eyes because the whole thing seems so...high school.

Garrett shoots a finger gun at me. "You and me. We need to talk."

Does anyone tell this guy no? "We really don't."

"After school. I'll be at the flagpole. Find me."

He did not just say that, did he?

I shoot a finger gun back at him along with a huge phony smile. "Yeah. For sure. Coolio."

The wave of his friends carries him past us and on toward the cafeteria.

Mai fixes her dark brown eyes on me. "Did you say 'coolio'?"

"Laid it on too thick?"

She shrugs a shoulder. "I thought it was a nice touch."

"This is why you should never have anything to do with an athlete. They think the world revolves around them."

"But they do have nice arms."

The warning bell rings, startling me. *Oh hell. What am I doing thinking about his arms?* "We better run."

Happily, it's in the opposite direction from Garrett Reeves.

Chapter Five

I pull into the parking lot of the Page & Prose Bookstore, heading for my usual shady spot in the far corner. I shut off the truck, waiting for it to cough twice and then settle into silence. Mom and I share the truck, which is a pain, but we're close enough to school for me to walk and that leaves Mom the truck during the day. I take it for my bookstore shifts. It works for now, but we've got a savings account started for a second car. It's going to be our first major purchase when the business expands.

A key part of our plan is an updated website. I knock my forehead on the wheel in frustration. I finally dug into it during Independent Study, and it's worse than I imagined. The original site was designed by Mom's friend who built it on her own platform nearly a decade ago. It can't be updated. I'm going to have to start over.

Shoot me now.

As soon as I step out of the truck, I hear someone call, "Walters!"

Startled, I turn. Garrett is walking across the parking lot

swinging a key chain around his fingers.

Shoot me five minutes ago.

I blink in case my eyes are playing a mean trick on me. But no. Tall, messy blond hair, muscles everywhere. Confident swagger that eats up the distance between us until he's suddenly close. Too close. "What are you doing here?"

"I followed you," he says. "You were supposed to find me at the flagpole."

"You were supposed to wait there for me. For a long time."

He smiles, but this one is slow and hitches up on one side. "I like your mouth, Walters."

Flirt. He's so obvious, trying to lure me in with his charm. And oh he's good, the way his eyes lower to my mouth. Even I can't help but feel a little *zing* down south.

It isn't fair. I may hate athletes on principle, but I'm not blind. My eyes still work and, unfortunately, they send signals down to my other working parts. And Garrett Reeves looks as good as he thinks he does. The hair. The blue eyes and straight brows. The perfect white teeth and the tiny dent he's chewed in his bottom lip. I'm genetically wired to respond. Or maybe it's an evolution thing. Or, hell. Mai would know, but it's some kind of thing. I don't like it, and I'm not going to be swayed by it.

"What does it take to insult you?" I ask.

"Keep trying. I'll let you know when you do." He flips the key chain again. "We've got a game on Friday. I want you to do color. I already cleared it with Coach Richards."

Shaking my head at the arrogance of that, I start toward the bookstore. "And I already told you no."

He falls in beside me. "You don't have all the facts."

I reach the green awning, and it's immediately cooler in the shade. I pass carts of used books and stop by the front door. "How do you know my last name?"

"I asked around."

"Well, you wasted your time. I'm not going to change my mind. I hate baseball. Now would you go away, please? I work here."

He shuffles closer, one hand planted low on his hip. "You can't hate baseball. You know the game too well."

"Just because I know it doesn't mean I love it."

That seems to shock him, and for a second he stares at me with a slack jaw. "Then why were you at the game?"

"For a friend."

When I try and reach for the door handle, he shifts in front of me and grabs it first. He studies me intently, and I feel the pull of his restless energy. "But once you were there, in the booth—you were into it. I could tell."

"I was doing the job."

"And you did. You knocked it out of the ballpark." There's honest appreciation in his eyes. "Walters. Please. You've got a real talent for this."

I'm shaking my head before he can even finish his plea. "I can't. Even if I wanted to, which I don't, I haven't got the time. I've got school, a business I help run, a website to develop, not to mention a job that I'm going to be late for." I pointedly gesture to the door handle he's still holding. "Find someone else."

"I would if I could. In a *heartbeat*," he says as if it's that obvious. "I hardly know you and already I can tell you're a pain in the ass. But in three weeks, I've been through three color-commentators. None of them impressed me the way you did. I've listened to professionals who weren't as talented." He ruffles the top of his hair where it's longer and falls in messy layers. "You're good, Walters. And with a partner like me, you could be great. A thousand dollars great."

I cross my arms over my chest. "You're going to pay me to do color for a high school baseball team that might not even make the playoffs?"

"We are making the playoffs. We're winning State."

"We?" I ask. "Does that mean you're playing this season?"

"I wish." He glances at his arm as if it still pains him, muscles flexing so I catch the sheen of his long, thin scar. "It's not me who's paying you. It's the Walter Cronkite School of Journalism."

"At Arizona State?"

"It's the first year they're running a competition. The best high school broadcast team wins five thousand dollars for their school and a thousand each for the broadcasters."

"You're doing this for the money?"

"You kidding? I'm in it to win it."

I groan. "How did I know you were going to say that?"

Garrett shifts closer. "When you sat down... No." He stops himself. "When you pointed at Nathan and told him to get out of the chair, the little hairs on the back of my neck went wild." He turns around and shows me a tanned neck with wispy blond hairs disappearing into the neckline of his tee. "These guys, they never lie."

"You haven't named them, have you? Each little hair?"

He laughs and his eyes warm. "Quick wit. Good. You'll need that to keep up with me during the broadcasts."

So much for pushing him away with my sarcasm.

"We can win this thing, Walters. I mean, how can we lose? I'm charming and insightful, and you understand the nuances of the game. Plus, you're a girl."

I blink in disbelief. "That's what I bring to this team? I'm a girl."

"It's a bonus. Sets us apart. How many others will have a girl who knows her shit the way you do?" His head tilts as he studies me. "Especially one who's so pretty."

My jaw drops. "Am I supposed to be flattered? Because

that's incredibly sexist, not to mention patronizing and..."

"Demeaning?" he adds helpfully.

I have the urge to kick him.

He laughs. "It's just an observation. Right now our camera is fixed on the field, but there might be opportunity for video, too. And you have nice eyes. Except when you frown and you get these weird slash marks between your eyes." He points. "Yeah. Like those. I love the vintage tees, but your sandals are hideous. We'll cut those out of our publicity photo."

"Publicity photo?"

"We need to submit it with our game tape."

It's all I can do not to scream. "There is going to be no game tape. I'm not saying yes."

"Because I don't like your sandals?"

"Leave my sandals out of this!"

"That's my point exactly." His eyes gleam. "See, we're already in agreement. Say yes. It'll be fun."

"I don't do things because they're *fun*."

His grin hitches up on one side. "That's your problem right there."

I gasp. I don't even know what to say to that. To him. He's a force of nature, but I'm not going to give in. "Go away, Garrett." I put my hand on the door to the bookstore. It feels like a hold on reality. Books are inside. My StoryClub kids. Brandi, my no-nonsense boss. Bryan, the new hire, with the cute glasses and the shy smile who made me an origami owl on Saturday. He's the kind of guy I want to spend time with. Steady. Smart. Trustworthy. A guy who plays no games.

Not a guy who only plays games.

I pull open the door. "I'm not going to say yes."

He holds the door open as I walk in. I can hear the smile in his voice. "That wasn't a no," he calls after me. "I think we're making progress."

Chapter Six

"Hi, Brandi." I'm still breathing hard after jogging to the office to stuff my purse in a cubby and then searching most of the store before I find my boss. She's at the computer station in the picture book section, looking like a teenager in a *Lion King* tee with jeans and Converse high tops. You'd never know she runs the entire children's department. Well, unless you heard her pissed off. Then she's scary.

She smiles when she sees it's me. "Hey, Josie. You ready for Book Club?"

"Always."

"Don't be so sure." She twists her long brown hair into a bun and fans her neck. "The princess book turned out to be a hit. We have ten girls today and two boys."

"Twelve?" Usually, Wednesday's Book Club gets about seven or eight kids. I run the gathering every week and we read a book and then the kids do a craft. But once a month, we have a special story that the kids are encouraged to read on their own, like a real book club. Usually, I have the kids act out their favorite parts, but I'm wondering if that might be a little wild with a dozen bodies in the activity room.

"They're waiting for you," Brandi says. "Good luck."

I hear the buzz of noise before I even reach the room. Pausing behind one of the doors, I take a peek. Book Club is meant for kids in kindergarten through second grade, but there are a few preschoolers here, too. I smile when I see Ciera's sparkly pink dance shoes. She can't resist an opportunity to dress up. Talia is wearing a tiara and mimicking Ciera's pirouettes. My shy ones—Lola and Kate— are waiting in the safe zones of their moms' legs. Bryson is running in a circle around the room while Javier stomps his foot, trying to get them to settle down. He's my rule follower and he sees me first, his whole body going limp with obvious relief that I've arrived. My heart takes over, pumping warm, gooey happiness through my veins. Even the commotion makes me smile.

I step in, calling out, "Who read the book?"

There's a tiny breath of pause and then twelve voices chant, "*Josie!*" and "*I did I did!*"

I have to plant my feet to withstand the onslaught as half a dozen bodies hurl themselves at my waist. I dish out as many hugs as I can, smiling over the top of their heads and making eye contact with the ones who held back. I recognize them all, and I'm glad to see a few I wasn't sure would come again. "All right, everyone. You know the drill."

The parents wave goodbye as the kids run to the round rug. They settle themselves while Javier does a loop to be sure everyone is in their place. My seat is the throne at the head of the circle. I made it myself out of a straight-backed chair and an upholstered headboard I found at a garage sale. James cut the headboard for me and nailed it to the chair, and I decorated the material with cutout stars and hearts. Brandi gave it two thumbs up and declared that I was officially in charge of both toddler groups. That was a year ago.

It's what I'm going to miss most when I graduate.

Seated on my throne, I take a minute to commit this scene, this feeling, to memory. All eyes on me, a fizz of excitement in the room. The kids are ready to go where I lead. It feels good to be trusted that way. To be able to trust them, too.

"So," I begin, "today's book is called *Pizza Breath*."

Voices rise along with their little bodies. "Josie! Noooooooo!"

"Oh dear!" I clap my hands over my cheeks. "Was it *Socks for my Head*?"

There are hysterical giggles and a louder chorus of "Nooooooooo!"

"Then who can tell me what book we read?"

"*Princess Pudding!*"

"Yes!" I say, and I pull my copy from under my throne. "*Princess Pudding*. Who can tell me something special about the princess?"

"She loves pudding!" they all yell.

I lead them through a series of questions and lots of opinions are given, nearly all of which I agree with.

Yes, pudding is good.

Yes, it was funny when the dragon slipped in the pudding.

Yes, it was good that the prince had the princess to save him, or else he'd be dragon dinner.

I love how much picture books have changed since I was a kid. Girls aren't lying around in metaphorical sleeps waiting for a guy to wake them up. Today it's Power to the Princess, and not even the boys question it.

"Who's ready for snacks?" I ask. Again, they know the drill. They sit in their spots so I can hand out cookies. The bookstore crew usually leaves the package on an upper shelf. I look, but no cookies.

"Let me see if I can get Brandi's attention," I tell the kids. "Sit still for a minute." I walk to the door, and something flickers in my peripheral vision.

Blue.

Bright blue raglan tee over blue jeans. Brighter blue eyes.

My pulse jumps. "Why are you still here?"

Garrett is half sitting on one of the tables meant for browsers. "I'm waiting for you. You're very cute with the kids."

Heat stings my cheeks. "You were watching?"

"It's a bookstore. The door is open." He grins. "Do you have a tiara, too?" He wiggles his eyebrows.

I refuse to smile. I'm not going to encourage him. An un-encouraged Garrett Reeves is as much as I can handle. I point a finger toward the picture book section. "Go and find Brandi. Tell her I need cookies."

"I don't know who Brandi is."

"You'll figure it out."

"Do I get a cookie, too?"

"You're worse than the kids." I point again. "Go!" I walk back in and tell the kids, "The cookies are on their way." I hope I'm right. My heart is racing. I smooth my ponytail and then mess it up again when I realize what I'm doing. *What is wrong with me? I don't even like him.* I take deep breaths until my pulse slows.

A few minutes later, he's at the door, a stack of napkins and a package in his hand. "Sugar cookies, anyone?"

The kids clap and cheer, turning shining eyes on Garrett as he saunters in.

"You look like the prince in the book," Ciera says.

"Are you a prince?" Kate murmurs, her eyes like Frisbees.

He tears open the cookies. "I am." He walks around the circle, squatting beside each kid as he hands them a cookie and a napkin.

"You're big," Bryson says. "Are you a football player?"

"I'm a baseball player," Garrett says. "You like baseball?"

"I like football better."

"We'll work on that." He gives Bryson a wink.

Talia tugs on my leg. "Is he your prince, Josie?"

"No," I say. "Girls don't need princes, do we? We're like Princess Pudding."

"But who will kiss us?" she asks.

Garrett points a finger at Talia as if she's asked a very good question. "Yes, Josie. Who will kiss you?"

I spare a second to glare at him and then smile at the kids. "I'm not old enough for kisses."

"My brother kisses his girlfriend," Ciera says. "Sometimes he kisses her on her boobies."

"Ohhhkay!" I say, ending with a clap so loud my hands sting. "Well. That's all the time we have for today."

Garrett is trying so hard not to laugh, his whole body is shaking.

The parents are waiting near the door, so I excuse the kids. I'm surrounded by more hugs and thanks. Half the girls swarm Garrett, and he doesn't seem the least bit surprised or uncomfortable. He's probably used to female attention wherever he goes. He immediately gets into the swing of it, saying something sweet to each of them in turn.

Until it's just the two of us.

My pulse quickens again. He watches me while I shelve the book and toss out the cookie bag. He's making me nervous and that makes me mad. Mad is safe. Mad I can do. "You need to go. I have work to do."

"Another story time?"

"Unpacking boxes."

"Doesn't sound nearly as fun."

"It isn't." Through the open door, Bryson is playing imaginary hopscotch while his mom browses the books.

Garrett follows my gaze. "They're great, aren't they? Every summer, Coach Richards runs a baseball camp and I volunteer. Kids are about the same age as this group. Sevens and eights. But ball caps instead of tiaras."

He slides his hands in the pockets of his jeans, rocking a little on his heels as if he's reliving a moment of time. I knew a lot of ballplayers who volunteered because it was expected, but there's no arguing that Garrett was good with the kids today.

"The things they say," he murmurs. "And the way you feel when you show them something and they get it right. You know?" His gaze shifts to me, his smile genuine.

I scowl. Yes, I know, but I'm not going to admit it. I don't want to have this conversation with Garrett. He's looking for an angle—trying to wriggle his way into my—

"You lied," he says, shocking my brain into silence.

"What? What are you talking about?"

"You said you don't do things for fun. And this—" He gestures to the room. "You were having fun."

I flush, feeling exposed. "I get paid to do this."

"Yeah, but it can't be a lot. You could make more somewhere else." He eyes my throne. "This is something you love. You're lucky to have that."

"You're making too much out of a part-time job."

"Stocking books is a part-time job. You have a talent with those kids." His charming smile switches back on. "Seems like you're one of those people who's talented at a lot of things."

I react with a sniff of disgust. "Now you're laying it on too thick." I bend down for a heavy box of books that should go to storage.

Garrett takes the box from me before I have time to straighten completely. "Doesn't mean it isn't true."

"I'm not changing my mind, Garrett."

He balances the box in one arm as if it weighs nothing. "You are. I just have to figure out your *why*."

"I'm afraid to ask what that is."

"Why you do what you do. It's like baseball. Every guy on the team is there for a different reason. Some love to play. Some want the glory and the girls. Some are there because their parents want it. It's their *why*. It's what motivates them."

"And what's your why?" I ask. "The spotlight?"

"I look good under the lights, no question." His cocky flash of smile fades beneath something much more intense. Much more real. "But for me, I love the game. More than anything."

He's so much like my father that it hurts to look at him. "Maybe it's not a *why*," I say. "Maybe it's a *why not*."

"Because you hate baseball?" He does that lip-biting thing again. "You can't hate a sport that is everything good and beautiful on this earth. And how is it that you know so much about a game you supposedly hate?"

"I'm a woman of mystery. Now can I have the books back?"

He hangs on to the box. "Or maybe your dad taught you."

The word *dad* triggers a flow of ice through my veins. I yank the box out of his arms and set it on a table. "How do you know that?"

He pulls his cell out of his pocket. "My friend Google and I have been getting to know you. Your dad is Clay Walters."

Just hearing his name stings, and I struggle to keep the hurt from showing. "I know who my dad is."

"There's a picture of the two of you." He holds up the phone, but I shake my head.

I don't need to see it. I know the one he means. It's always the first photo to come up in a Google search. I'm about three. My father is walking out to the field and I'm carrying his glove. It's almost as big as I am. It was my favorite picture, the one thing I unpacked first in every new house. The picture I kissed good night whenever Dad was on a road trip. When

Mom and I left Florida for the last time, I broke a framed copy of that photo over my knee and nearly sliced off a finger when the glass shattered.

"I also know your name isn't actually Josie. It's Joe. After Joe DiMaggio." He rests a hand over his heart as he says the name. "Joltin' Joe. The Yankee Clipper. Married to Marilyn." He sighs dramatically. "Did you know he was actually named Giuseppe?"

"I'm aware." I fold my arms over my chest as a memory tugs at the never-healing scab on my heart. Dad playing catch with me in the backyard, grinning like he'd always be there. *My favorite girl, named for my favorite player.*

"Think how proud your dad will be when we win this thing," Garrett is saying. His gaze hooks mine, the blue irises liquid with dreams. "Clay Walters' little girl, calling the game that he taught her. Josie, you have to say yes."

It takes me a second to swallow the bitterness of the past. In an even voice I'm proud of, I say, "Here's the thing, Garrett. My dad is a selfish ass who never gave a shit about anything but baseball, so you know what? I don't care about making him proud."

Finally—silence. He slides the phone away as his throat works over a long swallow. "I see Google fell short this time."

"Just a bit. Now would you please leave me alone?"

He swallows again. "I'm sorry. Really."

I'm still breathing hard as he walks out. At least now I'm rid of him for good.

Chapter Seven

He's standing outside my house the next morning.

I'm in a rush as I pull the front door closed. I've got my teeth around a half-eaten slice of jelly toast while I struggle to slide my phone into the pocket of my skinny jeans. When I catch sight of him, I freeze.

My backpack doesn't.

It swings forward and knocks into my other hand that's holding a can of apple juice, spraying the liquid into the air and all over my fingers.

"Shit," I sputter around the toast, but at least it's jarred me out of my shock.

Garrett is wearing a black tee, jeans, and a smile as blinding as the sun. "I thought you'd be a morning person."

I glare, because my mouth is still full of food. Tucking away my phone, I grab the toast and shake juice off my hand. "I'm late and I hate being late. Whoever invented the snooze button should be shot."

"I'm guessing they're already dead. In case that makes you feel better."

His smile does not make me feel better. Nothing about him does. Last night, the old dream returned. The fear. The panic. *I need my suitcase—where's my suitcase?* Waking up to find myself breathing hard, my legs dangling from the bed as sweat chilled on my skin. Always that damn suitcase.

It's Garrett who's bringing it all back. Garrett with all his talk about baseball and his naughty-boy smile and wavy neck hairs. Now he shows up here looking all Mister Golden Guy and I'm breathing hard again. I need him to go away.

"What are you doing here, Garrett?" My gaze sweeps past him to the black four-door idling at the curb.

"Let me help." He takes my half-eaten toast, which throws me off, but I do have a juice disaster to deal with. I finish the can in two big swallows, set it at the corner of the driveway to trash later, and pour water over my hand from the bottle I always carry to school. Finally, I release a sigh and hold out my hand for my toast.

He's licking strawberry jelly from his thumb.

"You didn't!"

He bites his lip. "Sorry."

"You are not."

"I'm not," he admits. "That was really good."

"Garrett!"

"Let me make it up to you. I'll drive you to school."

"You're acting like we're friends and we're not. How do you even know where I live?"

"Google, again."

"That's creepy stalker behavior," I say as I brush past him. "You need therapy."

"And I'm going to get some as soon as you say yes to broadcasting."

"Listen up, Blondie." I spin to face him. "There. Is. No. *Why*."

He acts as if he hasn't heard, jogging ahead to open the

passenger door of his car. "Come on. I'll give you a ride."

"I walk with Mai."

"The girl at the baseball game? We'll pick her up, too."

I waver. I don't want to spend any more time with Garrett, but I'm also running late and in danger of missing first bell. "Fine. Six houses up on the other side of the street. She's standing outside."

I slide in the seat, and a second later he's beside me, buckling his belt. I set my backpack on my lap as I take a quick look. It's cleaner than our truck and smells good—like the cedarwood soap that Mom used to carry.

He puts the car in drive. "Nice shirt."

I have to look down to remember which one I'm wearing. There's a giant whale and above it the speech bubble reads: *"Who are you calling Dick?"* "It's from a book."

"I'm aware," he replies drily.

I widen my eyes and flutter my lashes. "You read?"

"Only if the words are written across a girl's chest." He widens his eyes and flutters goldish-brown lashes in the same exaggerated way.

Smartass. And quick.

Then he surprises me by adding, "Melville today and Orwell yesterday."

It takes me a second to remember that I was wearing a quote from *Animal Farm* yesterday. *And a reader, too?* "Well. Maybe you're not as dumb as you look."

"Thank you." His grin is good-natured as he rolls to a stop in front of Mai.

I like that he can handle my snark—and give it back. But I'm still not saying yes.

Mai pops open the back door. She's wearing lipstick again. "A chauffeur? You shouldn't have."

"He's trying to break me so I'll say yes to broadcasting."

"Has he tried drugs? I've heard those work."

As she slides in the back, I quickly open and close two doors, and in an impressively short amount of time, I'm sitting next to Mai.

Garrett slides an arm over the seat. "You're really going to sit back there? Both of you?"

"Drive on," Mai says with a little wave of her hand. Her glossy hair is a few shades lighter than the black upholstery as she leans back with an air of superiority as if she were born to be driven around.

Garrett sighs but maneuvers us onto the main street and into the line of cars heading for the school.

"So are you a baseball player, too?" Mai asks.

"I am."

"He was."

"Which verb is it?" she demands.

"I shattered my arm a year ago."

"He broke it in two places, tore his shoulder muscle and needed surgery to repair everything over the summer." When his eyes meet mine in the rearview mirror, I shrug. "You're not the only one who's friends with Google."

Mai is not done with the interrogation. "So which one were you?"

"Which one was I?" Garrett repeats.

"On the team. Were you one of the guys on the bases or with the bat?"

Garrett bursts out laughing. My brilliant best friend really knows nothing about the game.

"I was a pitcher," he says. "I stood on the mound in the middle of the field."

"Oh," she says dismissively. "I don't think it's fair that one player is higher than the others."

"Riiiiiight." Garrett meets my eye in the mirror, and a moment of shared humor flashes between us. He clears his throat, probably to cover a laugh. "I can see that. But it's, uh, helpful, when you're the guy throwing the ball."

"That's what you did?"

"Pure heat." There's arrogance in his voice. I'm expecting that—I've had a taste of Garrett's ego. But his left hand has snaked over to the scar on his right elbow, rubbing as if it still hurts.

"Oh, wait," Mai says. She smacks the back of Garrett's seat. "You were that guy. At the school assembly last year. You broke your arm right after a big game."

"We won the Division."

"They handed you the trophy. It was a pity thing, right? I felt sad for you."

"Does she have a filter?" Garrett asks me.

"Nope."

"And now you're announcing?" Mai continues.

He parks in the school's back lot. "That's right. And I'd like to earn a trophy the real way."

Mai elbows me in the ribs. "So he's not actually a baseball player."

"Ow," I mutter. I know where she's going with this. That lipstick she's wearing is a neon sign that she's still stuck on Anthony. If I say yes to Garrett, then I'm saying yes to more baseball. *Traitor.*

"She doesn't like players?" Garrett asks Mai.

"Hates them."

"Then I'm officially retired."

She shoots me a victorious smile. "We can double date," she says. "Do you play pool chicken?"

Her question has obviously confused him. "Remind me not to pick you up again before I've had caffeine."

I open the car door. "Ignore her."

"Don't ignore her," Mai says. She follows me out. Garrett is locking the car when a guy calls his name. Does anyone *not* know him?

"Give me a sec," Garrett says.

We nod and then immediately join the stream of other kids moving toward the south doors. We're nearly there when Garrett jogs up beside me.

"Don't you have somewhere to be?" I ask.

"I do," he says. "But I also have your why."

"You *think* you have my why."

"Hey, G!" A girl I don't know launches herself at Garrett and grabs him around the arm. "You're going the wrong way. Class is down here."

"My locker is that way," he says.

"No time." Another girl grabs his other arm, laughing.

He opens his mouth and then shrugs and lets them pull him back. "Let's do lunch, Walters. Off campus."

"I have second lunch."

"I'll make that work."

I roll my eyes. "Do you get to do anything you want? You play the athlete card, is that it?"

"There are cards?" he calls. "I just use my charm." He points another finger gun. "By the flagpole at the start of lunch. You're going to want to hear this. And if I'm wrong, I promise I'll leave you alone."

"You're wrong!"

"I'll see you at the flagpole. This time show up!"

He turns away, and I stare after him and the girls who are still hanging onto his arms.

"You hate ballplayers," Mai says.

"I do. I especially hate that one."

"Then why are you staring?"

I blink, fighting the burn of a flush as I wave off her comment. "Because I'm disgusted. Did you see the finger gun? It's truly awful."

"It is. But he bites his bottom lip when he does it. It's kind of sexy."

"It is not!"

My treasonous mind whispers, *It's a* lot *sexy.*

Chapter Eight

Lunch is a sub shop tucked into the corner of a strip mall. It smells like meatballs and fresh bread and my stomach rumbles. This is a big step up from the school cafeteria where Mai and I eat every day.

"You're buying," I tell Garrett as I study the menu. "I'll have the steak and cheese."

Garrett inches forward with the line. "Coincidentally the most expensive thing on the menu."

"And a large drink," I add. "And a brownie."

It's his turn at the counter, and he orders my lunch and a Cobb salad for himself. I fill my cup with a mix of Sprite and lemonade, collect napkins, and find us an empty booth. The bench seats are covered in red vinyl and squeak as I sit. With nothing to do, I find myself watching Garrett at the soda fountain. His hair has flopped over one eye and he pushes it back, even that small movement a mix of confidence and grace. My dad had that, too. He probably still does. I wouldn't know.

How did I end up here? When Garrett ordered me to the

flagpole this morning, I was determined to do anything but.

During first hour, it was *hell no.*

Second period, *absolutely not.*

Third period, *no way.*

Fourth period, *in his dreams.*

And then, inexplicably, I was walking to the flagpole. I scowled when I saw him, waiting for one smirk, one smug comment so I could bolt. Instead his expression lit up. He stepped forward, ignoring the group he'd been standing with. "Walters, you make my heart sing."

"Blondie, you're so full of shit."

He laughed and we fell into an easy rhythm on the way to his car. As pathetic as it may be to admit, I've never left campus for lunch. So yes, the whole thing was weird and kids were staring and I should have felt nervous or awkward, but I didn't. I'm not even nervous now. I think it's because I don't want to impress Garrett Reeves. He has me off-balance and I don't like it. I want to get him out of my life.

They call our number at the counter, and Garrett detours to bring our lunches. He sets down his healthy green salad and slides me a red basket with my meaty-cheesy-gooey sub. I breathe in the toasty bread and garlic. Mmmm. "Where's my brownie?"

Shaking his head, he hands it over. Even though it's wrapped, it smells heavenly. It's covered in powdered sugar and has my other favorite feature of a brownie: it's huge.

But first things first. I lift half of my sub, which weighs as much as a Harry Potter hardcover. Garrett is watching me like an exhibit at the zoo. "What?" I say. "You ate half my breakfast." I lick a trail of cheese that's leaked over my hand.

"You can't eat all of that."

"Wanna bet?"

"No," he says. "I spent all my money on your lunch."

I grin. "So let's get this over with. What's my why?" I take a huge bite and then nearly choke when he answers.

"Your dad."

I swallow. "Way to ruin my appetite. I thought we already went over this? I don't want to talk about my dad." I take another bite because even if this conversation is slightly nauseating, the sandwich is seriously better than anything I've eaten in weeks. Mom is a distracted chef, which means home-cooked is usually over-cooked.

Garrett's finally done pouring Italian dressing on his salad and mixing it up. "I promise it'll be worth it." He pauses to eat a forkful of salad. "So your dad's career is a yo-yo of moves from team to team. He hangs around the league for a long time but never reaches the majors. Finally, he's released and takes a coaching job. Seems like an opportunity to put down roots, but not long after, Clay Walters is offered a chance to play ball in Japan, halfway across the world. What about his family?" He eyes me speculatively. "That couldn't have been an easy decision."

My fingers tighten around the sandwich, squeezing cheese out both ends. "You'd be surprised."

Garrett nods as if that confirms what he's already guessed. "Two months later, the Japanese press introduces the Nippon league's new power hitter, Clay Walters. The next articles show him with various women and it's mentioned that he's newly single. I'm guessing you and your mom didn't want to go, and he left anyway."

It feels like a meatball is lodged in my throat. I lift a shoulder, let it drop like it's no big deal.

"And the reason he goes is because he thinks a big year there might prove he can still play in America. After everything, at age thirty-two, he still wants to play in the majors."

I shove the basket away. "What does this have to do with the contest?"

"Stick with me, Walters. I'm getting there." His blue eyes radiate intensity. "He comes back to the States two years later and gets a coaching job. But where?"

"In the minor leagues."

"Which is where he is today. Passed over again this season." Garrett leans forward, his elbows on the table, his fingers curved nearly into fists. His hands are solid—strong. I can imagine him gripping a baseball. I can imagine that it would have been a beautiful thing to watch him throw. "What if his daughter was the one to get to the majors first? What if the girl he left shows him up by making it to The Show?"

I lick my lips, tasting the sourness of the memories he's dredged up. "How is that possible?"

His smile sends goose bumps up my spine. "There's something about the contest I haven't told you yet. Another perk that goes with winning."

"Which is?"

"The winning team gets to call one inning of an Arizona Diamondbacks game."

I clean cheese off my fingers while my heart beats faster. "Regular season?"

"The real deal."

"At the stadium? In the booth?"

He nods. "If we were to win this, you'd make it to the big leagues ahead of your dad."

The napkin crumples in my fist. My breath comes short. I know it isn't healthy to hate your dad. It isn't healthy to want him to hurt.

That doesn't change the way I feel.

There's heat behind my eyes, but I won't cry. I'm not the needy kid I used to be. It's the one thing that haunts me: the memory of how pathetic I was. I thought we were a team when my father never cared about me.

But he cared about baseball.

Making it to the major leagues was the one defining dream of his entire life. Would it break him to see me in the broadcast booth of a major league game? To know I made it when he never did?

No. Of course not.

But would it hurt? Would it sting a little?

Yeah, it might.

Garrett smiles. "I found your why."

I nod because there's no denying it. "You found my why."

Chapter Nine

"I love being right." Garrett leans back. "You'd think I'd be used to it by now; it happens all the time."

I toss my napkin at him.

He laughs, catching it with a deft flick of his wrist and tossing it back. "Everyone has a why, even if they don't know it."

"Yeah, yeah, yeah." I drop the napkin in my basket. "Are you done gloating?"

Laughter seems to lighten the color of his eyes. "I will never be done gloating."

I'm distracted from replying by the sound of plastic wrap. I blink and point to my brownie, which is now unwrapped and in his hand. "Hey. You stole my brownie."

"We're partners now, Walters. We share everything. Even chocolate."

The word "partner" gives me pause, but I break off a corner when he holds out the brownie. "I'm still not saying yes. I don't have time for revenge."

"There's always time for revenge." He sets the brownie

on a napkin between us where I can reach for more. "Is it your job? Because I only need you for two home games a week, usually Tuesdays and Thursdays."

"It's not that," I admit. "Brandi is flexible with my schedule and my main shifts are Wednesday Book Club and Saturday Storytime."

"Then what?"

"I run a business with my mom. AromaTher skin care."

"Oh," he says, as if he's solved a puzzle. "That's why you smell good."

I roll my eyes but still feel an unwelcome spike of pleasure at the compliment. "You only *think* I smell good because you spent all that time in the booth with Nathan."

"Possibly." He splits the last piece of brownie and hands me half. "So can't she give you six weeks off?"

"I'm not an employee. I'm a partner."

"A partner?"

"It'll be official when I turn eighteen in May."

"Really? Is that your idea?"

"Why wouldn't it be?"

A tick beats at the corner of his jaw. "I've got a father who wants me to go into business with him. And it's definitely not my idea."

"What kind of business?"

"Accounting. He has room for another tax guy."

"And you're a tax guy?"

"I'm good at math."

"Is that the same thing?"

"No," he says flatly. "And I hate accounting. But that's a minor detail for my dad."

I can feel his tension across the table, and I'm curious in spite of myself. "So you have a better plan?"

"I did." He shakes the ice cubes in his cup, but I have the feeling he'd really like to launch them.

"Let me guess. Plan A was baseball."

"And Plan B and Plan C. But now I'm supposed to embrace Plan Never-Going-to-Happen and move to Dallas."

"Your dad lives in Dallas?"

He nods. "My parents are divorced."

"So what are you going to do? You can't pitch—not with a bad arm."

"There are other things I can do to stay in the game."

"Like broadcasting?"

"Broadcasting would be one option." His eyes lower, shuttering his expression. I wonder if this broadcasting contest is about more than winning. If it's a way for him to show his dad it's a better career path for him. No wonder he's been working this so hard.

Still. You have to know when to say when. Dreams are opportunities for disappointment—I'm an expert at that. I'm doing him a favor, even if he doesn't realize it. I open my mouth, but he speaks before I do.

"Please, Josie." His voice comes low, almost pleading.

My words dry up. My dad never once said please.

His eyes snag mine, holding me in the beam of his need. I feel myself waver. Beneath the Teflon charm, Garrett is actually afraid. He needs this.

Maybe I need this, too.

If I do it, maybe I can finally put my dad in the past. I can let it go once I show him his daughter is a winner, even if he never was.

My hands are sweaty as I clasp them together under the table. "All right. I'll do it."

A slow smile spreads across his face, showcasing perfect bone structure and a mouth that makes me think of kissing. He really is gorgeous, damn him. And he's looking at me with so much warmth, I want to melt.

Nope. No way.

Instead, I stiffen my spine and focus on his nose. It's an extremely average nose. "There are going to be rules," I blurt out.

"Sure," he says easily. "What rules?"

I pause. *What rules?* "Well. For starters, no extra games, no tournaments, no weekend showcases."

"No problem. You don't even have to call the playoff games. The contest entries are due May first at the end of the regular season so no team has an unfair advantage. You can be done once we turn in our tape. You won't have to see me again until June twenty-sixth."

"What's June twenty-sixth?"

"The Diamondbacks game where you and I will broadcast an inning." He blasts two finger guns at me. "What else?"

"We treat this like a business partnership. That's it. I don't like baseball players and I'm not making an exception for you."

That brings another smile to his face. "We don't have to be friends, Walters. We just have to kick ass on-air. So do we have a deal or not?"

I sigh. "We have a deal."

He smacks a hand on the table in victory. Of course he's happy—he got what he wanted. Me, I'm not sure how I feel. I want revenge, yes, but this deal forces me closer to a fire that already burned me once.

"We start tomorrow," he says. "We have a home game at three o'clock."

His gaze suddenly shifts toward the door and sticks. His expression turns serious. I follow his gaze and watch a man move toward the line to order. I recognize the logo on his shirt, but obviously Garrett recognizes more than that. He stands, giving me a quick, "One second." He approaches the guy and they shake hands and exchange a few words. When Garrett steps back, I hear him say, "See you Saturday."

Then he's back at the table, his face set with determination. *Determined about what?*

"You ready?" he asks, gathering our trash.

I can tell his mind is already somewhere else from the distant look in his eyes. I'm just not sure where.

"So who was that?" I ask as we head for the car.

"Kyle Masters."

"He had a Saguaro High shirt on. Isn't that Cholla's biggest rival?"

He nods. "He's a teacher there."

"That was a baseball shirt."

He clicks his key fob and his car squeaks twice. "He's an assistant coach, too. Also runs a training program for kids on the weekends."

"So what's Saturday?"

"Plan E."

"You have a lot of plans."

He opens his door. "I don't give up."

We listen to music on the way back, and though Garrett taps his thumb on the wheel, I can tell he's still far away. Plan E maybe? What exactly is he doing with an assistant baseball coach? Is he thinking about coaching as another way back into the game? I know he likes kids. Or is he still thinking that somehow he can make a comeback as a pitcher? I knew guys who tried it. Changed their delivery motions and ended up ruining their arms even more.

Doesn't matter what he's thinking, I remind myself. It's none of my business. We're partners and the only thing I want from Garrett Reeves is revenge.

Chapter Ten

"Seven facials," Mom says, punctuating her words with a sigh. She drops her purse and briefcase on the counter and sets down the heavy case of AromaTher samples.

"You're the one who wanted me to stay home tonight and work on the website."

Thursdays are always Party Night. Mom and I meet with various women's groups and demonstrate the AromaTher line of essential oils and skin care. But Mom was stressing, so I stayed home. Secretly, I'm happy. I knew tonight was going to be a lot of facials. I hate touching skin.

"Did you get a lot done?"

I stretch my arms and yawn. My eyes hurt from staring at the computer so it feels like I did, but I know it's not as much as Mom was hoping. "I researched other sites and made a list of everything we need."

"I thought you already had a list?" She pulls a stack of order forms from her briefcase.

"It's a better list."

I know I sound defensive, but it took forever to find sites

I like, bookmark elements we need, and sketch ideas for the home page. I'm also feeling guilty for offering to do this in the first place when now I'm not sure I can. It made sense at the time. Part of my job when I become a partner will be running the website—I should be the one to update it. Plus, we'd save money. But I didn't know I was going to be starting from scratch and I didn't know how hard it would be. I still haven't looked at my homework, plus I've got tomorrow hanging over my head. Another baseball game.

Mai is beyond excited about the whole thing. For the first time ever, she texted me two pics of tomorrow's outfit: sleeves rolled up, sleeves buttoned at the wrists.

MAI: Which one?

ME: What have you done with my best friend? This doesn't sound like her but those look like her bony wrists.

MAI: Sleeves down it is. See you in the AM.

"How was the party?" I ask. "Lots of sales?"

"Yes," Mom says, brightening. She sets the full kettle on the burner and turns on the heat. "Which reminds me. One of the ladies asked if we could make an exception and do her gardening group next Tuesday afternoon."

The Cholla Wildcat baseball schedule flashes in front of my eyes. "You can do it without me, right?"

"I'd rather not. It's too many ladies for one person. We wouldn't start until four. You'd still have time to get home and have something to eat." She pauses with two mugs in her hands, her eyebrows raised in question.

I shake my head, and she puts one of the mugs away while my mind races. I don't want to tell her about baseball, but I don't see how I can avoid it. It's going to last for six weeks. At least Mom has been breathing in lavender for the past hour. She's as calm as she's going to get.

"I kind of started this thing at school. I'm helping broadcast baseball games."

"Baseball?" Her voice is a roller coaster climbing to a peak. "Since when do you go to baseball games?"

"I don't. Ever. Except once this past week because of Mai."

She fills a metal infuser with loose-leaf tea. "What does Mai have to do with baseball?"

"It's a long story."

"Give me the synopsis."

I draw in a breath. "Mai has a crush so we went to the game, and the color guy was awful. Didn't know baseball at all. I couldn't help myself—I stepped in. And next thing you know…"

"You're broadcasting the games?"

"Home games only."

"Josie, what in the world." She rubs her hands over her face even though she's told me never to rub my face because it creates more wrinkles. "Why would you agree to this?"

"Because there's a contest sponsored by the broadcasting school at ASU. If our team wins, we get to call an inning of a Diamondbacks game."

"So?"

I realize I've twisted my hair in my hands and I'm holding on to it like a rope…or a lifeline. I let go. "If we win, I'll make it to the Bigs."

Her eyes darken as I repeat the words my dad used to say. "You're doing this because of him? Honey, you have nothing to prove."

"I know that."

"Then why?"

I have to wet my lips before I can get the words out.

"Because sometimes knowing something and feeling it are two different things."

She covers my hand with hers. Her skin is so much softer than mine. Smoother. I feel hard, full of rough edges. "But if you do this…at what cost to yourself?"

"It's not that bad. Without Dad there, it's just a game. A game I happen to know really well."

"But you'll have to be around those people. That world." Something flickers in her eyes. "Wait. You said color commentary. Who's doing the play-by-play?" The kettle whistles, startling us both. She turns off the burner, barely taking her eyes from my face. "Josie?"

"His name is Garrett Reeves." I feel my cheeks heating and from Mom's narrowed gaze she sees it, too. "It's not like that," I say quickly.

"Not like what? Is he a baseball player?"

"He was. He's hurt."

"For heaven's sake, Josie. Please tell me this isn't about a baseball player?"

"Mom, please. I would *never*. It's not like that."

"Not yet," she murmurs.

"Not ever. He wants a life in baseball. Even if I liked him, I could never trust him. He's too much like Dad. And no way would I go back to that world."

There's a sadness in her eyes I haven't seen in a while. "I know how it is, Josie. I lived it. High school sports—athletes—they live a charmed life and you feel charmed just being a part of it. It can suck you in if you're not careful."

"I'm always careful, Mom."

"Keep it that way. I don't want to see your heart broken again." She runs her fingers down my cheek, her gaze far away. "Don't fall in love with the wrong guy. Once you do, you're never really over it."

Chapter Eleven

I get to the game a little early, but Garrett is already there, setting up the equipment. Mai is in the stands, her chem book open on her lap, but she says she'll look up at all the Anthony parts. I've thought about teaching her baseball, but her head is filled with things that will actually improve the world, so I decide not to.

"Anything I can do to help?"

"All done," Garrett says. "I'm just checking the site to make sure the video is coming through."

Sure enough, I can see the field on his laptop screen.

I set my backpack next to his on the floor and drag my stool forward so I have a clear view of the field. Today we're playing the Arredondo Warriors.

"It's a big game," Garrett tells me. "The Warriors are always in the playoff hunt." He pulls his key chain from his pack and I watch as he rubs the M twice before setting it on the counter.

"What was that?" I ask.

Pink creeps up his ears. "Nothing. Habit."

I grin. "Garrett Reeves is superstitious?"

"Superstitions have been proven to build confidence and improve performance."

He can't quite meet my eyes, which is, well, kind of endearing. "They're also sweet," I say. "Like believing in unicorns."

"Who doesn't believe in unicorns?" He's full-on blushing now, but he rubs the M again, kissing it for good measure. "Don't disrespect the power of M."

"The power of M? That's a new one." My chest rumbles with a laugh. "I'd forgotten about the superstitions."

He hands me my headset. "But you like them?"

Faces flash in my mind—grown men who wouldn't wash their socks after a win or shave their faces when they were on a streak. Even my dad had to have a blue Gatorade before every game he played or managed. "Superstitions have a way of turning huge egos into humans."

Garrett's smile is somehow both pompous and sweet. "I knew there was something."

"What are you talking about?"

"Something you loved about the game."

I slip on my headset. "One thing. And it hardly counts."

"One thing now." He winks. "But we're just getting started."

He cues up "The Star Spangled Banner" and we both stand as it plays over the speakers. Then the umpire gestures the start of the game and Garrett turns up the volume on our mics.

"Welcome to Wildcat baseball," he says. "This is Garrett Reeves with Josie Walters. We'll be bringing you the game today between Cholla and Arredondo. Cholla comes in to today's game with a five and two record. The Warriors have the same winning record, which means we should be in for a good one." He reads through the line-ups of both teams and then the game begins.

Garrett's got an easy delivery. As the innings fly by, he calls the action clearly and without a lot of fuss. He's also ridiculously positive, spinning a strikeout as a good at-bat, and ignoring a wild throw by our pitcher to focus on our catcher's dive for it. Then Anthony is caught stealing in the fifth.

"Aggressive lead on the base path by Adams, but he's called out at second," Garrett says.

"Aggressive?" I repeat with a touch of snark. "Is that a new word for 'poor base running'?"

His eyes flash with surprise as he gestures to the field. "That was a great opportunity to take a free base. You've got a lefty on the mound with a terrible move."

"But you've got a catcher with a rocket for an arm. And I'm sorry, but Adams was so off-balance."

"Because he was shuffling."

"That was not a shuffle."

"You kidding? He could enter a dance contest with that move."

"And he'd end up exactly the same way he did here: out."

There's laughter outside the booth, and if Garrett has a comeback, there's no time for it because Everly, who's up to bat, hits a pop fly to short and the inning is over.

"That's the end of five," Garrett says, "and the score is tied two all. We'll be back after the break."

There's a bang on the door, and Rich, one of the assistant coaches, says, "I can hear you guys through the wall. That's funny stuff."

Garrett's grin is catching. By now, I've realized we've got a similar sense of humor and I expected there to be some back-and-forth, but I had no idea I'd feel this *rush*. I don't even know what it is, but I think Garrett feels it, too. We're in sync, and yet there's also a current of tension. A push-pull.

Maybe it's because this is so new, because we don't know what to expect.

Because we both thought it might be good, but not this good.

Uncomfortable with my thoughts, I reach into my backpack for my bottle of water. I find it, but end up knocking over Garrett's pack in the process. "Sorry," I say. As I straighten it, a paper sticks up from the unzipped main compartment. I don't mean to look, but the large 67 in red ink is hard to miss.

My eyes flicker to Garrett. "Ouch."

He shrugs at the math test. "Whatever."

Whatever? I double-check that I didn't misread the number. I also note that it's the same quarterly test I took and it's worth a chunk of our grade. "I thought math was your thing?"

"It is." He shoves the test in and zips up his pack. "School isn't."

I gape, not sure what that means. *He doesn't test well? Or he doesn't study?* I don't have time to think about it because he turns the volume back on the headsets and the next inning begins. I shrug off the uncomfortable thoughts and force myself to refocus on the game. It takes a little while, but we work back into a rhythm and before I know it, it's the seventh and final inning. I'm glad high school doesn't play nine like they do in college and the majors. I'm having too much fun. That wasn't part of the plan.

"The Warriors take the field," Garrett announces. "We're still tied at two all. The plate is in shadows and we've got Evan Harris up to bat."

I speak into my mic. "If this team has done their homework, Harris will see nothing but curveballs."

"And the first pitch is a curveball outside. Harris swings for strike one."

I lean forward. "Wait for it—number two is on its way."

Sure enough, another breaking ball whizzes by while Harris swings wildly. I shoot Garrett a smile. I love being right. But he's looking at the field. Worried. Or maybe pissed. I've never seen Garrett pissed, but a nerve is ticking in his jaw and his fingers are tapping a nervous beat on the counter. I'm guessing this is what it looks like. When Harris strikes out, I swallow back a snarky comment. I forget that these are Garrett's friends.

"Sorry," I say, covering my mic. "He's your buddy. It must be hard to watch him struggle."

"He'll get it."

"He won't."

"How can you say that?" he snaps.

"Because my dad was a power hitter in the minor leagues for the first eleven years of my life and a hitting coach after that. I grew up watching guys at the plate. Guys who can't see the curve can't hit it. Harris…" I shrug. "He looks lost every time one comes over the plate."

"Doesn't mean he won't get it. He just needs more practice."

Practice doesn't fix everything. I have an eye for talent the way my dad does, but I keep quiet. I don't want to rub salt in the wound.

Fortunately for the Wildcats, Anthony Adams hits a bomb over the left field fence, breaking the tie. Garrett is up with a fist pump, Harris completely forgotten, as he watches Anthony circle the bases. Cholla wins and Mai is going crazy on the bleachers, yelling loud enough for me to hear her over everyone else.

The teams are still shaking hands on the field when Garrett shuts down the equipment and I pack up my stuff. There's a thrum of energy in the stadium. It's that feeling of a close game—a last-minute win. It crackles in the air and even finds its way into the booth.

Garrett lets out a long breath. "That was fun. Fact, that was the most fun I've had at a baseball game since the last time I threw a pitch." He's biting his lip again, damn it, his eyes shining at me like I just handed him a World Series ring.

I'm off-balance again, caught in the tractor-beam of his happiness, feeling more than I want. I shrug. "It didn't totally suck."

He laughs as he shoulders his pack. "Can you meet this weekend? I want to fill you in on the contest entry. There are a few other requirements."

"Requirements?"

"We can figure it out in twenty minutes."

"How about tomorrow afternoon? I finish at the bookstore at one o'clock." I wonder what he'll say—Saturday is the day for his secret-whatever meeting with Kyle Masters.

But he nods right away. "I'll meet you at the bookstore when your shift is over."

I think about Saturday and story time. About the costume I'll be wearing. "Let's meet at the café next door."

"It's a date," he says.

"Ooh, it's a date," Mai repeats. I didn't hear her walk up.

"Not that kind of a date."

Garrett nods beside me. "Walters and I are buddies."

Mai raises her brows. "The kind that starts with f—"

"No!" I snap before she can say more. "We're not buddies. We're partners. You drank a soda, didn't you?"

She smiles and I groan. Mai is unfiltered in general, but on a sugar high she's frightening. "We're leaving," I tell Garrett. I take Mai by the elbow.

As we walk out, Coach Richards looks up from the field. "Josie Walters," he says.

Mr. Richards teaches history and though I never had him for a class, I know who he is. And now, apparently, he knows who I am.

He gives me an approving nod. "Nice job today. You two are a good team."

"Thanks, Coach," Garrett says, answering from behind. "We are."

I hate letting him get the last word, but even I can't argue that.

Chapter Twelve

The dinosaur costume is hot. And I don't mean sexy.

It's also itchy. Like, bug itchy.

Can ticks live on fake fur?

The thought makes me itch more.

"How are you doing?"

I recognize Bryan's voice. A second later, a hand waves in front of the eye slits. I get a flash of dark wavy hair and worried brown eyes.

"It's a thousand degrees in here and the head weighs more than a bowling ball."

"Hang on."

Something shifts and the pressure is off my neck.

"The head wasn't on right."

"Thanks! I must have knocked it loose during the dancing."

Today, I was Dina the Dancing Dino. It's a new costume character for story time. Doing the Hokey Pokey with miniature yellow arms and huge stuffed feet is a little humiliating, but so worth it. The kids laughed their butts off and so did I. "I thought Ciera was going to bring me down that one time."

"I was ready to catch you."

Inside my oversize head, I smile. Bryan is the kind of guy who would, too. "Is it time for me to reemerge as a sweatier and more dehydrated version of myself?"

He laughs. I like that about Bryan. He laughs when he's supposed to. Not when I insult him—as if I ever would. He made me another origami animal this morning. Something with a really long nose. Maybe an aardvark? I'm afraid to ask, because why would you make an aardvark? But I thanked him in generic terms.

"Two minutes. Brandi wants me to get some photos."

A low groan slips out. I'm not sure what time it is and I don't want to be late to the café. "I have a meeting thing, so as long as it's quick." I lift my flappy felt-covered hands. Dina the Dino is permanently smiling. "Should I move?"

"You're perfect where you are." I hear a click and hold still.

"Brandi had an interview this morning," Bryan tells me. "For your replacement."

"Oh yeah?" My voice sounds tight, and I clear my throat. I'm glad she's interviewing. My dancing dino days will be over soon, and I want to help Brandi train my replacement. "Anyone promising?"

"Not sure," he says, and I remind myself to stay still as I hear more clicks from his phone camera. "That should be enough."

"Thank God. Can you help me out of this?" I turn so he can reach the hook at the back of my costume. "Do you know what time it is?"

"It's one o'clock," a voice says.

Not Bryan's voice.

Shit.

"Blondie," I say.

"Deeno," he says.

"It's Dina," I correct with as much self-respect as I can muster. Then I turn and whack my tail into something.

"Careful," Bryan says.

"I'll meet you in the café, Garrett." My voice is sharp.

I hear a full-throated laugh in response. "Nice tail."

My face is burning. "Bryan, can you help me, please?"

His hand is on my arm as he leads me to the activity room. He undoes the top hook and unzips the costume while I twist the lumpy head free. The heavy yellow material puddles around my feet while deliciously cool air prickles over my arms and legs. My blue tank and stretchy gym shorts are both on the damp side. I push back sweaty bangs and unwind the messy bun of my hair, finger combing it quickly before pulling it into a high pony. "Thanks."

"So who was that?"

"A guy from school. We're doing a project together."

"Oh." I see the hesitation in his eyes. He's only a year older than me, but he's in college. He's not like the goofball boys at Cholla. I've talked to him enough to know that he's serious about school, serious about the future. And now he's wondering what kind of girl I am. What am I doing with someone like Garrett Reeves? But I'm not with him. And we're not doing anything. Except...how do I answer a question that hasn't been asked?

Apparently by babbling, which is what I begin to do. "It's a broadcasting project," I say. "He's a baseball player. Was. And there's a contest. It's sponsored by ASU, which is why we're meeting, because there are requirements. For the broadcasting thing." Before I can mention my father and revenge, I bite my lip. Hard. I want to pull on the dinosaur head and bury my face in itchy fur. "I'll hang up the costume," I tell him.

His smile is back. "I'll take it. You go."

"You sure?" I'm flushed with heat and embarrassment but he looks at me as if I'm, well, beautiful.

"I'm sure. I'll see you Wednesday?" he adds.

"Wednesday. And thanks again for the, uh...for the origami." I give him one last smile and head out. I make a mental note to look up a picture of an aardvark when I get home.

Chapter Thirteen

Garrett is sitting at a booth with two water bottles.

I slide in across from him, setting my purse and a cream cardigan down beside me. I planned on wearing it to meet Garrett, but I'm still too warm, even with the air conditioning on full blast. "You were supposed to wait for me here."

"You were supposed to be on time." He slides one of the water bottles toward me. "For you."

"Thanks." The icy bottle feels good on my fingers. "That was...nice of you."

"Relax, Walters. It doesn't mean you owe me a kidney. I figured you might be thirsty. After seeing you, I was having Halloween costume flashbacks." He downs half his bottle in one go. His hair is damp, too, but I'm guessing his is from a shower.

"So who was the guy in the bookstore?" he asks.

"Bryan? He works part-time in the office."

"Is he your boyfriend?"

I roll the cool bottle over my now even warmer cheeks. "No, not that it's any of your business."

He looks at me through slightly lowered lids. "Because he was giving you that look."

"What look?"

"The look of a guy who's interested."

"You can tell that after knowing him for two seconds?"

"I'm just saying. In case, you know, that's your type."

The way he says it is not exactly complimentary to Bryan. I set down the bottle, the plastic crunching under my grip. "Bryan is a great guy. He's smart and nice and very thoughtful and—"

"He giggles."

"He does not giggle!"

"I heard him. It reminded me of tea parties with my sisters."

I blink, my thoughts derailed. "You have tea parties?"

"Not recently. But my sisters, Lilah and Felice, are both older, which meant they were in charge of daily activities growing up. And it was the only way I got cookies." He lifts his bottle with a pinky finger sticking out. "But I never giggled."

"Please," I mutter. "I am not taking relationship advice from you. Have you ever had an actual girlfriend? And I don't mean a hookup."

"Walters!" He bats his eyelashes in mock hurt. "What kind of a guy do you think I am?"

"I've seen the ever-changing parade of girls at your locker."

"You've been stalking me?" He looks extremely happy at the thought.

"I walk by your locker on the way to mine. You probably haven't noticed, surrounded as you usually are."

"Friends, Walters. Can't a guy have friends?"

"Friends with benefits?"

"Every friendship is beneficial."

My laugh breaks free. "You are so full of shit."

He laughs with me as he leans back, sliding an arm over the top of the seat bench. I realize I'm as relaxed as he is. He's easy to be around. "To answer your question," he says, "I'm not interested in anything serious right now, but I have had an actual girlfriend. We dated most of our freshman year. Annette Cruz?"

I shake my head. I don't know her.

"Anyway. It got to be too hard. For some guys, baseball is a spring sport. For me, it's a year-round commitment. Doesn't leave room for a relationship."

"So now you just play the field?"

His expression lights up. "A baseball metaphor, Walters? I'm kind of turned on."

"Well, turn off," I retort. "You're not my type, Blondie."

"What? I'm everyone's type." He puffs out his chest.

"Put those muscles away before you hurt yourself." I roll my eyes. "You and me—we are strictly professional. We're about revenge. Money. Winning." I tick each item off with a finger. "There will be no flirting. Add that to our list of rules."

"You're cute when you're giving orders."

"That's flirting."

"Sorry. I'll work on it." But the knowing look in his eyes says, *No, I won't.* He's obviously having too much fun.

Worse than that, so am I.

He's so frustrating. And so... I purse my lips because I don't want to think about what he is. I'm already irritated that he's smarter and funnier than I expected. I should hate him—I *want* to hate him—and instead I...don't.

"Can we get to work?" I ask. "What are these other requirements?"

Chapter Fourteen

Garrett's gaze sharpens and the flirty playboy is gone. When it comes to this broadcasting contest, Garrett is 100 percent serious. I can't help but respect that.

"The most important part of our application is going to be the game tape," he says. "We provide the link to one regular-season game, our choice. We also have to complete an on-air interview. It can be with a player, a coach, or anyone else involved in running the team. Three to five minutes on any topic we choose."

"You know who you want to interview?"

"Not really." He picks at the label on the water bottle. "I've been looking for an angle. Someone with a story that will stand out."

"So you're thinking of a background piece? Is there someone on the team who's gone through a challenge?"

"Nothing comes to mind, but guys don't usually share the hard stuff."

"And if they did, would they share it on-air?"

He nods, conceding my point. "Maybe we need to go in

a different direction."

"Or maybe we choose someone other than a player or a coach," I suggest.

"What do you mean?"

"I'm not sure. Just thinking out loud. Like, maybe the equipment guy or the trainer? Find a behind-the-scenes story."

He chews a divot into his bottom lip until a sudden smile lifts the corners of his mouth. "That gives me an idea. We've got a guy, he's a senior now, but he's been helping out since his freshman year. Not a player, but he loves the game. His name is Scottie, and he does a little bit of everything. You get hurt and need an ice pack, Scottie is there. You need the field chalked, Scottie does it."

"What's his story?" I ask.

"I'm not sure," Garrett admits. "I've never asked him. We could do it together."

I twirl the bottle between my fingers.

He points to it. "You want something else? I would have gotten you a soda but they didn't have lemonade for a mix."

I stare at my unopened water as his question sinks in. "You know what I drink? How much information does Google have?"

"It's what you got at lunch the other day."

I'm still confused. "You noticed what kind of drink I made?"

"Observation, Walters. You got to read the field."

My father's words.

They take me back to that little girl standing at the fence. Wanting to be just like her dad. I unscrew the cap, my fingers turning damp with condensation. "My dad always preached that," I admit. "Field awareness."

His seat squeaks as he shifts. "I thought it would have been cool to have a dad in baseball. Guess it depends on the dad, huh?"

I shrug because what else is there to say? "Did your dad play?"

"Never. Hates sports unless it's NASCAR."

"Is that a sport?"

"According to him. He loves cars. My uncle Max was the ballplayer." He reaches in his pocket and pulls out his key chain. "This was his."

"That explains the M. I thought maybe you couldn't spell."

"I know all twenty-three letters," he jokes, but I don't miss the sadness in his eyes as he squeezes the key chain. "I got in a lot of trouble when I was little, and my mom didn't know what to do with me. Uncle Max told her I needed to hit something. He took me to the batting cages, but I didn't want to go. The way he tells it, I grabbed the first baseball I saw and threw it at him—hard. And that's how he knew I should be a pitcher."

"Did you really?" I'm smiling as I try to picture it.

"I really did," he says with an answering smile. "But I missed by a mile. Still, over the years, he would show me the scar from the injury. Every time it was in a different place."

"Sounds like a good guy."

"The best. And he was right about baseball. It gave me something to focus on. I loved the rules. The sense of order. But also how fast things could change. We'd go to games together and he'd make me keep score. You know how that is."

I nod. "You can't take your eyes off the field for a second or you miss something."

"It quieted my brain. Gave me something more interesting to do than get into trouble."

"Sounds like you spent a lot of time with him."

His eyes drift with his memories. "As much as we could.

He's the one who came to every one of my games—who took me to watch the Diamondbacks. We spent every spring break traveling around and catching preseason games."

"Not anymore?" I ask.

"He died of cancer last year."

"Oh, shit," I murmur, realizing that's why he's carrying his uncle's key chain. "I'm sorry."

He works his fingers around the metal, his thumb rubbing over the M. "He fought hard. Lived a year longer than the doctors expected, so I try to be grateful for that. And at least he died before I got hurt. That would have killed him faster than the cancer."

Both of us look at his scars. "How did it happen?" I ask. "Was it during the playoffs?"

"I wish. Maybe it wouldn't feel so senseless that way." Frustration bleeds through every line of his frown. "The truth is that I fell during a game of pickup basketball. I was charging the hoop against a guy fifty pounds heavier." He mutters a curse under his breath. "All these years, I did everything right to protect the arm. Always watched my pitch counts, never threw on short rest. I was playing the long game from the time I was ten."

"Even though most guys don't make it?"

His chin tilts up as his burning gaze locks with mine. "I hit ninety-two on the radar gun the week before the accident. I wasn't going to be like most guys."

I can't look away. Though I've heard similar words from ballplayers before, I've never believed them as much as I believe Garrett. It pierces my heart, but also makes me want to keep my distance. He's as focused as my dad. "I'm sorry," I say. The words surface from a place deep down. A place that still remembers how much broken dreams hurt.

His nod is slight, but our gazes stay locked. It's as if more passes between us than simply words. "I'm not giving up.

Uncle Max never gave up on the things he loved. He taught me to do the same. He always said you didn't have to be strong, tall, fast, or smart to play baseball. You just had to have one out of the four."

I find myself nodding. There's truth to that. "Is that why you love the game so much?"

"It's reason number nine."

"Number nine? You've got a list."

"All the way to one hundred."

My jaw drops. "Even when I loved the game, I couldn't have come up with a hundred."

"Ah," he says, cocking an eyebrow. "So you did love it."

"That was a long time ago."

"You still love it. You've just forgotten."

I hide behind a look of exasperation. "Please. You think you're right about everything."

"I am about this. I'll prove it in two words: Cracker Jacks." His grin erases the sadness. "How do you not love Cracker Jacks? Would we even know about them if not for baseball?"

I roll my eyes for effect, but he's managed to make me smile. "Okay, I'll give you Cracker Jacks. That's one good baseball thing."

"Two things. Superstitions," he reminds me. "By the time we're done with this contest, I'm going to have reminded you of all the reasons why you still love the game."

His eyes spark with so much expectation, I almost wish he could. "Save your energy, Blondie. Baseball is not part of *my* plan. Let's focus on how to win this thing."

"You should come over to Seger's house tomorrow night," he says suddenly.

"What?"

"Jason Seger. A few of us are going to watch the Diamondbacks game. Scottie will be there. We can ask him about the interview."

"A baseball party?"

"You worried about being seen with ballplayers? You can wear the dino costume if you want to come in disguise." He pulls out his phone. "Come to think of it, I got a great picture of you waving those cute, fuzzy hands."

"You did not!" I may not chase popularity, but that doesn't mean I want to commit social suicide two months before graduation.

He flips through a screen I can't see. "I wonder if it's too late to get this in the yearbook."

"Garrett!" In one quick move, I slide out of my bench and into his. I lunge for his hand.

"Hey!" He twists away when I grab hold.

He lifts his phone higher. I find the skin under his arm and tickle.

He shrieks and his elbows flap like chicken wings.

I'm shaking with laughter, but it worked, because I've got a hand on his phone. I grab it free and escape to my side of the booth. "Now who's giggling?"

"You tickled me!" He's still laughing, his big shoulders shaking with it.

"The great Garrett Reeves is ticklish."

He bites his lip as he leans in. "You think I'm great, huh?"

"I think you're a pain in the ass."

"Nah, you like me."

"Never! And stop flirting."

Laugh lines deepen around his eyes. "It's okay, Walters. I like you, too."

"Hello?" I say drily. "More flirting." I wiggle his phone, my cheeks hot, my mouth hurting from trying not to grin like a complete fool. "Now how do I open this?"

He laughs again and gestures to his phone. I hand it over and watch as he messes with it a second. When he hands it back, it's open to his contacts page. "Give me your phone number. I'll text you the address for tomorrow."

I tense, my fingers hovering over the screen.

My number in Garrett's phone? Am I really doing this?

I have forty-two contacts in my phone. With a quick swipe of my thumb, I scroll through a list of names. It looks like he has forty-two just between A and B. And most of them are girls. I'm adding my name to a list of names.

I don't want to be on Garrett's list. I don't want to know he can call me.

I don't want a day to come when I want him to call me.

But I add my contact info and hand the phone back, shaking my head at myself. "I doubt I can go."

"For the contest, Walters. That's all." We both stand. "And if you can make it, you should bring Mai. Anthony will be there."

I gasp. "That's bribery."

His grin agrees with me 100 percent. "See you tomorrow."

Chapter Fifteen

"I'm having an existential crisis."

I drop my purse on the carpet of Mai's bedroom and sit on her unmade bed. "I'm not sure what that is," I say.

"I'm not sure, either. I just heard it on a TED Talk." Sure enough, there's a man frozen on her computer screen, the TED background behind him.

"Well, can your crisis wait?" I ask. "I have something important to talk about." I've just come from the café and I'm still scrambled from the meeting with Garrett.

She spins in her desk chair. "An existential crisis is extremely important."

"Fine. Your crisis first." I lie back, loving the softness of her bamboo sheets.

"I'm working on my valedictorian speech. Would you say you're the author of your own ambition?"

I lift my head so I can see if she's serious. She is. "What?"

"This man thinks we're little better than robots, going through life doing what other people think we should do."

"Why are you watching that?"

"I started out watching graduation speeches and ended up with this." She leaves her chair and climbs up beside me, pulling the pillow under her head. "I always thought I had things figured out."

"Because you do."

"I know where I'm going and what I'm doing, but how do I know it's what I want? I'm seventeen. My mother still packs my lunch."

"I've known you for four years. You've always wanted to be a microbiologist."

"Because it's what my parents do."

"Calling bullshit," I say. Above me is a dark smoke stain from a science experiment Mai conducted when she was thirteen. "If you weren't into science, you wouldn't have signed up for all those extra camps and winter intensives. You wouldn't have picked one of the top universities in the country."

She sighs, and I know she's thinking back to what she doesn't actually remember. An orphanage in a small country in South America. A little girl with glossy dark hair and brown skin. A mix of features from everywhere and ties to no one anywhere. "They picked me out of all those babies. They brought me here and gave me every opportunity. How could I not push myself?"

I tilt my head to look at her. "You seriously want to do something else?"

"Honestly? I never thought about it until I was asked to give the valedictorian speech."

"Is that what's going on? Or does this have something to do with Anthony?"

"No. Well, yes. Maybe."

"I think that covers all possible answers."

"He's a part of it," she admits. "He's part of what I'm not choosing."

I shift to face her, and she curls on her side so our knees are touching. Moving around as much as I did, it was never easy to make friends. I usually didn't bother trying, but with Mai I didn't have to. We just fit from the first day we met at the school library. I'm not sure when we had our first heart-to-heart, but I know we'll never grow too far apart to have our last.

"When you choose one thing, it means you don't choose another," she says.

"I guess. But that's how it is with everything, right?"

"I just hadn't thought about it that way." Her brow wrinkles the way it does when she's working through a math problem. "When you think about it like that, it's scary. Or maybe it's sad. Knowing there are things you can't have."

I hate to see her second-guessing herself. "I wish they'd never asked you to give this speech."

"I know. I'm making too much out of it when no one's going to listen anyway."

"I'm going to listen."

She folds her hands under her cheek. "And what would you like to hear?"

I pretend to think. "Maybe something Yoda would say. Yoda is very inspiring." I deepen my voice. "The force will guide you. If not, a general business degree good will be."

"That's a terrible impression." She rolls to her back again, and I do the same. I smile at the stain on the ceiling. It's a sad smile, though, because I'm going to miss Mai so much. I'm going to miss staring at that blot on the ceiling with the only friend who feels like family.

But I'm in denial about her leaving, so instead I say, a little too loudly, "Now! Can we move on to a different existential crisis?"

"Absolutely."

I tell her about my meeting with Garrett. Except for the

tickling, I-like-you part. "He wants me to go to this thing tomorrow night," I finish. "To talk to this guy, Scottie."

"Why can't he talk to Scottie?"

"Exactly."

"You don't have to go."

"That's what I said."

"And what did he say?"

"He said Anthony Adams would be there."

She shoots upright.

"He's using your crush to get me to do his bidding," I say. "It's selfish and manipulative. And we're not falling for it."

"Are you sure we're not?"

"Mai, really?"

"Why can't we go? It would help you for the contest."

"Because I don't want to be around him. I don't like him."

"Calling bullshit. You don't want to be around him because you're afraid you *do* like him." Her eyes challenge mine, and all I can do is groan and flop back to the mattress. Her voice softens. "Would that really be so awful?"

"Yes!"

As we settle into silence, deep reverberating music floats up. Mai's mom and dad must be working in the downstairs office. It's meditative music that's supposed to help the brain focus. It would put me to sleep, but then again, they're both geniuses. Seventeen years ago, they went to Guyana to study water safety, taking their infant son with them. Eighteen months later, they came back with baby Maya, too. What if they had picked a different baby? She wouldn't be here and neither would I. I shudder over the stream of my thoughts. If you think about choices for too long, you can end up never making another one again.

"I think we should go," Mai says. "You can see Garrett in his natural environment, surrounded by pretty girls and a sense of entitlement. You'll immediately remember why you hate athletes."

"And what will you do?" I ask.

"See if I can get my thighs around Anthony Adams' neck again."

"You're such a big talker."

"I am," she agrees. "Another one of those choices I'm making."

The hint of sadness in her voice convinces me. I'm still not sure what's going on with Mai, but I'm hoping it's just the stress of graduation. I'm sure it's why I'm feeling off, too.

Chapter Sixteen

"This is weird, isn't it?" Mai asks. She's sitting beside me in the truck, and we're both staring at Jason Seger's house across the street.

"The two of us parked here like creepers? Yeah."

"I mean the two of us at Jason Seger's house for a party."

"It's not a party. It's a baseball game." As if to prove that, I do a quick glance at my faded jeans, plain black tee, and comfy sandals. My hair is freshly washed, but it's pulled back into a ponytail. No one, not even Garrett, could think I dressed up for this.

Mai is wearing a sleeveless tuxedo shirt over her leggings. She's beautiful and also a little scary the way she's staring at the house. "I've had one class with Jason Seger. It was ceramics my freshman year and I don't think I said a word to him."

"We don't have to go in." I check the clock on my dashboard. The Diamondbacks game started an hour ago. If we sit here for another hour...

Mai pulls out her phone and takes a picture of the house.

"What are you doing?"

"I want a visual record."

"Of a house? You know what we're going to find inside? A bunch of guys sitting on a couch watching baseball. You'll be bored in five minutes."

"Josie." She blinks at me. "I was just studying the chemistry of a shrimp. This is not boring."

"You love chemistry."

"Right now, I love a couch full of baseball players." She tucks her phone away. "Will they have Cheetos? I've always wanted to go to a party with Cheetos."

"You've been to parties before, Mai."

"When I was little. And I've been to your birthday parties, which are always movie-bingeing-sleepovers and have never included Cheetos."

"I don't like how they get all over your fingers."

Her expression says, *My point exactly.* "I've been to book club parties and parties for National Honor Society, Language Honor Society, and Science Honor Society. None of them with cheesy puffs."

"I'm going to buy you a bag of Cheetos," I say. "I'm feeling like a terrible friend."

She pops open the truck door. "We should go in."

My heart yo-yos uncomfortably. I'm more nervous than I should be, which makes me even more nervous. Laughing with Garrett, teasing, *tickling*—it left all kinds of holes in my defenses. I keep trying to rebuild and then his words topple them again.

It's okay, Walters. I like you, too.

"Oh, and call me Killer tonight," Mai says, pulling me out of my thoughts.

"Killer?"

"It was my nickname at the pool."

I shake my head, releasing an exasperated sigh. "When

you let loose, you go all out."

She stops at the open front door, only a flimsy screen in our way. Voices spill out from inside.

My heart takes another trip up and down my throat. "Hello?" I knock gently on the metal part of the screen.

Mai doesn't pause. She pulls it open and heads into an empty living room. The noise is coming from the family room just beyond. As predicted, there's a couch filled with guys, including Anthony. A huge L-shaped sectional of chocolate leather. There are a few girls here, too—I recognize them from school but don't really know any of them. A coffee table is covered in soda cans and bowls of popcorn and chips. Garrett is lounging on one of the floor pillow chairs at the far side of the room. He's talking to a brunette who's laughing at whatever he's saying. She's pretty in a way that makes me feel oversize and awkward.

"Hey," someone says, and I shift my gaze to a redheaded guy on the couch who doesn't look sure if he's welcoming us or not. He's one of the players, but he spends his time on the bench, so I don't know his name.

"Jason, right?" Mai says. "Garrett invited us."

"Killer!" Suddenly, Anthony is sitting forward, a surprised smile flashing white against his tanned skin.

We've just walked into an alternate universe.

Garrett looks up at that moment, and I feel his attention like a heat lamp. I ignore him, though, and study the TV as if I actually care. D-Backs are down by four. Sixth inning. I'm proud of my ability to absorb the score while following Garrett's every move as he unfolds himself gracefully from the floor. Which should not be humanly possible. He picks his path toward us while the dark-haired girl follows his progress. She's not the only one wondering who we are.

"Glad you guys made it." He turns to Anthony. "You know Mai?"

"Show some respect," Anthony says. "That's Killer, the world's best pool chicken player."

Mai raises one eyebrow in acknowledgment, but I can feel her vibrating next to me.

"This is Jason," Garrett adds. "It's his house."

"We had ceramics together," Mai says. She points to an ugly gray bowl on one of the shelves surrounding the widescreen TV. "I have the exact same bowl."

Jason laughs. "Freshman year. I remember you. You organized the Empty Bowls project. Dude," he says to Garrett. "She got the whole class to make soup bowls and we sold them and donated the money to a homeless shelter."

"You should have donated that one, too," Garrett says, pointing to the bowl on the shelf.

"That's art, man."

Garrett slugs him playfully on the shoulder, then says to me, "You missed most of the game."

"Diamondbacks are getting killed."

"Come on, ye of little faith. Plenty of time for a comeback." He points us to the kitchen. "Sodas and water are in the cooler. You guys want something?"

Mai leads the way and pulls two waters from the cooler and hands me one. She pauses at the orange bag on the counter. "They have Cheetos."

"She doesn't get out much," I tell Garrett as Mai grabs the bag and heads back toward the TV. I watch her, suddenly anxious. Mai's always been oblivious to guys. This crush is so out of character that I'm not sure what she expects will happen. I don't want her to end up hurt—don't want her to fall for a guy just because he's hot and calls her Killer. I've seen Anthony in full-flirt mode all year. For him, Mai is one more girl. But for Mai, it's her first crush. That can be intense.

Anthony nudges Evan to make room and Mai sits down, getting swallowed up between big bodies and deep leather.

"This was a bad idea," I mumble.

"Mai can hold her own."

"She can't. She talks big, but she's not used to this kind of thing."

Garrett frowns as he rests one hip against the counter. "What kind of thing? TV? Hanging out with friends?"

There's a sudden burst of laughter from the general vicinity of the couch where Mai is sitting. I take in the room—really take it in—and I don't know what I'm expecting. Mom told me stories about baseball parties. About beer and pot and sex. I saw signs of those things at stadiums growing up, too. Comparatively, this gathering does seem pretty tame. There are seven guys and six other girls—four of them, including the dark-haired girl Garrett was talking to, who have taken over the floor cushions by the back patio door.

"I'm not saying we don't have assholes on the team," Garrett says. "With a roster of twenty, there are going to be a few. But these are my buddies—most of them I've known since elementary school. They're good guys. Even if they aren't the brainy-elitist gigglers you usually hang with."

I burst out in a surprised laugh.

Garrett grins, the warmth in his eyes kindling an answering heat in the pit of my stomach. He pushes off the counter. "Come on. Let's talk to Scottie."

Chapter Seventeen

Garrett leads me to a bedroom at the end of the hall. There's another TV and beanbags. Three guys holding controllers are battling it out, fingers clacking over the intermittent cries and curses. Cyborg-looking creatures race across the screen.

There's an explosion on the TV and then a fist pump by a guy with curly brown hair.

"Scottie," Garrett says.

The victor tilts his head back. Along with the hair, I see freckles and glasses with black frames.

"Andy!" I say.

"Josie!" He sounds as surprised as I am.

"You guys know each other?" Garrett asks.

"He's in my calculus class. Why'd you say his name is Scottie?"

"It's what we call him."

"I made the mistake of saying I was born in Scotland," Andy says. He gets up, dropping his controller on the beanbag. "I heard you took over from Nathan in the booth. I've been meaning to ask you about it. I didn't know you were a baseball fan."

"I'm not."

"She is," Garrett says. "She's just forgotten temporarily."

"I grew up with the game," I tell Andy, who still looks confused. "What about you? How did the smartest guy in my hardest class end up as the baseball lackey?"

Andy's brows shoot past the edge of his frames. "Is that how you described me?" he asks Garrett.

"I said baseball god."

Andy laughs. "Blame it on my mom. She's got a rule. I've got to participate in one club and one sport every year." He holds out skinny arms. "The sport thing is a challenge. I stumbled on the idea of baseball lackey and Mom said yes, so here I am, four years later."

Garrett and I exchange a look. Not the drama we were hoping for.

"You sure baseball isn't your dying sister's wish?" Garrett asks.

"What?" Andy scratches at his jaw. "I don't have a sister."

"How about an immigrant grandfather who fought in two wars to come to America to play baseball and breed a love of sport in his grandson?" I ask.

His eyes flicker from me to Garrett. "Yeah, uh. I'm going back to my game." He gives me a nod. "See you tomorrow in class."

"See ya."

Garrett and I turn back to the hall. "That was disappointing," I say.

"Extremely."

"Maybe one of the other guys?"

There's a cheer from the living room. Garrett perks up. "A comeback!"

"No way."

I follow him to the family room, and sure enough the

D-Backs have scored two and are threatening to score two more.

"What did I tell you?" he says.

"They're going to choke."

He laughs, and I know I shouldn't like it so much when he laughs. When I'm the one who makes him laugh.

I search for Mai—she's not on the couch and neither is Anthony. I spot them outside, sitting around a table on the back patio.

"Come on, we'll take the floor chairs," Garrett says.

"They're occupied."

The brunette is still there, talking with a friend. Probably waiting for Garrett.

"I'll introduce you. That's Annette and Kim."

"Your ex?"

He nods. "She'll move. She doesn't care about the game."

"No, I'm not—"

But he grabs my hand, shocking me into silence. His fingers are warm, the palms calloused as he draws my hand in tighter. He does it so matter-of-factly, I let him. As if I need help climbing over a few legs. As if we hold hands all the time. As if he's mine. And I'm his.

Oh, jeez.

I reel in my thoughts and drop his hand. He's already making introductions.

"I don't think you guys have met yet. Annette and Kim, this is Josie. Josie, this is Annette and Kim."

"Hi." I wipe my tingling palm against my leg.

"Hey," they say in unison.

I give Kim a quick smile, but Annette is the one I want to study. She's pretty but not all done up, which is what I pictured when Garrett said he'd had a girlfriend. Her brown hair is lighter than mine and tied back in a messy knot. She's dressed almost exactly like I am, except her jeans are darker and her shirt is white. Now that we're face-to-face, she does look a little familiar. "I think you had a locker near mine last year."

"I've definitely seen you around." Her smile is wide and friendly.

How did she and Garrett date for a year and stay friends? That almost never happens—not at our school. Another way Garrett doesn't fit the mold of the ballplayers I grew up around. A lot of them were good-looking and charming but also self-centered assholes. Or maybe that's just the guys Dad hung around. Guys like him.

"You don't mind giving up your spots, do you?" he asks Annette. "D-Backs are about to go on a run, and I've got a bet with Josie. She's my new color commentator for the contest."

"What happened to Nathan?" Kim asks.

"Josie happened to Nathan."

Annette rolls her eyes, but they both hold up a hand and Garrett pulls them to their feet. Annette's legs seem to go on forever. It probably takes her an hour to shave them. I decide to feel sorry for her. All that time lost.

"What's the bet?" one of the guys asks.

"She has to wash my car if we win."

"I do not," I say. "He's lying."

The guy laughs and shifts to make room for Annette and Kim on the couch. "I'm Cooper, by the way."

"I know who you are. You're the catcher." His brown hair is wavy without a baseball hat on, but I recognize the scraggly fuzz on his chin. "That was a nice throw down you made Thursday."

"Thanks. I heard you gave me some love on-air." He grins. "My grandpa lives in Chicago and listens to the broadcasts. Says you guys are really in sync. You going to stick with it?"

"Yes, she's sticking with it," Garrett answers.

I'm introduced to Eddie and Tucker and Evan, along with two girls I think are part of the cheer squad, Steph and Cassie. My head is spinning with all the introductions and compliments. I wasn't expecting everyone to be so nice.

Then the game is back on, and in a crazy string of plays, the D-Backs tie it up. There are cheers and claps and beefy boy bodies rising so everyone can high five everyone else. Optimism pulses through the room. The D-Backs weren't expected to be good this year, and so far they're playing like they are. But I've been around baseball long enough that I've seen this, too.

"Settle down, boys," I say to the room in general. "They haven't won yet."

"Who is this girl?" Cooper says to Garrett. "What's she doing with her mouth all over my team?"

"Watch it," I say, "or I'll broadcast the fact that you wink when you're up to bat."

"I do not!"

"Yeah, you do," Tucker says. He could be Cooper's twin except he doesn't have the chin fuzz.

"It's cute." Garrett makes a smoochy sound and everyone busts up.

I'm laughing, too, when my gaze meets Garrett's. It's a shared moment of fun—nothing more. Except...there's a warm, tight feeling in my chest that says, *you like these guys, Josie. You like* this *guy.*

"You know who we could interview?" he says suddenly. I swear I can see the idea traveling from his brain to a grin as slow and sweet as the Manuka honey Mom adds to her tea.

My heart reacts without even knowing why. "Who?"

"Mai."

"*My* Mai?"

He laughs. "Bet that was a fun name in middle school."

"She didn't get that evil glare without practice. But that's a terrible idea. Mai knows nothing about baseball."

"That's the point." He shifts his chair closer. The edge of his armrest bumps mine, and his shirt brushes against my shoulder. My shoulder wants more. I edge back. "I was thinking about what she said in the car the other day. About how it isn't fair that pitchers stand on a mound. It got me thinking."

"About dumb questions?"

"About dumb rules. Is there another sport with as many rules as baseball? And ones that seem random. Like the pitching mound. It's ten inches higher than home plate, but it also has to be sixty feet and six inches from home plate. Who came up with that?"

I nod as his idea sparks my own. "We use Mai's questions as a way to explain some of the arcane rules of baseball."

"And do a little social commentary on recent rule changes."

"Like the no-pitch intentional walk!" I swivel, crossing my legs as I face him. "It doesn't have to be just Mai. We can find plenty of clueless kids—have them ask their question on video, then cut back to us for the answer and an explanation."

Our eyes lock, and the tremors are back, sparking through nerve endings I didn't even know I had.

"It would mean spending more time together," he says. "Asking questions. Doing research. That's probably against your rules."

I smother a smile. "Are you making fun of my rules?"

"Would I do that?" His face is the picture of innocence. Up close like this, I decide he's less overwhelming. Easier to handle one feature at a time. Eyes. Nose. Mouth. A tiny scar at the edge of his eyebrow. Nothing all that special. "I'm making a new rule. No making fun of the rules."

"Why do you get to make all the rules?"

"Because I'm the brains of this operation."

His smile sends tingles down to my clunky sandals. "Does that mean you like the idea?"

"It means we might win this thing."

There's a sudden loud cheer and we both turn to see what happened.

"Walk off double," Tucker cries. "D-Backs win."

"How about that?" Garrett says. He pushes to his feet for the replay.

I scramble up, too, and Garrett turns to me with the grin I'm expecting. "And that's another thing I love about baseball. Number seventeen on my list. Comebacks."

"Yeah, yeah," I say. "Study the stats, Blondie. Comebacks only happen about thirty percent of the time." But I can't hold on to my scowl—not when he's smiling at me like that. Like he's having the best time. Like we're having the best time *together*.

A flush burns through my cheeks. *He's a baseball player.* Even if he is a nice guy, he's as wrapped up in the game as my dad ever was. Nothing and no one will ever be as important. And I know better than to be feeling like this. "I gotta go."

"Already?"

"School tomorrow." Weak, but also true.

"You want to ask Mai if she'll do it for us?"

"I'll ask her later." I turn to the patio door and tug open the sliding glass.

She's sitting on a cushy chair facing Anthony. She's got the bag of Cheetos in one hand and her feet on Anthony's lap. His hand is resting on her ankle. It's a strange sight— her petite foot and his rough fingers, the thick metal chain hanging from his wrist. I'm struck with the thought that neither of us is safe.

"We need to get going," I tell her.

She pulls her feet down and slides them into her flip-flops. Her fingers are bright orange as she leaves the Cheetos in Anthony's lap. "See you at school."

"I'll look for you," he says, smiling.

Talk about alternate universe.

Garrett walks us to the door. "See you tomorrow."

"Yep, see you tomorrow."

When we reach the truck, he's still standing there, silhouetted by the screen. My heart pounds like it wants out. Like it wants *him*.

I look at my best friend and sigh. "I'm in deep shit, Mai."

She nods. "So am I."

Chapter Eighteen

The next morning, I make my usual late entrance to the kitchen and find Mom standing at the counter, sipping coffee and looking through her calendar.

"Sleep well?" she asks. She watches as I head for the fridge and the orange juice. If she was worried that a night with the baseball team would change me, she has to be relieved. I generally pull on whatever tee is on top of the stack, but today I purposely chose my vintage Orange Crush that ought to be burned. It's so faded, and does anyone really look good in orange? But I'm convincing her—and maybe myself—that I'm not dressing to impress anyone else.

"You okay?" she asks.

I pause to sigh. Loudly. "Are we playing Twenty Questions again?"

"I didn't ask you twenty questions last night, and for the record, you gave me no answers."

She'd been waiting when I got home and stopped an episode of *The Great British Baking Show* to ask, "So?" Even curled on the couch in pajamas, she still managed to look tense. Mom went through her own personal hell with my dad; I'm sure she was reliving all of it while I was at Jason's house. She doesn't want me to be a part of that world—neither do I. Yet there I was, and the worst part of it was I had a good time.

I had a good time. With baseball players.

A baseball player.

I pull a glass from the cabinet. Shocking, yes. Unthinkable two weeks ago, yes. But it was one effing baseball game on TV. I know who Garrett is and what he wants. I know what *I* want. This is a convenient arrangement for us both with an expiration date. Like a library book. You have fun while you're reading but when you reach the end, the book goes back to the library.

"There isn't anything to tell," I say. "It was a bunch of guys watching baseball and girls talking about people I don't know. Mai had Cheetos, which was probably the most exciting part of the entire night."

"And Garrett Reeves?"

I pour juice in the glass, splashing a little on the counter. "You remember his name, huh?"

"I listened to one of your broadcasts online."

My breath catches. "You did?"

"You two are a good team."

I drag a finger through the juice on the counter and lick the tart orange flavor. "We are. On the air."

"And off the air?"

I meet worried brown eyes. "Honestly, Mom. He's a decent guy, but all he cares about is a future in baseball. I'm not going down that road. I know better."

"I thought I did, too." Her eyes get that unfocused, distant look. "I knew who your dad was before we met. He was the school's star athlete and the girls were all crazy for him. But not me. I was more serious, focused on school. Then one day, I was walking back from the library during the middle of class.

Your father was hanging out in the hall, ditching. I turned my nose up at that, until the minute he jogged to my classroom door and held it open. The way he looked at me...something in his eyes made me feel different. Special. My heart jumped so high in my throat, I couldn't even say thanks."

I shift to face her. "You never told me that before."

"Because it sounds ridiculous. One look and I'm suddenly enamored?" Her smile is wry. "I told you we met in high school."

"You said he invited you to a game."

"He did. He was waiting outside the door for me when class ended. He walked with me to lunch, sat with my friends, ate half my French fries and had all of us laughing. Asked me if I'd come to the game that afternoon."

"And he hit three home runs."

She nods. "I was his blue Gatorade. He had to have me at every game after that or else he didn't feel right. It was heady at first. Made me feel important and...necessary. I mistook that for love."

I rub my toe at a spot of juice on the floor. "He never loved either one of us, did he?"

She's quiet for a long moment. "Not the way we deserved. His heart was already too full of other things."

She doesn't need to say baseball.

It's nothing I don't already know, and it only stings a little. Barely a nick on the toughened outer wall of my heart.

"You'll do better than I did," she says. "You'll find a soul mate worthy of you."

I know I'm supposed to want a soul mate—the one guy I can't live without. But I don't want that. I don't ever want to love someone that much. I want a guy who can't live without *me*. Someone who loves *me* best.

I down the juice and set the glass in the sink. "I'd better go."

Her nod is filled with all the other things she knows I don't want to hear right now. "We'll do prep around five p.m. today. That work for you?"

"Sure." Mondays we look at the week's schedule and put together sampler gift bags. I sling my pack over my shoulder. "I'll be home."

"Can we go over the website?" she adds. "I'd love to see where we're at."

I manage to meet her gaze for one long second. "Definitely." When the door closes behind me, I allow my face to fall. Where we are is a very basic template because I can't figure out how to add the features we need. I rub my stomach. Guilt is not a good mixer with orange juice. I really need to find someone to help. On the way to meet Mai, I work out a plan to visit the computer lab.

Mai is in her usual spot, but sipping from a travel mug.

"What is that?" I ask.

"Coffee."

"You're drinking coffee now?"

"I was up late doing the work I should have done while we were at Jason's house."

"You sound happy about it."

"I am. I feel so normal. Staying up to do homework."

It's a sudden relief to stop worrying about my problems and shift focus to Mai.

We head toward school, moving slowly, since Mai hasn't quite mastered drinking and walking. "I'm not sure how to say what I'm thinking," I begin. "I don't want to sound insensitive."

"Since when?"

She gives me a smile, and I have to laugh. I can be pretty blunt, but so can Mai. It's one of the things I love about our friendship. We call each other out on our bullshit, even if it can seem harsh. It gives me the courage to say what I'm thinking. "Are you serious about Anthony?"

She sips from her mug. "I'm serious about climate change. About shrinking polar ice caps and pollution in our waterways. I'm not serious about Anthony Adams."

"Then what were you doing with your feet on his lap?"

"Trying to feel his package."

I stumble as we hit the curb that marks the beginning of school property. The two-story brick building casts a cool shadow across the walkway. A row of droopy palm trees lines the path leading us toward the entrance and a glowing sign announcing HOME OF THE CHOLLA WILDCATS.

"I'm teasing," she says. "We were talking. He's funny." A small smile plays around her mouth. I wonder if she even knows it. "And he's nice." She pauses and adds in a quieter voice, "I like him."

"But he's so different from you. What's he going to do after graduation?"

"He's not sure. He says that's what your twenties are for."

"He needs a whole decade?"

"It's a harmless crush, Josie. I know it can never be more than that. My parents would disown me if I brought home anyone less than a Rhodes scholar. Anthony is a little fun before I graduate from high school. If I don't do it now, what stories will I tell my test tube babies when they grow up?"

"Test tube babies?"

"I'm never going to have sex. I don't see how I'll have time." She sips again and makes a face. "How do people drink this stuff on a daily basis?" She stops to dump the rest in a pile of gravel. "What about Garrett?" she asks.

"What about him?"

"Have you felt up his package?"

"I'm sure it's small in comparison to his ego."

After that, there's no time for conversation because we've joined the masses who are in the process of unloading from the buses. This part of the walk always makes me feel like a salmon flowing upstream. Mai feels it, too, I know, and our thoughts shift into school mode.

There's a lot of pressure when you're special like Mai. Sometimes I'm jealous because she's going to do something that matters and I'm going to be selling skin care. But mostly I'm proud of her. I want her to have fun, but I don't want her to jeopardize her future over a fling.

"Killer!"

Speak of the devil.

Mai turns, and in an instant, the school pressure is gone, shaken off with one flick of her hair. Anthony isn't as tall as Garrett, his build more on the stocky side, but he walks with that same confident swagger. His brown hair is wavy and long enough to reach the frayed collar of his tee. His chin is up as if he wants to look down on the world, but his dark caramel eyes are warm enough to rival the sun as he watches Mai. Watches her as if *she's* the sun.

I'm wondering if I'm reading him right when another voice chimes in and my pulse skips.

"There's my broadcast buddy."

Chapter Nineteen

Garrett walks up with Cooper and Tucker. He's wearing a white V-neck. He should look awful in white with his coloring. And a V-neck. I hate V-necks on guys.

God, he looks good.

His eyes smile into mine. My heart, which a second ago was right where it belongs, is now in my throat, choking me with an unexpected response.

Shit. I'm just like my mother.

Alarm vibrates in the pit of my stomach along with an answering chorus in my brain of *No-No-No-No-No.* I scowl at Garrett. *I cannot fall for this guy.*

"Someone angry at their snooze button again?" he asks in a mild voice.

"Um. I'm late. I have to go." Not smooth, not even true, but I turn, needing to get away. I told myself I was standing on the edge of quicksand—close to trouble but in no danger of falling in. Now I realize I've been sinking for days.

Tucker comes up beside me, and I'm flanked by him and a grinning Cooper, who have no idea that I'm in meltdown mode. "G told us you were named after Joe DiMaggio."

"He was my grandpa's favorite player," Cooper adds. "I got to tell him that—he'll like you even more on the broadcasts."

"I hate my name," I say.

Tucker looks shocked. "But it's perfect for you."

"I think she's perfect for me," Cooper teases.

"Sorry," Garrett says, appearing right beside us. "She doesn't date ballplayers." There's an edge to his smile and something watchful in his eyes that makes me feel too exposed.

"I'll change her mind about that."

"You know what they say," I tell Cooper. "Big ego, small—"

"Josie!" Cooper places a hand over his heart. "I'm insulted. But I'm prepared to prove you wrong any—"

I interrupt. "Save it. Not interested."

Garrett opens his mouth, and I snap, "Definitely not interested."

There's a tiny moment of shocked silence and I realize how harsh that sounded.

Mai's expression says *WTF?*

"I'll see you guys in a few," Garrett says, not taking his eyes off me. "Walters and I need a minute."

"We do not."

Mai gives me a meaningful tilt of her eyebrows and then heads off with the others.

I fold my arms over my chest and face Garrett. I know him well enough by now to know he won't give up until he has his minute. "What?" I say, my eyes avoiding his.

"You mad about something?"

"No."

"Then what's with the attitude this morning?"

"I always have attitude."

"Come on, Walters. No bullshit." He moves closer,

smelling of soap and sun and crackling with barely suppressed energy that has my nerves crackling, too. "That's not how we work, you and me."

I have nothing to say to that because he's right. And because I can't tell him how good he looks in that V-neck and how I'm mad at myself for noticing. For liking him when I swore I wouldn't. For wishing he was anyone but who he is. "I don't want to be late," I mutter.

"I'll walk you."

He's still waiting for an answer, so I give him the first excuse that pops in my head. "I'm tired," I say. "And stressed. I have a lot going on."

"Like what?"

"Like it doesn't have anything to do with you." Unfortunately, my history class is only a few doors down, and I have no choice but to stop.

"Come on," he urges in a singsong voice. "Tell the nice Mr. Reeves what's wrong."

"Is that how you talked to the kids in summer camp?"

"Yes," he says. "But first I had them sit on my lap. Wanna try?"

A smile sneaks out, fighting me until there's no way to hide it.

He smiles back as if I've made his day. I hate how good that makes me feel.

The halls are emptying, only a few kids hanging out by their doors for a few last minutes of freedom.

"I'm serious, Walters," he urges. "Maybe I can help."

"Why would you want to?"

His expression is a little surprised. "Because we're friends." He says it as if it's obvious. As if it's a done deal. As if it's no big deal.

"That's not part of the rules," I say, but it sounds lame even to me.

"Is it really going to kill you to have a friend who's a baseball player?"

"Maybe," I mumble.

He laughs, and I start to feel a little ridiculous. I'm the one turning this into a thing and it doesn't have to be. He's still a library book that's going back on the shelf in a matter of weeks. "I'm just busy," I say. "I told you before we started that I had a lot going on. I'm in charge of designing a new website for our company and I've got nothing to show my mom today."

"You can't handle WordPress?"

I bat my eyelashes in pretend confusion. "Is that like Word, only ironed?"

His smile is crooked and adorable. "There's that unsophisticated wit I know and love."

I stick out my tongue. "I've got a basic template, but I need dropdown menus and sidebars. I can't figure that stuff out."

"Is that all?" He leans against the wall, bracing his weight on one hand. Not only a stupid V-neck but one that's too tight. I can see every one of his ab muscles shift and strain against the shirt.

I'm careful to look directly in his eyes. "I also need secure ordering pages and multiple options for accepting payments."

"I can help you do all of that."

His muscles are forgotten in a momentary burst of hope. "You speak HTML?"

"My mom works in advertising. Half her business is developing websites." He shrugs like it's nothing. "We can do most of it in a couple of hours. How about after school today? My house is a mile from yours. I'll drive you home after."

"Your *house*? I can't go to your house."

"Walters. Really? Are you afraid I'll take advantage of you?" He's looking down at me, all blond and tan and flashing white teeth.

My heart somersaults. "No."

"You think you're so irresistible I won't be able to help myself?"

"No!"

"That if I get you in my room, I'll lose complete control in your presence and—"

"All right!" He's making me feel stupid. And a tiny bit hurt even if I don't want him to like me in that way. "I think we've already established that you're not my type and I'm not yours."

"Did we?" His eyes lazily move up and down all five eight of me. An unwanted flush covers my skin everywhere his gaze touches. When our eyes lock, there's something different… uncertain…in the way he's studying me. "You smell good."

I swallow. "You shouldn't be smelling me."

"No," he says. "I shouldn't be." Then he smiles and whatever was there is gone, like a sound you're not really sure you heard. "I'll see you after school."

Chapter Twenty

Garrett lives in the custom neighborhood where the houses are a little bigger and a lot older. They sit back from the street with big yards and trees that have had time to grow thick and tall. They feel settled. Permanent.

Garrett's walkway is lined with potted flowers and fairy lights. There's even a couch outside the front door. I make a mental note, not that we have room for a couch, but maybe a bench. An old one that's weathered.

My love of vintage isn't just T-shirts. We left almost everything when we moved from Florida and found most of our furniture at consignment stores. Filling our house with older things gave us a history, even if it wasn't our own.

"Come on in," Garrett says when he unlocks the front door. "My mom's at work, so it's just us."

"Your sisters?"

"Both at ASU—they live near campus in an apartment."

A moving shadow catches my eye. "Someone is home."

A small gray cat saunters around the corner of the foyer, meowing loudly.

"There's my girl." He squats by her. She looks at me suspiciously. "This is Wild."

"You named your cat Wild?" I squat beside him.

"Officially she's Wildcat, named for the University of Arizona's mascot because that was where I wanted to play college ball."

"Oh." I glance at him, but he's focused on Wild. Does that mean he's given up on the idea of playing?

The cat sniffs my fingers and then nudges my hand with her nose.

"Demanding," I say, complying with a rub around her pointy ears. "My mom and I might get a cat this summer."

"Before you go to college?"

"I'm taking online courses from ASU, so I'm going to live at home. And before you ask, yes, it's my idea." Wild purrs and gives me greater access to her neck. "What about you? Know where you're going yet?"

"Not sure." His mouth thins with frustration. He scoops Wild into his arms, standing as he rubs her belly. I stand, too. "I told you my dad wants me to come to Dallas. In May, it'll be a year since the injury. He thinks it's time I give up my boyish dreams and get a job." He says the last word like it's a disease. "He's been pushing that since I was sixteen."

"A job?"

"I never had time for one." His eyes meet mine. "You know how it is. If you want to compete in baseball, you got to play summer club and pitch on travel teams. He doesn't get that. He's insisting I spend the summer in Dallas working in his office as an intern. In August, I'm supposed to enroll in college there and get my accounting degree."

Wild meows in complaint as if he's squeezed her too tight. "Sorry, girl," he murmurs, setting her down softly.

"What does your mom think?"

"She's backing him up."

"Even about college? Why can't you stay in Phoenix for that?"

His eyes shift away. "He thinks I need more structure than I'm getting here."

My mind flashes to the math test I saw in his backpack. *Just how bad are his grades?* Instead I ask, "So what are you going to do?"

He starts toward the kitchen. "Still working on that. You need anything to drink?"

"I'm good."

We pass through the kitchen and family room, and into a hallway full of photos. I slow to look—most are family pictures of him, his mom and two sisters. "Your mom never remarried?"

"Not yet. She's dated the same guy for years. He has a daughter who's a freshman in high school so they're waiting until she graduates."

"What about your dad?"

"He got married a year after the divorce. Heather is his wife. She's okay. I have a half brother, Chase, who's eleven now. I don't see him very much."

I slant him a look. "Is that weird?"

He straightens one of the frames. "It is what it is."

I take a few more steps and come to a strip of handwriting on the wall with black slashes and dates. "What's this?"

"My mom used to measure us every year, growing up. She marked our heights and ages along with the date." He points to a fading black marker and I follow the lines down, sinking into a crouch. The penmanship at the very bottom is different. I glance up and Garrett must read the question in my eyes.

"My dad started it."

"You were two?"

He nods. "Felice was six. She wanted to know how tall

she was before a trip to Disneyland. That gave him the idea and my mom kept it up over the years."

The very next line was written by his mom. His next words confirm what I'm thinking. "My dad quit on us when I was three."

Maybe there are no charmed lives—not even the ones that look like they are. I trace a finger up the line of Garrett's history, standing as I do. "But this is cool. One day I want a wall like this."

"You moved around a lot?"

"Never stayed in a place more than two years."

"Must have been hard."

"It is what it is," I say, using his earlier words.

A smile flickers over his lips. "What was it really like?"

I lean against the wall, letting myself remember. "It was hard starting new schools, hard to make friends. But I hung out at the stadiums as much as I could, so it wasn't as if I was lonely."

"You were close to your dad back then?"

"We were a real father-daughter duo for a while." I hate the bitterness that's crept into my voice. "Anyway. I'd had enough of baseball when we moved here. I always liked to read so I joined the school book club for something to do. That's how I met Mai."

"And how you ended up at a baseball game."

"And how I ended up here, shocking as that may be."

"Not shocking," he says with one of his easy smiles. "Fated. Come on. Computer's in my bedroom. You're going to have to brave the Room of Sin."

I roll my eyes. "I'm surprised you don't have that engraved on the door."

"Good idea, Walters."

I'm back on solid ground when he leads me into his room. There are no piles of clothes to climb over, but he does drop his pack next to a desk and quickly straightens the comforter on his bed.

"Oh my God, is that a stuffed bear?" I ask.

He's tucking something under the comforter but he pauses and a second later, turns with it in his hand. It *is* a stuffed bear. He's wearing a Cubs baseball jersey and hat. "His name is Wrigley, if you don't mind." He sets him back on his pillow. "Wrigley belonged to my uncle Max."

My smile fades, but a knot of memory loosens in my chest. "I had a Cubs bear, too. Mine had a batting helmet." I take a look at the rest of his room and realize I had a lot of the same kinds of things. His room is painted a deep blue and covered in posters of the Arizona Diamondbacks and a framed ticket from the 2001 World Series. There's a shelf of baseball bobble head dolls, team pennants, a crate full of baseballs, tattered gloves, and an old wooden Louisville Slugger bat. But what holds my attention are two rows of framed jerseys on the wall behind his bed.

"Are those yours?"

He slides his hands into the pockets of his jeans. "My mom can't throw anything away."

"Yeah, I think my mom has a bunch of mine stuffed in a closet somewhere."

His face lights up. "You played?"

"Oh yeah. T-ball, Pee Wee, Little League, even some club ball. I was good, too."

"That I believe." The look in his eyes warms me. "What position?"

"Pitcher. I had a good fastball."

"I bet you did."

I wait for a teasing smile, but the look in his eyes is sincere. I flush, his appreciation affecting me more than I want it to. I turn my attention away, focusing on the frames as a distraction. I realize they're really shadow boxes, each holding a jersey from a different team. The jerseys are all different sizes—the smallest looks like it would fit an infant. "Very sweet," I say.

"I prefer to think of them as the physical manifestation of a sporting passion."

"Have you been talking to Mai?"

"It's the title of my final essay for English."

I widen my eyes. "Who helped you with the big words?"

He gives me an angelic smile. "The cheerleading team. They do that kind of thing for me."

"Oh, please. You like playing up the stereotypes, don't you?"

"Only because you like believing them."

I hesitate—unsure what to say. He folds his arms across his chest, eyebrows raised, blue eyes challenging, and waits. He knows he's got me. The truth is, I would have believed that about him a few weeks ago. Now, I know better. I know *him* better.

"Fine," I admit. "I might have judged you a little quickly, but I do have a locker near yours, remember? And you were acting the part, too. Ordering me around and shooting your finger gun and flipping back your hair."

"I don't flip my hair," he says. "I ruffle it in a manly way." He demonstrates. "And to be clear, I think what you're saying is that I'm a great guy, and you're sorry for ever doubting it."

"Don't push your luck." But there's a smile under my grumble.

He disappears into the hall and comes back a minute later carrying a chair. He sets it beside the one already in front of the computer.

"The wall of jerseys might make a good backdrop for our interview," I say.

He glances over his shoulder. "Sure. I'll tell the guys you were making excuses to get back into my bedroom."

"Garrett Reeves," I say, with evil in my voice. "You are not going to ruin my reputation."

"You don't have a reputation, Walters. In fact, you're in desperate need of one, but don't worry. You've come to the right place." He clears the desk of a few textbooks and a stack of notebook paper. "You can thank me later."

"I'm not adding my name to your list of castoffs."

"They're not castoffs." He sits beside me. "They're happy runners up."

I gape, torn between laughing and groaning. "Do you say this crap to other girls?"

"Of course not. But I feel like I can say anything to you." He pauses, as if thinking that through. "Is that weird?"

My brain immediately pulls apart what he just said, rearranging the words until they say, *You're special, Josie.* I hide the thought behind a shrug, wishing I could shut my brain off for good. "I say weird shit to you, too."

"You mean you *give* me shit."

His smile eases my tension but does nothing to stop the flutter in the pit of my stomach along with an unbidden thought: *You're special, too.*

I half stand, moving my chair over a few inches. I need a reset. I am not going to think about Garrett like that. He's already in love—with baseball. If I need more reasons to keep my distance, Garrett can recite a hundred of them.

"So you ready for the link to my site?" I ask, pointing to the computer.

He slides his hand over the mouse. "Let's do it."

Chapter Twenty-One

An hour later, Garrett has done more than add some sidebars. He took the template I started, improved the graphics, changed colors and fonts, added features I didn't know were possible and put together a newer, cleaner site. He's got a better sense of design than I do, which he said was obvious to anyone who sees the way we both dress. It was hard to argue since I am still wearing Orange Crush. He's linked our featured products to buying pages and incorporated all the ordering information.

"What title do you want for the sidebar?" he asks.

"Just put skin care for now. It's my mom's niche."

"She has a niche?"

"You have to. Lots of people sell essential oils, so you need a specialty. Cleaning products, or health care, or oils for moms with new babies."

He wiggles the mouse and a box pops up. He starts typing. "So what's your niche?"

"Skin care. I just told you."

"That's your mom's thing."

"Her thing *is* my thing. It's going to be our business."

"You can't take her niche. You gotta pick something that matters to you."

"Like what?" I ask drily. "Essential oils for baseball players? Healing rubs that regrow elbows and cartilage?"

His hand freezes. "They have that?"

"No!" I smack his shoulder, and then point to the computer screen. "Save that before the power surges."

"The power isn't going to surge." But he saves it, and then finishes creating the sidebar. "There has to be something you love about AromaTher. Otherwise it's just a job."

"That's the point. It is a job. And it comes with a paycheck."

He shifts back in his seat. "That's…sad."

"What's sad about doing a job well and getting paid well? Not everyone has a passion, Blondie. If you ask me, you're better off if you don't." I can see he wants to argue, so I speak before he can. "I grew up with a dreamer, and he surrounded himself with other dreamers. I saw it play out a hundred times. All you're doing is setting yourself up for failure."

"Jeez, Walters. You sound like my dad."

"Is he really so bad?" I ask. "He wants you to have something to fall back on if baseball doesn't work out."

"He doesn't *want* baseball to work out."

He's getting angry, and with all I've been through with my dad, I'm having a hard time feeling sorry for him. "At least he wants you with him now. He wants you to come and work with him."

"Now, when it's convenient for him." His eyes narrow. "You think you were the only one without a perfect father? When I was little, my sister Felice was in and out of hospitals. The three of us kids were under seven and my mom was barely holding it together. That's when I needed my dad, and you know what he did? He left. He quit because it was too hard for him."

His words land on my lungs like bricks. In his eyes, I see a reflection of everything I still feel. Anger. Sadness. Betrayal.

"I didn't know. I'm sorry."

He turns away a second, his voice rough. "It's not something I share. Not usually."

The words seem to cost him something. Maybe that's why I'm able to open up. "It was easier for my dad to leave, too. He didn't even consider staying. And when he got to Japan, he told reporters that he would have made it to the major leagues if he hadn't had the distraction of a family."

His head shakes with the same sense of helplessness I feel. "That was one of my dad's tricks, too. Blame it on us. On the kids."

Our eyes meet. We're sitting so close I can see flecks of green in his blue irises.

"How does a parent do that?" he says. "Make a kid feel like they're to blame. What are we supposed to do with that? Feel like shit every time we open our mouths or need a Band-Aid?"

"You think if you're good, if you're worthy, it'll be okay."

"And then they leave anyway."

His words are followed by a heavy silence. The fronds of a bush brush the window glass. The wind must have picked up while I've been here.

"I'm sorry," he says.

"Not your fault."

"I mean that I keep bringing up your dad."

That causes a small smile. "You didn't know."

"Do you…" He pauses. "Do you talk to him?"

The computer screen flashes black and then the screen saver comes on. A swirl of baseballs in a field of green. They bounce from corner to corner, locked in a never-ending loop.

"I haven't in about two years." In my mind I see my

suitcase toppling down the incline. Yankees blue and covered in fading baseball decals. Side over side, dust shooting up as it bounced and skidded and tore out of my life. I'm shocked to feel tears dangerously close to the surface. I blink hard, my eyes stinging.

"I did it again," Garrett says. His hand rises to smooth back loose hairs over my ear. "Sorry, Josie." I shake my head, and I know I should pull away, but I don't. It feels good, this connection. I've never talked about my dad with anyone who really got it.

"It's their loss," he says.

"Damn right."

His eyes roam over my face. I start to smile, but my breath catches as his gaze settles on my mouth.

All the emotion, so close to the surface, slowly shifts, bubbling into something new. Heat rises in me—sudden and hot as if it's been simmering there and the look in his eyes has brought it to a boil.

His thumb moves over my cheek, but it's not comforting.

It's questioning.

It's wanting.

His eyes are so dark I think he's boiling, too. "Josie," he says, barely audible, and yet my name is a roar in my head.

My face lifts, my breath fast, but not as fast as his. Our lips are close. So close we're sharing the same air. So close I can almost taste him.

Can taste how much I want to kiss him.

Want him to kiss me.

Stupid bad idea. Oh God. Kiss me. Please kiss me.

No!

I yank myself back with a sharp breath of sound that breaks the mood. He jerks away. My heart hammers at my own fierce emotions.

His hand, the one I can still feel on my cheek, is rubbing

over his mouth as if wiping away a kiss that never happened. His eyes meet mine, stricken. "I'm sorry. I didn't—I shouldn't... It's not—" He swallows. "I—" He dips his head and runs a hand through his hair. "Shit."

I know exactly how he feels. "Garrett." I lick my lips and then wish I hadn't when the movement draws his gaze to my mouth. My pulse is sprinting. The question I blurt isn't planned or thought out, but it's the only one that matters. "What are you doing on Saturdays? With Kyle Masters."

It takes a second for him to look me in the eye, but he's not surprised, that's obvious.

"You're training with him, aren't you? You're still hoping to play." I hold my breath because his answer determines this. Determines *us*.

His nod is small but certain. "My dad has agreed I can have until graduation to make a comeback. If that doesn't happen, I do it his way. College. Accounting. I can't afford to live on my own."

"What about your mom?"

"She's always supported my dream, but after my grades dropped..." He blows out a long breath. "He's got her convinced this will be good for me. So I'm down to my last shot."

Disappointment curls my fingers into fists. Without admitting it to myself, part of me has been hoping he'd given up on playing again. That he might find a way to stay in baseball without stepping on a field again—without living that life. "What about your arm? The bones might have healed, but what about the torn labrum in your shoulder? That's not an injury most pitchers come back from. How can you create the velocity you need?"

"Not every pitcher relies on speed."

"Oh, so you're going to be the one successful sinker ball expert?"

"Not the only one. Brandon Webb. Derek Lowe."

"There's also Braden Garnet. Ever heard of him?" But of course he hasn't. "He was on my father's Double A team. He messed up his arm, just like you, and tried coming back as a side-arm pitcher. Then he tweaked that to throw submarine style. Ended up wrecking his arm even more, and he never made it back."

"At least he tried."

My voice rises. "Did you even hear what I said? He fucked up his arm. That means lifelong pain. You really want that?"

His jaw hardens. "It's one story."

I want to shake him. "And your arm is holding up?"

He looks away, but not before I see a flash of pain. So *no*, the arm is not holding up. "What's your brilliant Plan E, Garrett? You gonna try pitching leftie next? Is that it? See what you can do to your other arm?"

"Other guys have made the change."

"Are you serious?" Tears hover behind my lids. Angry, frustrated tears because he's never going to give up, and that means everything I'm starting to feel for him is a mistake. "There's always some other guy, Garrett. Always. It doesn't mean it's going to be you."

"But you don't know that it won't be me."

"You have no idea how much I know." My voice trembles, but I don't care. "I lived that life. Rookie ball, Low A, High A, Double A, Triple A. Up and down and down and up. Lying awake at night checking stats on my computer because if my dad had a hit then tomorrow would be a good day. And if he went enough nights without a hit, then it meant we might have to move again."

I close my eyes, swallowing against the rise of other, darker memories. When my gaze finds his again, my eyes don't waver. "I will never get involved with a guy chasing that dream."

He doesn't look away. "And I will never get serious with anyone until I'm done chasing." He slides his chair back, putting more space between us. "What almost happened—it won't happen again."

I nod in agreement. I feel like I was standing too close to the edge of a cliff and barely saved myself from going over.

"Friends?" he asks.

"No," I say. "Partners."

The word expands between us, creating distance. "Partners" is safe. "Partners" is the way we planned it. We're together for the contest, for a chance to prove myself. For Garrett to find a way back into the thing he'll always love more than anything or anyone.

"I should get going," I say. I busy myself with my backpack, though there's really nothing for me to do. I never even unzipped it.

"I'll drive you home. Let me find my keys."

"Thanks."

"And I'll get you a flash drive with everything we did here tonight."

"Thank you for the website, Garrett. You didn't have to do this, and I, well, whatever our disagreements are, I want you to know I appreciate it." He nods, and I follow him out. My heart, safe behind its protective wall, still feels the loss.

Garrett Reeves is a good guy.

Just not the right guy.

Chapter Twenty-Two

People have the mistaken belief that anticipation is a good thing. But really, if you look up the definition, all it says is "the act of anticipating something."

It could be good.

Or it could be humiliatingly bad.

Such as, let's say, when you have an awkward almost-kiss with a guy and then have him drive you home in complete silence while you pretend there's something so fascinating on your phone that you can't possibly look up. When you get out, you mumble a goodbye without meeting his eyes. Without knowing if he was willing to meet yours. And then you see him the next morning in the halls, and do you acknowledge his existence? No. You pretend not to see him.

Now it's three in the afternoon, school is over, and here's what I've discovered: the longer you say nothing, the more you anticipate having to say something.

Even though Mai and I are walking very slowly toward the baseball field, we'll be there in a few minutes. I'm going to be stuck in the broadcast booth with Garrett for two hours. I can't *not* speak to him. Once the first word is out, I'll be fine. It's just that first word.

"Hi," I say.

Mai shakes her head. "Bitchy."

I clear my throat. "Hi."

"Surprised."

I stop walking. The grass is wet around my sandals and seeps into my toes, making me even more irritated. "How did you get 'surprised' from that? I was going for 'casual.'"

"Wrong inflection." She rolls her eyes as if it's so obvious.

"It's not that easy," I say defensively. "The word is only two letters—it's not as if there's a lot to work with." We start again, and I spare a glance at the cloudless blue sky. Where's a big thunderstorm to cancel a game when a girl needs it? "I'm not even sure what I should be going for. Friendly. Bored. Cool. Cold."

"You're going to give a weather report with one word?"

"Don't make fun of me. This is important." We round the fence and head up the metal ramp toward the booth. "What if I get the inflection a little bit wrong and he thinks I'm upset?"

Or that I'm still thinking about a kiss that didn't happen?

She straightens the hem of her sleeveless gray button-down. "You're making too much out of this."

"Of course I am. Because that's what happens with ballplayers. All those muscles in one place turn our brains into gelatin."

"Scientifically speaking, I'm pretty sure that isn't true."

"It turned *your* brain to mush."

She glances out to the field where Anthony is warming up his arm. "But look at those biceps. Can you blame me?"

"Thank you for proving my point." I hesitate outside the broadcast booth, my hand on the door. "Hi," I murmur, refocusing. "Hiiiiii."

Suddenly, the door jerks open and I stumble back.

Garrett appears. His eyes meet mine for one undecipherable heartbeat before we both look away.

"Hey," I say.

"I need another cable," he mutters. He takes off at a run toward the school.

My heart is pounding in my ears, but not loud enough that I don't hear Mai's disappointed sigh.

"We didn't even work on 'hey.'"

The good thing about the missing cable is there's no time to talk before the game starts. Garrett is busy doing his thing, and I'm busy letting him. I study the line-up sheets each team has provided for today's game. I recognize one of the coach's names for Saguaro: Kyle Masters.

It only takes a second to spot him by the visitors' dugout. He's wearing a ball cap and the team uniform, but it's the same guy who came into the deli when Garrett and I were having lunch.

I glance at Garrett and catch him staring at me. A look passes between us. It's one of those: *I-see-what-you're-seeing-and-I-know-what-you're-thinking-and-I-know-that-you-know-what-I-see-and-I'm-thinking.*

Our mouths tighten at the same moment, and we both look away. It feels as if battle lines have been drawn. It's stupid. I have no need to fight with Garrett. If he wants to ruin his arm, then fine. He'll end up like coaches I knew from the minors. Guys with such bad arthritis from overuse injuries that they moved like their joints were made of metal. Probably they were.

Not my problem. I'm keeping my distance. Metaphorically speaking, since he's just finished all the tech work and is now sitting next to me, his stool so close I could spit sunflower seeds ten feet past it. And I was always the worst spitter on every team.

"Welcome, Wildcat fans," Garrett begins. He's wearing a maroon baseball shirt with gray sleeves and his last name stenciled across the back as if he's someone special. *You're not*, I want to say. *I've known a hundred guys like you.* But that's a complete lie, and it makes me sad and angry at the same time. It's such a waste. Another guy chewed up and spit out by a sport that doesn't give a shit.

He leans forward, elbows on the counter. As he runs through the opening routine, introduces the players and covers the team records, his fingers massage along the line of his scar. I don't think he knows he's doing it.

"This is an important game for the playoff situation," I say, focusing on my job. "But it's also a big rivalry. Saguaro is only five miles away, and each school wants bragging rights."

"A lot of these guys grew up playing each other. Don't expect them to be fooled by Scott Kingston's breaking ball."

"Even knowing it's coming, the question is whether they can hit it," I add. "Kingston has one of the best arms in the league."

Garrett stiffens, tension radiating from him. His fingers press into his shoulder, and I wonder if he's reinjured his arm. I try and focus on the game, but we're stilted and clumsy as we get through an uneventful first inning.

"Well, that was good," I say sarcastically.

"You're flat today."

"*I'm* flat? You sound pissed off."

"Well, I'm not. I'm having a great time." He flashes a fake smile and turns up the volume so our microphones are hot.

I bite back a retort. *Let it go, Walters.*

Jeez. Now I'm calling myself "Walters."

We make it through the next four innings the same way. Between changeovers, when Garrett usually turns off the volume, he leaves it on. *Good. Fine. We don't have to talk to do our job, and that's what this is. A job.*

After the sixth inning, Scottie bangs on the wall. "What's up with you two today? Sounds like you're calling a funeral, not a game."

I bang the wall back. "Your funeral, if you don't be quiet!"

There's a muttered *jeez*, which I'm pretty sure I deserve.

Garrett says nothing but quickly lowers the volume. The booth is so thick with tension it's a wonder we're able to breathe. The teams switch positions on the field, and we both watch as if a bunch of guys jogging across grass is exciting stuff.

"So," Garrett finally says. "I jotted down a few ideas for interview questions today. I thought I could get some video on my own."

"And I can use my phone to record Mai asking about the pitching mound. You don't need to be there for that."

"Good." He doesn't look away from the field. "We also need to schedule pictures."

"What?"

"Pictures. I told you about that."

"When you insulted my sandals? I thought you were kidding."

He ignores that. "Can you do it Friday after school? That works for Annette."

"Annette?" I repeat. "Your ex-girlfriend."

"Annette, my *friend*."

Hurt wraps around my lungs, stealing my breath. The way he says her name—the way he says *friend* as if he's reminding me that they are and we aren't. The way they must obviously be more than friends if he's scheduling his Friday around her. Pretty fast work even for him, since yesterday he almost kissed me. "Sorry," I snap. "I didn't know we were working around *your friend's* schedule."

He looks at me, his eyes as cool as glass. "She's going to take the picture. She's into photography and she has a nice camera. Is that a problem for you?"

"No problem."

"Fine."

"Fine." I turn back to the field, but I don't see anything more than the stiff outline of Garrett beside me. "You're the one with the problem."

"What?"

"You've been rubbing your shoulder ever since we sat down, so either you think if you rub hard enough a genie is going to appear, or else you're in pain."

"My shoulder is not your problem."

"You're right, it isn't. It's none of my business if you ruin your arm with your stupid Plan F or G or whatever it is now."

"I'd rather ruin my arm than spend my life in a cubicle."

I bark out a disbelieving laugh. "You think you're too good for a regular job? And when baseball doesn't pan out, then what?" I glance at his backpack and notice it's zipped shut today. "How are you going to get a job as an accountant if you're failing tests?" I pause as a thought flickers in the back of my mind. "Or, is that the plan? Make sure you *can't* work as an accountant?"

His lips press together, but the answer is clear in the defiant glare of his eyes.

"Very mature, Garrett. Flunk out on purpose. That's brilliant."

"I'm not flunking."

"You sure? Or are you *dreaming* that along with everything else about your future?"

His mouth twists. "At least I won't live a soulless life."

"Soulless?" The word stabs at me. Hard. "You think I'm soulless?"

The volume goes up on our mics.

Conversation over.

Stupid jerkface. Tears burn behind my eyes. How could I have thought I liked him for even a minute?

Thankfully, it's a relatively quick game. We lose, three to one.

It only takes a second to grab my backpack and slide my stool in place. I reach for the door, but before I leave, I say, "Bye."

I'm pretty sure it sounds like *Eff you.*

Chapter Twenty-Three

"I'm wearing tutu undies," Ciera says. "Want to see?" Without waiting for an answer, she flings up her pink skirt and yes, she is wearing undies with a fluffy white netting that looks tutu-ish.

"Ciera," I say. "Pull down your skirt."

"But aren't they cool?" she asks.

"I like them," Kate says. "Mine have butterflies on them."

Annie looks worried. "I don't know what's on mine." Her head dives down between her legs to check.

There are only six girls this week, and none of the moms are in the room right now. This one is on me.

"Girls!" I say, and all eyes pop up. "It's not polite to show your underwear."

Ciera drops her skirt. "Why do they make them so pretty if no one else can see?"

I pause for a second, because that's actually a good question. "Well. *You* get to see them. And you know they're pretty."

"But I want everyone to know."

"I understand, but underwear is private."

"Because it covers our private *parts*?" Annie's eyes are wide.

"Yes, that's right!"

"Boys don't have pretty underwear," Julia says. "But they have privates."

I am now officially out of answers. I'm also smiling ear-to-ear on the inside because how can you not?

"Time for cleanup," I announce. "And then cookies."

Immediately, the girls are in motion, scrambling for the art supplies scattered across the table. Thank heavens for short attention spans.

We made our own stories with finger puppets, and it turned out to be a tea party with puppies, kittens, and one monkey. The best part is that for the past hour, I haven't thought about Garrett once. Our argument yesterday left me miserable all day. *Soulless?!* Because I know the dangers of dreaming? Because I'm choosing to keep my feet on the ground and avoid the hard falls? That's smart, not soulless. But I was so worked up, I even snapped at Mai. I wince as I think back to our short conversation this morning.

"No finger gun?" Mai questioned when we saw Garrett before first period and he barely acknowledged me.

"We're not on shooting terms anymore."

"Anthony said Garrett is in a crap mood. He thinks it has something to do with you."

"It doesn't," I said flatly. And then I turned the spotlight on her. "And what's up with you and Anthony?"

"We're still having fun." She shrugged lightly. "I don't want to be one of those girls who kisses and tells. But." She shot me a grin. "I am no longer in danger of reaching the age of eighteen without ever having been kissed."

"Mai—really?" Excitement warred with surprise. She'd been flirty with guys before but never let it get that far.

"He is an excellent kisser."

That's when worry joined the mix. Flirtation was one thing, but was she getting her heart involved? I let my bad mood and every bad memory I had of baseball players crowd my mind. "Probably because he's had a lot of practice." It wasn't fair and wiped the smile off Mai's face. "I don't want to see you hurt," I added, my heart in my throat.

She'd stopped and waited until I faced her. "If you actually looked, Josie, you would see me *happy*."

"Josie, we're done," Ciera says.

I blink, a little surprised to find the art table completely cleaned. "Wow. You guys are fast."

"Do we get a prize?" Annie asks.

"Absolutely!" Some days I have little extras for the kids. Stickers or bookmarks, that sort of thing. Today I grabbed a stack of pencils that were donated.

"Kissing pencils," Ciera says when I hand her one. They're white with red lips running down the barrel. She proceeds to kiss each set of lips.

Julia clutches hers in both hands. "Where's the cookie man?"

Annie nods. "The one from last week."

"Could he have a kissing pencil?" Ciera asks.

My traitorous brain conjures up an image of Garrett's lips. Almost kissing my lips.

Almost, I remind myself. *As in didn't happen, will never happen.*

"No," I snap, more sharply than I mean to. "He wouldn't want a kissing pencil."

"I think he would," Ciera insists.

"Well, he isn't here, and he isn't coming back." I force a smile to soften my words. "That was a one-time thing."

"If you gave him a kissing pencil, he'd come back," Kate says. She's the shyest and the one I've been trying to bring out. She's clutching her pencil tightly over her heart as if she can wish him here.

God. He's got them mooning after him along with half the population at Cholla.

"Cookie time," I deflect with a big smile. Their expressions say, *Fine, we'll take a cookie. But we'd rather have the cookie man.*

Traitors. All of them.

We finish up as the parents wander back in. "Until next week," I say, "find magic in books and in the world."

I'm dragging the throne back to the corner when a familiar face sticks his head in.

"Hey," Bryan says. "How'd it go?"

I hold up a pencil and smile. "These were a huge hit."

"What's not to like about lips?"

His grin is a little flirty, and so are his words. *Is this the next step after origami?* There's an awkward pause because I don't know if I should flirt back. "So what have you been doing this morning?" I ask, taking the safe route.

"Logging in the trade books and updating the schedule."

"Anything good coming up?"

"Actually." He steps closer and leans against the opposite side of the door. He shifts the folders in his arm and crosses one black loafer over the other. He's preppy but not in a stiff, starchy way. And there's something unruly about his curly brown hair that makes me think he has an unbuttoned-down side, too. "There's an author coming next Wednesday."

My heart skips. *We* are *moving on from origami.*

"No dinosaurs or little kids, but the author who's speaking is supposed to be interesting. She writes sci-fi. I don't know if you like science fiction, if you like events, or if you're free..." He trails into silence.

He's obviously a little nervous but mostly adorable. This is what I *need.* Book-loving, origami-making Bryan. "I haven't read a ton of sci-fi, but I like it, and I like events, and yeah, I'm free."

His eyes smile into mine. He has nice eyes. Brown and wide-set. His smile makes me like him even more—it's relieved and hopeful, the same things I'm feeling myself.

"It's at seven. I'm working until then, so maybe we can meet here?"

My heart lifts. "It's a date."

Chapter Twenty-Four

"My hands feel like they're covered in skin."

Mom laughs as she puts the kettle on to boil. "They are."

"Not my skin. Old skin."

"One day your skin will be old."

"And I probably won't like touching it, either."

"Oh for heaven's sake. It wasn't that bad." She sets out all the tea things. Mugs, spoons, metal infusers for the loose leaf and a plate to place them on when we're done steeping our tea. I like our Thursday night ritual. What I don't like is old person skin.

"Why'd you make me do the moisture mask?" I ask. "You know I hate that the most."

"Because you're going to be my partner on May fourth, and you need to be comfortable doing everything."

"There's plenty of other stuff I can do. I don't need to rub all that goo into bony, wrinkled necks."

"Either they're bony or they're wrinkled." Her gaze narrows in disappointment—with me.

"Sorry," I say. "It's just not my thing."

The kettle whistles loudly and a burst of steam announces the water is ready. Mom slides off her stool. "It should be one of your favorite parts of the job—applying products that offer real-time results. Knowing you're helping people."

She pours the boiling water in our mugs and I set my infuser in the water. Instantly, the scent of orange and nettle rises with the steam.

Mom sits again, kicking off her ballet slippers. "What is your favorite part, by the way?"

I wiggle my infuser. "What?"

"Of the job." She leans over the tea, letting the steam mist her cheeks. She claims it's good for the skin. It just makes me hot. "What do you love most? I don't think I've ever asked you that."

I study the swirling leaves. It makes me think of people who read fortunes in tea leaves. To me, they look like wet weeds.

"Josie?" My mom's voice prods me. "What are you thinking?"

"I'm looking for my future in the tea leaves."

"And what do you see?"

A pair of angry blue eyes. "Do you think I'm soulless?"

Her eyes widen. "Of course not. Why would you ask that?"

"Because I don't like applying moisturizer to people's faces. Because I don't care that I'm helping them with skin care issues." I push away the tea, my hand shaking with anger, confusion, and a fear I don't understand. "What's wrong with a paycheck? What's wrong with wanting a career in a business that's growing, that has a solid client base and a great work environment? What's wrong with that?"

"Josie!" Mom looks shocked. "What's going on, honey?"

"Nothing." I stand, frustrated with myself. I was perfectly happy wanting the things I wanted until Garrett made that stupid comment. Now I feel like somehow it's not good enough. Or just not...enough. "Sorry, Mom. I'm tired. I'm going to head to bed early."

"What about your tea?"

"I'll take it with me." But somehow, I don't think this is something that healing herbs are going to fix.

. . .

I'm still in a bad mood after school on Friday. Mai offered to come with me to the field but I said no. I want to take the pictures and get out of here.

Annette and Garrett are already standing by the backstop. They could be posing for a picture themselves. Garrett's got one hand against the fence, a fitted blue Henley shoved up his forearms and muscles on display across his shoulders and back. Annette is looking up at him, somehow leaning in and arching back at the same time. He looks like he's never been happier.

Why not? She probably thinks it's great he wants to keep playing. She can massage his arm every night and kiss his scars.

Annette sees me then, and she shifts away. I notice a camera bag hanging over one shoulder as she smiles and waves a hand.

I still kind of hate her.

When I reach them, Garrett's got his hands in his jeans pockets, but I can feel his tension as if we're tuned to the same station.

"I see you're wearing my favorite sandals," he says.

"I live to make you happy." They're words we might have said teasingly a week ago, but now they sound flat. Empty. The way I feel. "Where do you want us?" I ask Annette.

"Let's try it with you guys in the broadcast booth."

Garrett gestures for me to go first. He's careful not to touch me as he takes a seat on his stool. I move mine a few inches away, and we get settled while Annette unpacks her camera.

She finally takes a look at us and shakes her head. "You're too far apart."

"It's how we sit when we broadcast," I say.

"Nope. Garrett, slide closer."

I hear the stool scrape along the ground, and the hairs on my neck rise to attention.

She takes a look through her viewfinder. "Closer."

Another scraping sound. The leg of his stool is so close I can see it out of the corner of my eye.

"That's better."

Garrett shifts on the stool, and my pulse quickens. "Josie, can you lean right a little? Yep. That's it." She lowers her camera to give us a smile. "You guys fit together perfectly."

No, we don't.

But I can feel that we do. I roll my shoulders, shaking off the thought that if I just leaned back...

His breath is warm on my cheek, reminding me of the other day in his room. I swear I hear him inhale as if he's smelling me. Heat shivers down my spine. "Are you done?" I blurt to Annette.

"I haven't started." She laughs. "You both look like you're delivering bad news."

"We're serious broadcasters."

She snaps a series of pics, shifting one way and then the other. I hold my breath, which is probably why a few minutes feels like an hour. "Let me check and make sure I've got something here." She turns her back to us, finding some shade to review the photos. "Don't move," she adds.

Shit.

A minute passes. Then another. I flash back to the

Haunted House at Disneyland where the walls start to press in.

He clears his throat. "Did you video Mai?"

"I did. She asked the same question she did in the car."

"You want to prepare the answer for that? Or should I?"

"I can do it. I also got her dad on video asking why some baseballs have colored laces."

"Good."

I nod stiffly. All of me is stiff as I try not to move. Not to let an inch of me touch an inch of him. It feels like it's a million degrees in here.

"I tried a few practice questions in the cafeteria. We'll have to plant some so we can cover the topics we want, but I think it'll work."

"Excellent." I sound like a recording of a robot.

"Can you meet after school on Monday to put them together?"

"I've got inventory on Monday."

"Tuesday we have a game. What about Wednesday?"

My throat is suddenly so tight it actually hurts when I swallow. "I can't on Wednesday."

"I mean after your Book Club."

"I have a date."

His breath sucks in, and the tension flares between us. My shoulder blades feel like they're on fire. I don't care what Annette says. I slide off my stool and move to the doorway. Crossing my arms over my chest, I breathe Garrett-free air.

Annette leans in. "Hang on. Don't go anywhere. I've got one I like but I'm trying to see if I can adjust the lighting."

"I'm sure whatever you have will be fine." But she's already hunched over her camera again.

"A date?" Garrett's face is unreadable. "With who? That guy at the bookstore?"

"His name is Bryan."

He leans to his side and rests one hand on the counter, but it's an awkward movement. Or maybe it's that I feel awkward. "You guys are dating now?"

"It's our first date. We're going to an author event."

"Oh. Sounds...fun."

"It does." I ignore the sarcasm in his voice. "Which is why I said yes."

"Great." He stands and shoves his stool under the counter. "Really great."

"Okay," Annette says. "I think we've got a couple that will work." She pauses as she looks from Garrett to me, and her smile vanishes. "What's wrong? What happened?"

"Nothing," he says.

In near perfect unison, we say, "Everything is great."

Chapter Twenty-Five

"Should or must?" Mai demands. "I'm taking a vote."

"I abstain," Avi says.

"Me too," Jasmine adds quickly, raising a hand to make sure she's officially off the hook.

Mai points a finger at me before I can say a word. "No abstentions."

We're sitting in the cafeteria, and I'm munching leftover meatloaf in a tortilla. It's better than it sounds. The four of us have been eating lunch together since our sophomore year when we bonded during a Walk for the Cure. Circling the school track for six hours can do that. Avi and Jasmine are brains like Mai, and though we don't do much outside of school, I'm glad they're both staying in-state for college.

"You first," Mai says to me. There's a plea threaded with the demand. The days are flying by. March is now April, and Mai thought she'd be done with her valedictorian speech by now.

I try to ignore the scent of tuna coming from the next table. "You know what I think. You do what you *should* do and find a career with opportunities and get a job. Dreams are nice, but they don't pay the bills."

"They do sometimes." Avi's gaze is disapproving through square black frames. "Look at *American Idol*."

Jasmine's pointy chin gets a little pointier. "And even if you don't end up on a TV show, you can live a dream and make ends meet. My sister works two jobs but she's managing."

"She's in fashion design. That's a real thing."

"Who gets to decide what's 'real'?" Jasmine is always up for an argument. Her parents really blew the name thing when she was born. Jasmine, in the world of essential oils, is known for its sweet scent and calming properties. *Ha.*

"I just mean that there are actual careers in fashion design," I say.

"There are careers in art and theatre," she retorts.

"But do they pay the rent?"

"So you find roommates. You take odd jobs. You make it work."

Her words take me back to the year after Dad left. I was so lost when he took off. So hurt I couldn't face it for a long time. Maybe that's why it affected me so much when I realized Mom was worried about losing the house. How could I stand to lose one more thing? Jasmine's words stick because they're the truth. You do what you have to do. You make it work. But having been through it, I never want to go through it again. I take a long pull on my drink and nod at Jasmine. "You're right. I'm just saying *I* don't want to live that way."

Mai holds up a finger as she takes out her phone. "Wait a second. I want to record this."

"I'm still abstaining," Avi says.

I smile, glad to put the dark thoughts behind me. "Chicken." I've barely said the word when it feels as if a shadow passes over me. Except...it doesn't pass. It stops. There's an actual shadow hovering over our cafeteria table.

Which is weird because we're sitting inside.

Jasmine looks up and squawks like a bird.

When I turn, Cooper and Jason are standing there, trays in their hands. Tucker and Anthony aren't far behind.

"Hey." Cooper nods with his tray. "Got room?"

Mai's sitting beside me and immediately gestures to Jasmine and Avi. "Move over."

"What?" From the shocked surprise in Avi's eyes, I think it's pretty impressive he's managed a syllable. In all the years we've been eating together, we've never once had four baseball players speak to us, much less want to sit at our table. Their lofty place is normally on the covered patio.

In the time it takes to think this, the guys have already moved in.

Anthony sits next to Mai, Tucker next to him, while Cooper and Jason take the newly vacated spots and Avi and Jasmine shift over, dragging their lunches with them.

"You can't just squeeze in here. I've barely got room," I say. It's not a lie. I've got one butt cheek off the bench.

"You want to sit on my lap?" Cooper offers.

"Ha."

Jason rips the paper off a straw and puts it in a carton of chocolate milk. "So what's it like at the nerd table?"

I kick him in the shin.

"Ow! It's painful at the nerd table."

Mai and I both laugh.

"Careful," Cooper protests. "You don't want to injure our players. At least wait until we've won State."

"Pretty confident, aren't you?"

"We've got the bats working," Jason says. "Anthony's going to have at least ten more home runs. Right, dude?"

"And that's just next week." Anthony grins and leans over the table to high five Cooper. I can't help but notice how close he presses against Mai as he does. How she doesn't bat an eyelash. *Just how much kissing has been going on?*

Jason and Anthony start spewing stats while Mai looks on. I go back to my meatloaf burrito, but it's lost its flavor. I give up when Cooper catches my eye.

"What?" I ask.

"That's what I'm wondering. What's up with you two?" His eyes are serious, worried.

"What are you talking about?"

"You and G. Something happen?"

I start wrapping my uneaten lunch, lowering my face to hide the red creeping up my cheeks. "Why would you ask that?"

"G got pissed when I asked him that, too. But then, he's been in a generally pissed-off mood all week." His fingers play with the scruff on his chin. "He's had a shit year, Josie. This broadcasting thing…it was starting to work. Starting to change things for him."

"It's still working."

"You guys were off yesterday in the booth."

"It happens."

"Happened last Thursday, too." He leans closer. "Listen. Garrett's one of my best buds. And I know we don't really know each other yet, but I like you, Josie. I like the two of you together."

I wipe my fingers on my napkin, my stomach going from mix to churn. Cooper seems like a good guy and it's sweet that he's so concerned about a friend, but this isn't just about broadcasting. Yeah, I'm still hurting over the *soulless* comment, but the scary truth is I could like Garrett way too much. I already do. I have to protect my heart. "What's your point?"

"The point is that whatever is going on with you and Garrett, you need to figure it out."

"There's nothing to figure out."

"Funny," Cooper says, but he isn't smiling. "Garrett said the same thing."

Chapter Twenty-Six

I'm nervous.

Mai says it's normal. It's my first real date, and butterflies are part of the deal. But they're not butterflies. They're the size of vultures, circling my stomach in a death spiral.

This is why I should have dated more. I'm seventeen, and my only experiences are a first kiss at age twelve (followed by a squeeze of my breast and a punch to his gut) and a flirtation sophomore year that ended in a kiss so sloppy I felt like I'd rubbed faces with a bulldog. So basically, I'm starting from scratch. I really want this to go well, but how do you impress someone you don't know well enough to know what they find impressive?

I pull into the Pages & Prose parking lot for the second time today, but it's dark now. The store name is lit brightly and fairy lights twinkle in the trees. It adds to the sense that tonight is a special occasion. I dry sweaty palms on my jeans and try to psych myself up. *I'm going to have a great time!* Immediately, I regret my choice of words.

"Great" has been our little buzzword this week. Garrett's

and mine. Along with "giggler," which is how he likes to refer to Bryan and "jiggler," which is how I like to refer to the girls I've seen hanging all over him.

Has something happened to the world's supply of bras?

Each time I've passed him in the halls—which has been a surprisingly large number of times—he's had some girl with him. Cassie once. Steph once. Annette twice. Two girls I didn't know. *Funny how he has so many friends who are all pretty girls.*

My whole body is tense again just thinking about him. I let out a long breath and "gather my calm," as Mom would say.

Once I'm out of the truck, I give myself a critical once-over. I have no idea what people wear to an author presentation. I borrowed one of Mom's flowy blouses to pair with my favorite skinny jeans. My hair is down and I've done up my face for a change, not that I think Bryan is shallow enough to only care about looks. Not like some people who I'm not thinking about.

Bryan is waiting for me by the front doors. He's dressed the same as I see him every day, but I still find myself looking at him differently. He's not smart, nerdy, book-loving, origami-making Bryan. He's Bryan, my date. (I really need to come up with a new nickname for him.)

He hands me another origami made of purple and brown paper and folded into a...into a... I turn it over in my palm. I'm not sure which way is up, so I keep turning it. "Wow," I say. "This is..." I blink at him. "Thank you."

He looks from the origami to me, and I know I should say something else. But I have zero idea what it is, other than an oval blob with three possible ears. Or tails. Or snouts.

He saves the awkward pause from getting any worse. "You look really nice."

I smile. "Better than the dino costume?"

"A close second." He pulls open the door and gestures me in with a flourish of one hand. "Shall we? I saved us two seats up close."

There are around forty people in folding chairs. The author, a woman with spiky hair and red glasses, is sipping water behind a podium. Bryan's hand skims my back as he leads me to our chairs. It's nice. *He's* nice.

I realize this is partly why I said yes. I want to stop thinking about Garrett. Feeling things for Garrett. I want to feel those things for Bryan—for someone I could actually have a future with.

I settle in as the author begins speaking. I'm not sure what to expect, but it's pretty cool to hear how someone comes up with ideas and makes up an imaginary world. By the time it's over, I'm already checking out the schedule for who else is coming. Mai would like the author of a book about global warming. And there's a meditation expert Mom would enjoy. My gaze snags on the author of a series about mysteries in baseball stadiums. *Nope. Not going there.*

Purposefully, I step closer to Bryan. We're in the line for an autograph and he smiles when I brush his arm. After the author signs the book, we head to the café and join the line waiting to order at the counter.

"What did she sign in your book?" I ask.

He shows me the title page. In black Sharpie she's written: *Pray for the power of plasma.*

"I thought we lived in a scary world," I say, "but I'm feeling much better about our planet now."

Bryan grins. "I told you the book was a little out there."

We get cookies and sodas and then look for an empty table. He points to a booth where a couple is getting up. "How about that one?"

Of course it's the same table I sat in with Garrett. A ghostly image of him smirks at me from the bench.

I'm banishing you, Blondie!

"Perfect," I tell Bryan.

We settle at the booth and I set my origami on the table. "It was cool that the book is about a different universe, but it sounds a lot like our own society. Like how they turned people into slaves with opioids."

"That's what I love about sci-fi," he says. "It gives you a different world to look at, so you can see this one more clearly."

I nod and smile because he's so right and so...smart. *How can I not like this guy?* I reach for my drink and accidentally knock over the origami. "Oh. Sorry!" I set it right again.

"Actually, that's upside down."

Embarrassment floods through me. "It is?"

"It's the spaceship from the book. I figured you would ask me about it."

"Oh. Crap." I smack a hand against my forehead. "I didn't want to be rude, so I didn't ask."

He straightens the spaceship. "It's okay. Origami is a new thing. My mind is always racing, and I read somewhere that it helps if you give your hands something to do."

"Yeah? That makes sense. I should try it. It's probably better than biting my nails." I show him the evidence.

"What's got you worried?"

"School. Finals. What I'm going to do with my life. The usual."

He laughs.

"So what do you worry about?"

"School. Finals. What I'm going to do with my life." His grin is sweet. "A first date." He stretches his hands on the table. My hands are a few inches away, our cookies forgotten. My heart skitters in my chest. I could slide them a little ways... just a little...and he'd meet me halfway.

"I'm glad you could come tonight," he says.

"I am, too." Bryan is the exact right guy for me. Thoughtful. Kind. He's got a good sense of humor and he loves the same things I do.

My throat tightens.

And he isn't the guy I'm wishing was sitting across from me.

The vultures are back, swarming my stomach, my chest, my head. I hate myself right now. I don't want it to be Garrett. I want it to be Bryan. But there's no room inside me for him. Not with Garrett taking up all the space.

I pull my hands back.

Bryan watches until my hands have disappeared into my lap. "So you had a good time, but...?"

"But...it's complicated."

He pulls back his hands. "I don't really do complicated."

"I never used to, either."

"It's okay. That's how it goes sometimes." He stands. "Come on. I'll walk you to your truck."

Chapter Twenty-Seven

When I park in the garage and turn off the car, my phone buzzes with a text.

And another.

And another.

And another.

It gets set to silent while I'm driving, so multiple texts aren't that unusual, but I'm immediately worried something's happened with Mai and Anthony. I free the phone from my purse. My breath catches.

Garrett.

Can we talk?
Text when you're home.
Are you home?
Can I come over?

Five minutes between the first two texts. Then three. Then two. As if he couldn't wait. I press a hand to my chest where my heart is racing. Stupid heart. Nothing has changed. Garrett hasn't changed.

I type: **Yes I'm home. No you can't come over.**

My thumb hovers over the send button.

What does he want to talk about? Why does he want to come over? What if he's been thinking about me the way I've been thinking about him?

The truck's headlights flick off, and it's suddenly pitch black. My heart goes from racing to pounding. My thumb wobbles. Shifts. Deletes.

ME: Yes I'm home. Thought we already said everything.

GARRETT: There in 5

I drop my cell as if it's the phone's fault, then sink lower in the seat. *So, so stupid, Josie.* But my mind is already whirring ahead to what he'll say. Maybe he wants to clear the air? Stop fighting? Maybe he's felt the strain, too, and he wants to be friends again. Maybe he'll say, *I miss you, Josie. I like you, Josie.* Or...oh God. Maybe he's coming over to end the whole broadcasting experiment. Call it a failure and get Nathan back. *It's not working, Josie. Sorry, Josie.* And if he does that, then fine. I'll listen. *I totally agree, Garrett.* Or—no, I'll pretend not to even know what he's talking about. Like I haven't noticed. Like—

A car door slams.

Shit.

I step out of the truck as he gets out of his car. We meet on my driveway with plenty of space between us. He's completely still, and yet I can feel the thrum of him...the thrum in myself because he's near.

Why him? Why is it him who makes me feel like this?

His face is in shadows, his hair dark gold in the porch light. I don't want him here, and yet there's no one I'd rather be with.

I try to read his expression, prepare myself for what's coming. He looks as tense as I feel.

"So he didn't drive you home," he says.

My mouth opens, surprise filling my lungs and silencing my voice. He sounds upset. *Jealous.*

"Did you have a good time? With Bryan." He's in front of me, his shape blocking the light, casting us both in darkness. There's something sharp beneath the words. Something close to breaking. "Did he kiss you? Did you let him kiss you?"

"Garrett." His name is a plea, but I don't know what for. I'm balancing on a high wire and on either side of me is a long fall. Do I want him to leave and end this before it can start? Or do I never want him to leave? Either way, I pay a price.

"Did you?"

My throat tightens with indecision.

"Did you?" He reaches for one of my hands and rubs his thumb over my knuckles. "Did you?"

I close my eyes against the dizzy rush of blood ignited by his words. His touch. "No," I say.

His breath gusts out as if he'd been holding it. He widens his stance and pulls me closer, or maybe I step closer. I'm like all the other girls pressed against Garrett Reeves. I'm exactly where I said I would never be.

"What does it matter, Garrett? If I did or I didn't? Nothing's changed."

"I know what I said at my house." His cheek is warm against mine as he bends his head to whisper in my ear. "But I was a fucking idiot. I should have kissed you. It should be me kissing you, not that asshole." His hands skim up my arms to my shoulders and then into the loose waves of my hair. "You shouldn't be going out with him, Josie. You should be going out with me."

I want to shake my head, but I'm caught in his hands. In the pull of everything I don't want to feel for him and can't help.

"You're still chasing baseball, Garrett."

"And I'll never catch up. My arm is a mess. Plan E is a joke."

I pull back until there's space between us again. It's easier to think when he isn't touching me. When I don't want to be touching him. "Then you'll come up with Plan F. There will always be another plan."

His eyes close for a second, and when they open, I can see exhaustion in their depths. "I don't know what's going to happen. I've got one more month paid with Kyle Masters, and I'm going to try whatever I can. That's just who I am. What I need to do. But after that? I don't know where I'm going to end up. If I'll have to go to Dallas, if I can make this broadcast thing work. I don't know shit right now."

He takes a breath and steps close again, his fingers tugging at mine until our hands are laced together. "I just know that every minute we're not together, I want us to be. And that kiss we didn't have? It was the best kiss of my life."

His words shred the last of my defenses. And when he bends to kiss me, I rise up on my toes to meet him. His lips are soft. Careful.

I think I might die from soft and careful. I put my hands on his chest—not to push him away but to bring him closer. And when he moans, I stop thinking of anything at all.

We kiss until my lips feel swollen and new. Until I know the texture of his face under my fingers and until I never want to taste anything but Garrett again. We kiss until I pull back because it feels so good that I'm scared.

"Jesus, Walters." He's panting as if he just ran the bases.

I want to smile because I'm happy it's not just me, but fear is expanding with my lungs. How can I trust in this? In Garrett? He's a guy with one foot out the door and I'm a girl who knows what it means to be left. "This is such a bad idea."

"I think it's a great idea. I think it's right up there with the wheel, and chicken on a stick, and the infield fly rule." He runs his fingers through my hair. "I hate that you got dressed up for someone else."

"I'm in jeans."

"You're beautiful." His touch is restless, skimming my hair to my shoulders and down my arms.

"Garrett, stop. This is crazy."

"Why? We've got a month before graduation. Before anything has to change, before any decisions have to be made. A month to see what happens."

"A month for it to end badly."

"Why are you thinking about endings?" His blue eyes shine like an endless sky. "This is a beginning. First inning, first at bat."

"You're not seriously giving me a baseball analogy right now?"

He brushes a grinning kiss over my mouth. "We'll hang out, Walters. Where's the danger in that? And you'll tell the giggler to keep his hands off."

"He's not like that. He's a gentleman."

"Quit saying nice things about him. You're denting my massive ego." When I laugh, his eyes flare with a look that would melt a metal bat. "You have the best laugh."

"Yeah, yeah," I grumble. And because this is all too much and I need time to process and maybe to crawl under the bed and scream with happiness, I shove at his chest. "You have to go now. I'll see you tomorrow at school."

"I'll pick you up."

"No. I'm going to walk with Mai."

He looks as if he might argue for a second and then sighs. "All right. Wait for me by the flagpole."

He turns away and he's jogging to his car before I can sputter a *no*. Did he really order me to the flagpole? I fold my arms over my chest and watch him drive away. No way I'm going to be waiting for him.

Effing baseball player.

Effing lungs that are still breathless.

Effing lips that are still throbbing.

Effing heart that already misses him.

Chapter Twenty-Eight

"Cooper Davies is coming to the plate." Garrett's voice is thick with worry. The Cholla Wildcats are down by one in the final inning against a team we should beat. A team we have to beat. The playoff picture is tightening, and Garrett isn't the only one worried. I've come to like these guys, and I want them to win.

"Davies has popped up both times at bat today, but now would be a great time to make contact," I say. "The Wildcats are down to their last three outs."

There's a sudden pressure on my hand, and my heart leaps with a whole different kind of feeling. Garrett works his fingers over mine and squeezes.

Last night is still replaying in my head—has been all day—and I'm trying to adjust to this new reality. Whatever it is. Garrett's grin was a little wider when I walked in today, but he's been nothing but professional in the booth. So holding my hand is a little surprising and a lot, well, wonderful.

Not that I'll tell him that.

He's already acting way too smug. It's amazing he could

walk at all with the swagger in his step when I turned up at the flagpole this morning. But I couldn't stay mad at him when he left the group—including Annette—to meet me halfway and thread his fingers through mine.

Mai was with me and groaned in disgust. "You're not going to be one of those gross couples who kiss all the time, are you?"

"We're not a couple," I said.

"Define all the time?" Garrett said.

I've been stupid-happy ever since.

Now, Garrett leans forward, his hand still clutching mine. "The pitcher is on the mound, toeing dirt off the rubber. He looks down to the catcher, watching for the signal."

I breathe in the hush of the stadium, the collective tension of nine players on the field, and the one at bat. The rest of Cholla's team is lined up along the dugout fence, eyes fixed on Cooper. Logically, I know the white chalk lines mark a game diamond, but it feels like more than that. Like it's a battlefield. It's man against man even as it's team against team. It all rests right now on one pitch. One swing.

"Here it comes," Garrett says, "and—" His voice drops. "It's a fastball down the middle. Davies doesn't take a swing. Strike one."

I swallow a frustrated groan. "That was the one he wanted, but Davies froze. Now the pitcher is ahead in the count and the pressure shifts squarely on Davies." My blood feels fizzy and thin. There's a tight, nervous ache in the pit of my stomach. The feeling takes me back to nights I sat in the stands watching my dad at the plate. Nights when the game rode on his bat. There were times when I couldn't watch—when I had to pace beneath the stands—when I waited for the roar of the crowd to tell me what had happened.

Garrett wets his lips. "Davies gives us his trademark wink as he sinks into his stance."

There's a whiz of the ball leaving the pitcher's hand and then a solid *crack*.

Garrett stands so fast, the stool overturns and crashes behind him. "That's going deep—it's over the head of Brewster in left field," he cries. "Cooper is in to second base with a stand up double!"

I'm on my feet, right next to him. "He hit that fast ball right on the screws!"

"The guys in the dugout are going crazy." Garrett pauses so the outdoor mic can pick up all the cheers. "The Lions coach is coming out to the mound. Looks like a pitching change."

I nod even though the audience can't see. "You can't blame that one on the Lions' pitcher. He hit his spot, but Cooper Davies went after it and crushed that ball."

"By the way," Garrett says, "sorry about that crash, folks. That was my stool doing a cartwheel." He rights it, and we both sit again.

"That was...*wow* good," I say.

"*Ridiculous* good."

"*Stupid good*."

Our adjectives are rapid-fire, and I love how in tune we are with each other—how I don't always know where he's headed but I can jump in and we find a way to play off each other. According to Scottie, the number of listeners for our broadcast has tripled in the past week alone, even with a couple of clunker sessions. Everyone is asking for more.

Normally, when we go to a pitching change, Garrett turns off the mic. But he leaves it on now, and I know we're in for more fun. "*Crazy* good," he says, keeping it going.

"*Oh my* good," I add.

"That's how the late, great Dick Enberg would have called it." He puts a hand over his heart in respect. "For those of you who know your broadcast legends, you know that was his signature line."

"Why don't we have a signature line?" I ask. "We're great."

He laughs into his mic. "You're right, Walters. We need a catchphrase. How are we going to be legends without one?"

"Oh, so now we're legends?" My grin is a match for his.

"As soon as we come up with a phrase, we are. Stuart Scott had *boo-yah*, Chris Berman had *He could go all the way*, and Walt Frazier's was *Posting and Toasting*."

"Really? I thought that was Dr. Seuss."

I wish the audience could see Garrett's smile. "Clever, Walters. Now apply that thinking to a catchphrase."

"I'll put it on my to-do list, right after 'call the game.'" Laughing, I point to the field where the new pitcher has finished warming up. Garrett quickly runs through his stats while Anthony strides to the batter's box.

Behind the fence, I see Mai sitting with fingers crossed. Inside her black leather lace-ups, I'm guessing her toes are crossed, too.

All business now, Garrett says, "First pitch is a ball, low and outside." He's got his fingers gripped under his chin, his elbows resting on the counter.

I copy his position so that my elbow touches his. He nudges me back and turns my insides into melted butter. We're connected like that when the next pitch comes in. Garrett stiffens. "It's a high fast ball. Anthony throws every ounce of strength into his swing...and fouls it off."

"You know he wants that one back."

"The count is one ball and one strike," Garrett says.

"It's all riding on his bat. Can he lift the ball and this team?"

As I say the words, the ball comes in hot from the pitcher, but Anthony is ready this time.

Garrett jumps up again, and when the stool crashes, I

don't hear it because he's shouting, "That ball is out of here. Anthony Adams hits a home run!"

I join in. "Davies is across home plate for the tying run. Here comes Adams for the win!"

"A walk off home run, folks. How about that!"

"And Adams' tenth home run of the season. This one couldn't have come at a better time."

Garrett runs a hand through his hair, looking dazed and relieved. "Cholla Wildcats win a big game. Our playoff hopes are alive and well."

"That's a feat you can't beat."

"We'll end our broadcast there, everyone. Hope you'll listen in to our next home game where we'll call all the action and try out more signature sayings. Until then, signing off for Cholla Wildcat baseball, I'm Garrett Reeves with Josie Walters."

He yanks off his headset and reaches for me, hugging me so tight my feet leave the ground. "I didn't think we were going to pull that one out."

"I would have chewed off my nails if I had any left."

He sets me down and glances out the window. The teams have exchanged handshakes, and now our guys are celebrating on the field. His gaze moves from them to the counter with all the equipment and cables. I don't have to hear him sigh to know he doesn't want to be here, packing it all up. I know where he wants to be. Where he wishes he still was.

"Go out there. I'll get started on this."

He shakes his head. "You don't know where anything goes."

"I'll figure it out." I wave him toward the door. "Go on."

He's like a kid who's just gotten everything he wanted for Christmas. He stops at the door. "My house after we're done here? We can brainstorm more sayings." He unholsters his finger guns and adds a wink to the lip bite.

"You know you look ridiculous when you do that, right?"

He laughs. "You know we could be legendary? We're good together. Good enough to win this contest."

"We'll find out in May."

"Don't need to wait. I've willed it to happen. It's a vision quest."

"A what?"

"Like the movie." When I stare blankly, he says, "You've never seen *Vision Quest*?"

"I've never heard of it."

"Then it's a date. Saturday after your shift at the bookstore. How can we attain true greatness if you don't understand the power of a vision quest?" He leans further in the door. "Plus, we can make out during the credits."

"Oh," I say. "Well, in that case."

And then he's gone, his laughter echoing in tune with the pound of his shoes on the ramp. A minute later, I watch him jump into the circle of guys. They swallow him up.

Tears press against my eyes, sudden and hot. His joy hurts because I know it's for baseball. For a sport he'd choose over me every single time. A fierce possessiveness rises in me. Because he may not have a choice. If he can't miraculously pitch again in the next month, baseball won't get Garrett Reeves.

But maybe I will.

Chapter Twenty-Nine

Brandi's found my replacement. I knew she was looking for one—I am leaving at the end of May. But I'm still surprised when I get to the bookstore on Saturday morning and meet her in person. Lianne is sixteen with auburn hair, freckles, and bright green eyes. Brandi tells me she's been part of the teen reading group and she volunteers at an after-school program, so she has lots of experience with kids.

"I know I can learn so much from you," she says a little shyly.

It's the right thing to say, but I'm still sad. I don't like the idea of someone coming in and taking over *my* group.

My kids.

It's a stupid reaction—even I know it. They're not mine and I'm leaving. So I smile and lead Lianne back to the room. But for the whole hour, I'm heavy with a feeling of sadness I can't shake. I've always hated goodbyes. Why should I expect this to be any different?

• • •

It's a little past noon when I knock on Garrett's front door.

We've hung out during the week at school, we've texted and talked, and though I told him he couldn't pick us up yesterday, he cruised by while we were walking, offering us candy to climb in. Idiot. We were saved by other drivers yelling at him to get moving.

"So are you guys officially boyfriend-girlfriend?" Mai asked yesterday. When I said no, she tried to pin me down on what exactly we are. "I can ask my mom for some euphemisms," she offered. "Naked friends. Bed buddies. Private-parts partners."

"Stop!" I begged, and then we spent the rest of our walk coming up with more. It was fun, laughing about it, but her question has stuck in my head. He's still training. He spent the morning working with Kyle Masters. What if he had a breakthrough? Then what? He starts down a path I won't follow. That's why we can't be boyfriend-girlfriend. Why this isn't a date. Why I promised Mom I was only going over for the afternoon. And I didn't use the word "date." I said hanging out. I said contest-related. I said doesn't-mean-anything.

But my heart is pounding now as if it means everything.

Garrett answers the door a second after I ring the bell.

"Hey. I heard your truck." He's wearing the blue shirt that does sparkly things to his eyes. "You ready for movie magic?"

"I'm withholding judgment."

Wild greets me with a loud meow of displeasure and a dismissive swish of her tail.

"Your cat reminds me of you."

"Regal?"

"Full of herself."

There's a laugh from the kitchen. I slap a hand over my mouth.

Garrett grins and heads that way. I follow more slowly.

My face, I'm sure, is the flattering color of a Red Hot.

"Mom," Garrett says. "This is Josie."

His mom is standing at the counter, filling out what looks like a shopping list. I'd recognize her even if I hadn't seen pictures. Garrett has her eyes and wide smile.

"Hi." I give her an embarrassed wave. "Sorry about that."

"You mean insulting my son?" Her eyes are a lighter blue than Garrett's and so warm that I like her immediately. "I enjoyed it."

"Mahammmm!" Garrett says with mock affront.

She pulls him close and gives him a quick peck on his cheek. "What are you two up to?"

"Movie." He shifts past her to a pantry door. "We got any popcorn?"

"We will when I get home from the grocery store." She looks my way. "I've really been enjoying your broadcasts."

"Oh. Thank you."

"Garrett was very lucky to find you."

"I didn't find her." He tosses a new bag of Lays on the counter. "She barged in on me. Practically begged me to take her on as my partner." He pulls two cans of bubbly water from the fridge. "I thought she was going to cry if I said no."

My gasp is impressive.

"Save that story for someone who wasn't listening the day Josie barged in," his mom says. "Poor Nathan really was out of his element. The job requires someone who loves the game."

I can't help shaking my head. "I know the game, but I actually hate it."

"I'm changing her mind." Garrett holds out both cans. "Lemon-lime or cherry?"

"He's *failing* to change my mind." I take the cherry.

She gives us an amused look. "I can tell you two agree on just about everything. I'm only sorry I can't stay for the debate on what movie you'll watch."

"No debate." Garrett pops open his can. "*Vision Quest.* She's never seen it."

"Shocking," his mom says in a voice so dry, I laugh out loud.

"You mean it isn't the greatest sports film ever?"

She reaches for an oversize gray purse and pulls it onto her shoulder. "You'll have to let me know what you think." She takes the list. "It was nice meeting you, Josie." She turns to Garrett. "I've got a few errands to run before the store. I'll see you later?"

"Poker tonight at Cooper's house. We'll probably get pizzas."

"Sounds good. Text me if anything changes."

"Nice to meet you, too," I say as she disappears through a door into the garage. I turn back to Garrett. "Geranium and mandarin orange."

"What?"

"Her perfume. Both scents reflect calm and balance."

"Which she is." He sniffs, leaning closer to me. "I could make a comment about how good you smell, but I'm not going there. See?" He sticks out his chest. "I'm reformed."

"Yeah, right," I scoff. "Are we going to watch this movie or are you going to blather all afternoon?"

"Blather? Grab the chips, Walters. And get ready for epic."

Chapter Thirty

There's a TV in the family room, but he bypasses that for another room tucked at the back of the house. It's got brown shag carpet, a foosball table, and an overstuffed couch with a flat screen on the wall.

He sets up the movie while I sit on the edge of the couch and try to keep my knees from shaking. I was never nervous around Garrett when I didn't like him, but there are moments now when I objectively think about his perfect looks, and his popularity, and how much more experience he has. I feel like I've come in to pitch to Babe Ruth. I got no chance.

Garrett settles beside me and lifts an eyebrow when I put the bag of chips between us. "You okay?"

"Yeah," I lie.

"You can use the whole cushion, you know. Sit back. Put your feet up." He drags over an ottoman nearly as long as the couch. I shimmy back and put up my sneakers.

"A little better," he says. He shifts closer, and surprises me by planting a kiss on the side of my jaw. "You smell like boysenberries. Or maybe rhubarb."

"Rhubarb?" I push him away, but the silliness of his words relaxes me. "I thought you were reformed?"

"I've relapsed." He tosses the potato chips to the end of the couch and settles beside me—not quite touching, but too close to pretend we're just friends. As the opening credits roll, he hits a remote and the panel of curtains slides shut until the only light is from the TV, and a movie that appears to have been made in a different century.

Ten minutes later, my face hurts from rolling my eyes. "Can I get a cracker with this cheese?"

"Give it a chance."

"That wrestling outfit..." I wave a hand at the TV where Matthew Modine is in a slinky one-piece that shows off his bits and pieces.

Garrett hits the pause button. "It's not an outfit. It's a uni. Come on, Walters, I expected better from you."

"I expected better from this."

"You have to focus on the story. Not the low budget eighties filmmaking. Now can I hit play again?"

"All right, but who is this Shute guy?"

"You'll see. It's going to take a vision quest to beat him."

Though I hate to admit it, I do get into the movie. It's one where you know exactly what's going to happen, but it's still fun to watch. By the end, I'm grinning as the Shute kid goes down.

"Tissue?" Garrett asks.

"What?"

"You look a little teary."

"I do not." I shove my shoulder into his. At some point during the movie, almost touching turned into touching. After I remembered to breathe again, it felt good. So good I think I'm going to miss the feel of Garrett every time I watch a movie.

He laughs and hits the mute button. "Admit it. You liked

it."

"It wasn't horrible. But as sports movies go, it wasn't the best or even the second best."

"Not even top ten, but it still fires me up every time. I first saw it with Uncle Max. It was after a club game where this kid hit for the cycle against me. After he had a single, double, and a homer, I got smart and decided to walk the guy. He caught a low pitch with the end of his bat and ended up with a triple. He was my Shute that day, and I got my ass kicked."

I scoot over a cushion so I can see him as we talk. I like looking at him. He's still too pretty, but now I can see the disappointment behind his smile. The fear that pushes him. The scars that don't show on the outside. "Did you ever get revenge?"

"No. He got a homer off me the next time I faced him, and then he moved out of state. But I still think of him sometimes when I work on my drills."

"What kind of drills does Masters have you doing?"

He shakes his head in slow motion. "I don't want to talk about that with you."

"Why not?"

"Because you tense up. And then you get mad."

"I do not." But I already can feel how tight my shoulders are. "You'd tell me, wouldn't you? If anything changes? If it looks like you might have a shot?"

"I'd tell you."

My eyes search his. "Because you wouldn't have to be all that great to play at a junior college or even a D3 university. They always take a lot of pitchers."

"Josie—"

"You don't have to throw hard if you can hit your spots. They need—"

"Josie!" He puts his fingers over my lips. "I don't want to play D3 just for the hell of it. I don't want to play unless I have a chance to go all the way. That's what it's about for me. I'm not trying to stretch it out so I can sit on a bench for another year. Okay?"

Something unfurls in my chest. I think it's a tiny blossom of hope. "Okay."

The TV shows a stripe of white static. Garrett reaches for the remote and hits the stop button. "Next movie we watch is *One on One*. College basketball."

"Is that from this century?"

"Nope. It's even older than this one."

I sit up and stretch. "Why not baseball? I would've thought that would be your go-to."

"I love baseball movies, but you've probably seen them all."

"Probably. My dad and I watched a bunch." I smile in spite of myself. "He was awful to watch movies with. Spent the whole time critiquing the baseball parts—but every once in a while he'd make me pull up his training journal and add a note about something to try."

"He kept an online journal?"

"Never missed a workout. Kept track of his exercise routine, training drills and reps, even what kind of protein shake he had afterward. I did a lot of the typing for him."

"It sounds like you were close."

"Sounds like it."

"You going to tell me what that means?" His voice is soft. His hand on mine is tentative.

"It means he left without looking back."

His thumb smooths a path across my knuckles. "You didn't want to go with him?"

The truth presses against my throat, burning. *More than anything.* I swallow, hard. "He didn't deserve us, not after everything we'd already given up. After the promises he made."

"So you cut him out?"

"He's the one who left."

"But that's baseball. What about us?" Garrett presses. "What if we're together and I have a chance to keep playing only it means moving across country?"

Go back to that? My head is already shaking. "I'll wish you well."

Garrett's hand slackens on mine. "That's cold, Josie."

"I'm sorry." There's heat behind my eyes because I'm not cold, only careful. "It's just the way it is."

When our eyes meet, his are cloudy with indecision. I try and tug my hand free, and that seems to settle something for him. He grips me tighter.

"We said we'd see what happens. So let's see. I'm not going anywhere right now," he says. "And neither are you."

There's a husky note in his voice that unravels me. "Why do you like me, Garrett?"

"Because you're smart and funny. You challenge me and you frustrate me and somehow even that's a good thing." His fingers wind between mine. "Because under all that sarcasm, you have a smile that gets to me." His throat works over a swallow. "You're like baseball, Josie Walters. Hard to get to know—lots of rules—but you bring out the best in me."

Tears swim in my eyes. No one's ever said anything like that to me before.

I kiss him. I press my mouth hard against his so that nothing can get between us. Not even the future.

A breathless time later, we end up with our foreheads touching, our hearts racing.

"I should go," I say. "I promised my mom."

"Not yet. Stay a while longer."

As much as I like the idea, I pull back. "You have poker, remember?"

His fingers slide from my hand to my forearm. "I can skip poker."

"You can't. What will the guys say?"

"Lucky me?"

"Ha." But his words and his touch send another wave of warmth through my veins.

"Speaking of the guys, they're really impressed with how good you are on-air."

"You're not bad, either."

He widens his eyes. "Gee, Walters. I'm overwhelmed." His fingers skate further up my arm. "Cooper's grandfather thinks we could have a future in broadcasting."

"What does he know?"

Garrett surprises me by saying, "A lot. He was a TV sports producer before he retired. Which makes me think…" His fingers still. "If I can't play, broadcasting might be the perfect fallback plan. For you *and* me."

"Me?"

"You like fallback plans. They're very practical."

I'm scrambling to catch up. "You're talking about broadcasting. For reals?"

He purses his lips. "Reals is not a word, Walters. I'm not sure if I want a partnership with someone who is unfamiliar with the English language."

"Smart-ass." I flick his chest with a finger. "What about your grades? Can you even get into a broadcasting program?"

His expression is part irritation, part exasperation. But he says, "It's possible that I did a little better on this week's quiz."

"Ninety percent or better?"

"Did I say I liked that you challenge me?" But his expression softens into something I think is embarrassment.

"You were right, okay? As good as it felt to get back at my dad, it wasn't my best idea. Besides, the bad grades were hard on my mom. Dad made her feel like they were her failure, too."

"So if you bring up your grades, you can stay here for college?"

"As long as I have a plan that includes a potential paycheck, my dad won't fight it. I'm still not going to settle for a cubicle. But a booth—with you—that's got potential."

I'm excited for him, but... "I already have a partnership. With my mom."

"Do you love it?" He doesn't wait for an answer. "Think about it. It's just an idea. We'd have to get better first. Have to work at it to see if we could."

"You mean, treat broadcasting as more than a contest?"

"Why not? The winning team gets admission to ASU's School of Broadcasting. I was never going to go that route, but what if I did? What if you did?"

My throat is tight as I put the thought into words: "What if *we* did?"

He smiles. "I like how you say *we*."

"We?" I repeat.

"Your lips get all puckery."

"Puckery is not a word, Blondie. I'm not sure I want a partnership with someone who's unfamiliar with the English language."

His eyes spark with humor an instant before he grabs my shoulders. "That's it. You're getting tickled for that."

I shriek as I'm suddenly flipped on my back. He doesn't have to tickle me, though, because I'm already laughing. I'm laughing at every ridiculous thing he's said to me since we met. At the realization that I'm going to get to hear whatever it is he says next.

He's laughing, too, his chest shaking until he finally buries his head in the curve of my neck. We lie like that until the laughter dies away, and I have to wipe tears from the corners of my eyes. His weight feels good, and I'm sad when he finally moves, shifting until he's propped up on one forearm.

His eyes are still full of laughter, but there's also a stillness to him that speaks of something important. "So what do you think?" he asks. "About the broadcasting? You want to try it?"

My heart thuds with a mix of fear and excitement. My fingers are a little sweaty as I find the edge of his shirtsleeve and grab hold. "I guess it can't hurt to try."

I ignore my heart that's saying, *Yes, it can.*

Chapter Thirty-One

I'm in so much trouble.

"Let me come with you," Garrett says.

We're standing in front of his house, by my truck. In the dark.

Full dark.

My heart's beating faster with each passing second. "Are you crazy? My mom is already going to be so mad."

"Let her be mad at me. I'll take responsibility."

"No." I unlock the door and toss my purse in. "It'll be a million times worse if you're there."

"I'm good with mothers. Really." His smirk is full of self-satisfaction, which is one of the things she'll hate most about him.

I give him a quick kiss that catches the corner of his mouth. "I have to go. Now." I hop in the truck.

"Fine. Call me later?"

If I still have possession of my phone. "Yes. Bye."

I've heard of the walk of shame—this definitely feels like the drive of shame. I keep hoping the porch light will be off when I get home. That Mom won't have noticed how late it is. But when I round the corner of my street, the light is on.

Of course she noticed.

This is not still afternoon, which is when I promised I'd be home. Not dusk when I told Garrett I had to go. Not pre-moon, which is a new category Garrett made up as an excuse for me not to leave. An excuse I jumped on.

It was such a perfect day, I didn't want it to end. After *Vision Quest*, we watched a baseball movie after all, *Sandlot*, reciting most of the lines with the characters. We even did some work, brainstorming questions for the baseball feature. Somewhere along the way, we ended up sharing our most embarrassing moments. (Garrett farted before delivering a speech in fourth grade English. I accepted a perfect attendance award in third grade with the back of my skirt stuck in my underwear.) We shared *mosts* and *leasts* and *bests* and *funniests*. Mrs. Reeves made us meatball subs and salad for dinner.

Garrett blew off poker.

I blew off my mom.

He's going to get ribbed a little, and me? I don't know. I've never been late. Never ignored a phone call or a text. I did reply to the second text—but only to say I was fine and would be home soon. That was over an hour ago.

Rather than come in through the garage like I usually do, I fit my key into the front door. Maybe I can sneak by her. Pretend I've been home for a while. I turn the knob so slowly it doesn't make a sound. Even I don't hear the door as I push it open. The TV is on in the family room—perfect. I close the door with a tiny click and...*silence*.

I peek around my shoulder and...*oh crap*.

Mom is standing in the hall, her feet bare and her arms crossed. There are splashes of red on her cheeks, and it's not blush. "Where have you been?"

"At Garrett's." I swallow. "I texted you."

"You texted that you were coming home." Her chin trembles, and I realize it's not anger laced through every tense muscle. It's fear. "And then you didn't. I was worried, Josie. This is not like you."

"I know. I'm sorry." I feel queasy at the hurt on her face. "I kept meaning to leave and then...I lost track of time."

"Lost track of time?" Her throat works over a swallow. "Were you having sex with that boy?"

My mouth drops open. "Mom!"

She strides toward me where I'm frozen by the front door. She reaches for my upper arm and smells me. *Smells me?*

"Mom!" I pull free. "That's disgusting."

"You smell like him."

"I smell like his cat. Her hair was all over the couch."

"Which means you were all over his couch."

"Not doing *that*!"

I'm shocked when a tear runs down her cheek. "I'm so afraid you're going to make the same mistakes I did." She covers her mouth with one hand while more tears join the first. The sight triggers a pang of guilt. I've seen her cry before, but it's never been because of me.

"Mom, don't. It wasn't like that."

"You said you'd be home this afternoon. My mind has been racing."

"Can we at least talk in the kitchen? It feels weird here by the door."

She looks around and seems to realize we're both in the small entryway. "I need a cup of tea."

I follow her to the kitchen, where she grabs a tissue from the box on the counter and then pulls open the drawer of tea leaves. "You want one?" she asks.

"No, thanks."

She busies herself with the tea, but it's only a few seconds before she says, "Are you going to tell me what you were doing all this time?"

"We were watching movies. That's it. And then we got hungry and his mom made us dinner. She was there nearly the whole time."

"She made you dinner?"

An awful feeling makes me turn to the sink, and I see the pots on the draining board.

"I made you stroganoff," she says.

It's one of my favorites, but Mom rarely makes it because the prep takes forever. "I didn't know. You should have told me."

She forgets the tea and faces me. "I tried to when I called. You didn't pick up."

"I'm sorry. I should have. We weren't doing anything," I finish lamely.

Her eyes search my face, and I try not to look away. "You've never lied to me before."

"I'm not lying."

"You didn't come home when you said you would. You didn't pick up when I called. Things like this never happened until you met that boy."

"His name is Garrett," I say, though she already knows that. "You know we're doing this contest. You've listened. You've heard how good we are."

"Is this still about proving something to your father?"

I swallow, my throat chalky and dry. This is the moment to tell her what Garrett and I were talking about tonight. That we're going to take it seriously. But how can I do that now? She's already upset, and she'd go off the rails if I told her I was even considering a future that included baseball and a baseball player. Plus, we only just agreed to *try*. There's a good chance it won't come to anything. I hesitate and then settle for partial honesty. "It's turned out to be more fun than

I expected. And we're better than I expected, too. We have a real chance to win, so why not go for it?"

"And when it's over? Is it...will it be over with the two of you?"

My shrug is uncertain—that's 100 percent honest. "I'm not sure. It depends on him and whether he's going to play baseball. But his arm is a mess, and I really think he's getting it out of his system."

New tears seep from her eyes.

"Why are you crying?"

"Because we went through so much with your father. I stopped keeping track of the times he said he was ready to leave baseball. The promises made and broken. I don't want you to put your trust in a boy you told me yourself is just like him. I don't want you to end up with the same regrets I have."

"I won't."

"You tell yourself that, but I know what it's like to be attracted to the wrong guy. You can lose sight of common sense and a whole lot more."

I nod because I do know what she means. Because it scares me, too. "I'll be careful. I promise."

She nods, but her chin trembles. "Protect your heart, Josie. I couldn't stand to see it broken again."

Now I'm the one who's leaking tears.

When I hug her, she hugs me back so hard I feel the bones of her wrists pressing into my back. It reminds me how strong she is—how strong she had to be when Dad left. He didn't love me, but she always did. Whenever she had a choice, she chose me.

I push aside thoughts of Garrett and broadcasting. "So are there leftovers?" I ask. "Or did you eat all my stroganoff?" I'm not hungry, but I'm glad for whatever impulse made me ask. Mom gives me her first faint smile. "I saved you a plate. I'll heat it up."

She goes to the fridge, and I pull up a stool at the counter. That's when I spot a small box with a red bow by the coffee pot.

"What's that?"

"Take a look," she says. The box has a white cardboard top that slowly lifts from the heavy bottom. Inside are business cards. Hundreds of business cards. I pull out one and read:

Josie Walters

AromaTher Co-President

New tears spring to my eyes. "Oh, Mom."

"You like them?"

I nod. It's the future we've been planning for more than two years. It's not a risk like Garrett. It's not an unknown, and it doesn't require a fallback plan. I should never have told Garrett I'd think about broadcasting.

It scares me that I did.

It scares me even more that I don't want to take it all back now.

Carefully, I replace the card and close the box.

Chapter Thirty-Two

Our lunch table has gotten a little more crowded over the past week. Cooper, Tucker, Jason, and Anthony keep appearing as if this is the baseball player table now. Avi is still suspicious of the new species sitting with us. Jasmine, on the other hand, keeps sneaking looks at Tucker as if she wishes he were on the menu.

Today it's Cooper, Tucker, and Anthony, but they have enough food to feed a dozen people. It's Southwestern Fare Friday, and our table is covered in paper trays of tortilla chips drenched in nacho cheese and sprinkled with slices of green jalapeños. My eyes watered at the smell, but the guys have nearly downed four trays along with beef tacos and chicken burritos. It's like watching an episode of National Geographic where the lions take down an antelope.

Mai and I have our Contraband Quesadilla, which is what we call the cheese-filled tortilla, because her mom would shudder to see Mai eating cheese so orange it probably glows in the dark. Mai is also eating her packed lunch so that the healthy balances out the unhealthy.

"Try this," Mai says, handing Anthony one of her green veggie sticks.

"That looks gross," Cooper says as he tears open a packet of sugar and pours it into his mouth.

I gag. "You did not just do that."

"Where did you even get that?" Jasmine asks.

"I stole it from the Bagel Barn."

"This doesn't look like a French fry." Anthony sniffs at the stick.

"You're going to be arrested," Mai tells Cooper.

"And it's the wrong color," Anthony adds.

"If you get busted, I'll bring you a bird in prison," Tucker offers.

"Why would you bring him a bird?" I ask.

Tucker chews through a taco. "It's from a movie. *Birdman of Alcatraz.*"

"Dude!" Cooper fluffs his chin hair. "That movie was awesome."

Anthony finishes chewing. "It wasn't horrible."

"Now you can have an orange one," Mai says. "They're better."

Mai is expanding Anthony's world, or so she tells him. I think she's trying to pawn off the veggie sticks.

Tucker and Cooper are still going on about the movie. I'm getting good at multiple conversations.

"The scene where he tells the bird to leave?" Tucker begins. "You remember that?" He throws a hand over his heart and I think he's trying to impersonate an actor. Or maybe a statue. Then he starts talking in a gangster voice. "You don't wanna be a jailbird all your life, do ya? You're a highballin' sparrow. So you fly high, old cock. Go out there and bite the stars—for me."

Mai and I exchange surprised glances. That actually...impressive.

"Wow," Jasmine breathes.

My voice is a little awed too. "Tucker. That's poetic. I can't believe you memorized that."

Tucker gives me one of his dimpled smiles. "I was a kid when I first saw that movie. I got to say cock out loud and my mom couldn't yell at me."

Mai and I groan in unison.

Cooper gives him a high five. "Gotta love a good cock quote."

Heads turn at the loud word. Avi hides his face in his hands.

"What?" Cooper says, looking around at the neighboring tables. "It's a bird word."

"Hey, that rhymes," Tucker adds. They both grin like they're Shakespeare.

"Orange is better. But still not a French fry," Anthony says.

Mai nods. "But now you've had your vegetables for the day."

Anthony lights up with a slow grin. He's nothing if not chill—his word, not mine. I'm not sure how this is still a thing. Mai's list of qualities for a potential boyfriend includes Ivy-league brains, goal-oriented, and ambitious. Definitely not... *chill*. And here they are, still hanging out. Nothing official, Mai says. But they text, they go for drives. Mai met him at the school last night for ice cream sundaes, which she said were delicious—and gave me a smile that made me think she wasn't talking about the ice cream.

I'm trying to be cool with it. The girl traffic around his locker has stopped, which is great, but it doesn't change the fact that they come from different worlds and they're headed in opposite directions. I think his friends are just as confused by it as I am.

"You and Garrett have been lighting it up this week,"

Cooper says now.

We have been, but I try to look humble.

He scrapes the last bit of cheese off a paper tray. "G said it's getting serious with you two."

My heart clenches mid-beat. "It is not."

His smile hooks up on one side. "Broadcasting, I mean."

"Oh. Well." I swallow my embarrassment and attempt to form a complete sentence. "We're playing around with the idea." I haven't said anything to my mom. I still can't bring myself to do it. Mai has agreed to support me in my plan of denial and lying.

"Josie is weighing her many options," Mai says, making it sound oh-so-impressive.

"Does she weigh herself naked?" Tucker asks.

I throw one of Mai's veggie sticks.

"Hey, not a potato one," Anthony says.

That gets the table laughing—including me. I like these guys more and more. Too much, maybe, because now I'm nervous at every game. I want them to make it to State. I want them to win. They don't talk about it a lot, but I know how important it is. Especially the seniors who aren't going to keep playing. Like Tucker and Anthony. They want to leave Cholla with a State trophy and enough memories to last for whatever comes next. I hope they get it. They have a shot if they can keep the bats hot.

The guys gather their trash and there's some talk about Fridays and lockers and laundry. *Please tell me they wash their gym clothes more than once a week?* On the other hand, I don't want to know.

They get up to leave and that reminds Avi and Jasmine about some notes they were going to exchange. It's suddenly Mai and me as the table clears.

"Later," Anthony says, and gives Mai a slow smile that raises the temperature of the entire cafeteria.

"That was hot," I say when he's out of earshot.

"He's very hot."

"Maya Senn!"

"Stop worrying."

"I can't help it. How far have things gone with you two?"

"Just kissing. *Lots* of kissing."

"Really?" I bite my lip. "You know I like Anthony. But is he really boyfriend material for you?"

"No," she says. "But I'm not looking for a boyfriend. I just wanted to have some fun." She lets out a long exhale. "But it's getting…complicated. I have to break it off."

Before I can press her for more, my phone vibrates with an incoming text. I pull it from my back pocket and see Garrett's name on the screen. I tilt it so Mai can see. "He shouldn't have his phone in class." I click open the text.

GARRETT: Meet you by the math wing for kissing and groping?

"Aww," Mai says. "That's sweet."

ME: Get your mind out of the gutter.

GARRETT: I've tried. Can't.

ME: I'm wearing my sandals.

GARRETT: That worked.

I laugh out loud as I slide my phone away.

"You can thank me now."

"For what?"

"For getting you to the baseball game that first day."

"Uh-huh," I say. "And what happens when the whole thing goes to shit?"

"Who says that it will?"

"He's still working every Saturday with Kyle Masters."

"Because the lessons are paid for. He's going through the motions."

"But he's still going through them." I like him so much and the uncertainty scares me. I can see us together. I can see us broadcasting games, working together. I can see a future I want more clearly every day we're together.

And I can see myself standing with a packed suitcase while he walks away.

The warning bell begins to ring. As we gather our stuff, I hope to hell it isn't a sign.

Chapter Thirty-Three

"I think we should have a party for you."

Lianne says this as we're putting away the art supplies. Her voice is hushed, but I still look over at the kids who are arranging themselves in our final circle. They have supersonic hearing when it comes to the word "party."

It's Saturday morning, and the room feels like summer with a big vase of freshly picked flowers that Brandi brought in. It's two weeks into April and wildflower season. Though I love when the desert blooms, I hate how fast the days are flying by.

"I'll do everything," Lianne is saying. Her voice is a little hesitant—her eyes hopeful. She's just so nice. She's always here early and asking how can she help. I shouldn't be surprised by the idea of a party, and it would be fun for the kids, but for me?

"I'm not big on goodbyes," I say.

"But it's not really a goodbye. It's more of a good luck party."

"Yeah, I've heard that before."

After pre-school.

Midway through first grade.

The semester break in third grade.

The worst was fifth grade. Mrs. Cline threw a party with red velvet cupcakes. Everyone made a card, and I could barely hold back tears. But the awful part was the end of the day because when everyone was ready to go home, they stopped being sad. They started talking about the next day. I couldn't join in because the next day I wouldn't be there. It was the first time I understood that they would forget me before I forgot them. It made me wonder why I'd bothered making friends at all.

Lianne is still looking at me hopefully. "It'll be a nice way for the kids to make the transition. A passing of the throne."

Though I still hate the idea, she's right. It would make it easier for the kids and for her.

She fishes glitter glue out of the crayon tub. "I'll bake a cake."

How do I say no to that? "If you want to, then sure. Thanks."

Her smile is immediate. "We'll do it your last Saturday. It'll be here before you know it." A quick frown shifts her expression. "You okay?"

I'm spared from answering by a shout from Ciera. "It's the cookie man!"

Garrett is standing at the door. I'm not sure how he became the cookie man, but the circle collapses into chaos as kids rush to him. These are my regulars—Ciera, Fiona, Kate, Julia, Javier, and Bryson. They only met him the one time, but you'd think he was Santa Claus. Javier and Ciera each grab a hand and pull him toward the circle.

"You have to sit," Javier says.

"Did you get the lips?" Ciera asks. "Josie was supposed to give you the lips."

His eyes are laughing as they meet mine. "She was?"

"Pencils with lips on them," I explain.

"Kissing pencils." Kate turns as pink as the bows in her hair.

"Oh, those." He nods, serious. "I use them to draw hearts on all my school papers."

The girls giggle. "We want to see."

"I draw snakes," Bryson says.

Lianne claps to get the kids' attention. "Why doesn't everyone settle down, and while I pass out the cookies, you can tell the cookie man what you like to draw best."

The kids love the idea, and I'm left to watch the whole thing from outside the circle. It's good, though. It's time. This is what all of us want. For them to move on so that I can, too.

It's Lianne who greets the parents and says goodbye to each kid. Garrett stands beside me, and we watch the process.

"She's good," he says.

"Yeah, she is."

"Can you head out now? Seems like she can manage without you."

I stiffen. "It's still my job. What are you doing here anyway?"

"Surprising you."

I slant him a wry look. "You came for the cookies, didn't you?"

"That, too." He rubs at a chunk of silver glue stuck to the back of my hand. "You coming over when you're done? We need to practice. And I want to put together a final tape of our feature."

"But it's Saturday."

"We said we were going to get serious about this."

"We said we were going to try."

"There's no try in a vision quest. Only do." He heads for the door but stops and shoots me a wink over his shoulder. "Oh, and Walters? Bring the lips."

Chapter Thirty-Four

"That ball was smacked up the middle," I say, my eyes glued to the TV. "Harris saves an easy double with that diving catch."

Garrett hits the pause button. The screen freezes, halting a game that happened yesterday. Garrett showed me his DVR list when I got here today. He's recorded six baseball games, and the plan is that we watch the games on mute and try to do the broadcast on the fly. It's nearly impossible, I've realized in the past hour, because I have no idea who all these players are.

"That's not Harris at short," he corrects. "Harris is at first."

We're both sitting on the edge of the couch, our knees touching because he's man-sitting, his knees spread so wide he's in my territory. I'm not giving an inch. I'm already at a disadvantage.

"How am I supposed to remember that?" I complain. "I haven't watched a game in years. We should call all the players Smith. Otherwise it's not fair."

"It's not a contest, Walters."

"Then why are you gloating every time you get it right and I don't?"

"I'm appreciating the vast superiority of my brain."

I elbow him in the ribs. "You're such a bad winner."

"I am not."

"Winners are gracious. They downplay their glory in deference to the tender feelings of their opponents."

His brows lift, his eyes widen. "Did I hurt your tender feelings? I'll kiss them and make them better." He leans in and brushes a kiss over my cheek.

"Stop it, Blondie."

"Am I missing the right spot? You keep your tender feelings...lower?"

My snort turns into a laugh as he kisses me again, this time on the mouth.

"Stop trying to distract me."

His smile makes it hard for me to breathe. He's just so...everything. Funny and sweet and smart and sexy and outrageous and ambitious. And he's looking at me as if I'm the one who's everything.

"I like you, Josie Walters," he says.

My heart turns to oatmeal, warm and smushy. "I like you, too, Garrett Reeves."

"I have something for you."

From under the couch he pulls out a folder that he must have stashed there earlier. With a flourish, he presents it to me. The folder is black with a strip of white that holds the ASU logo and beneath it a line that reads: *Walter Cronkite School of Journalism and Mass Communication.*

"It's an application packet along with a course outline."

My hand shakes a little. "You went to ASU?"

"My mom did. She picked up one for me, and I asked her to get one for you, too."

"But." I swallow. "We're just trying this, Garrett."

"I know."

"If I did this…" I'm not even sure how to finish the sentence. It's too big of a thought, too much to even comprehend. Too *real*. "I never said I would."

"It's just so we can read about the program. See if it sounds interesting."

I open the folder a few inches, wide enough to see official-looking documents and a blank schedule for choosing classes. "What do I do with this?"

"You don't have to do anything."

My gaze flies to his. "Did you fill yours out?"

"No."

"But you're thinking you will?"

Our eyes meet. Hold. My heart reacts, beating faster. Heavier. "I have a plan. A future I've been working toward. My mom…" My breath shudders as I think about her. "She's made an appointment with the business lawyer. We're going to file the partnership papers on my birthday, even though it's a Saturday. She's ordered a cake. I saw it by accident. 'Happy Birthday, Partner.'"

"You don't think she'd understand?"

"Understand what? I don't know if *I* understand."

"People change, Josie. Dreams change."

I know he's thinking of himself. But me? My skin feels hot. "I don't have dreams. I have plans."

"Why can't you have both?"

Because plans I can control. Dreams I can't.

I open the folder, my eyes skimming over the papers stacked on both sides. He's serious. Garrett is serious about this. About us.

"We could go to your house. Talk to her about it. Together."

I close the folder, set it aside on the couch. "No. I couldn't do it that way."

"Then what way?" He cocks his head and I know what this is really about. He confirms it when he says, "Does she even know about me?"

"Of course she knows."

"Does she know I'm your boyfriend?"

"You're not my boyfriend. We're just hanging out while you try and make a comeback. That's what we agreed on. Remember?"

He looks so hurt. "Things have changed for me. I thought they'd changed for you, too. Or is this it, Josie? Is this all you can give me? That we're just hanging out?"

My eyes fill with tears. "I'm afraid to trust this."

"You mean trust me?" The couch squeaks as he stiffens and puts space between us. "Because your dad left?"

"It's not just that."

"Then what, Josie? What did your father do that you can't forgive me for?"

Chapter Thirty-Five

"Don't get mad."

"Too late," Garrett says. "You're comparing me to your dad. Blaming me. How is that fair?"

"It isn't. I get that. But if you're standing in the batter's box and you keep getting hit in the leg by wild pitches, you start wearing an ankle guard. You learn to protect yourself."

"From what?" He reaches for my hand. I'm not at all petite, but his hand is bigger than mine, light hairs showing against the tan of his skin. The palms are calloused, and absently I wonder why they're so rough. Why rough feels so good. "Tell me what happened."

"You know what happened. My dad went to Japan."

"You said it was more than that."

I sigh. I know I have to give him more, but how much? "You already know most of it. We had a plan, my dad and me. That while he could play, he would. And after, he'd take a coaching job and eventually I could help. And that's what happened when he got released. He took a coaching job and I got to help run mini camps. I was good at it, too. Then, the spring before he left, he asked if I wanted to coach Little League as a father-daughter team."

"And you wanted to?"

"More than anything." My throat fills. "By then, I knew I wasn't going to play much longer, but I loved the game. I could totally see it happening. My dad and me starting with Little League and then running a club and one day coaching in The Show." I glance up, expecting to find him laughing over the ridiculousness of that. But he isn't.

"So you did have a dream," he murmurs.

"I did. Right up until my dad got the offer to play in Japan. He didn't even pause to think about me—about us. He chose Japan."

"Yeah, but..." His eyes flicker to mine and then down. He rubs at a dark smudge on the couch.

"What, Garrett?" Because there's obviously something.

"Don't take this the wrong way. But it's not like he could have told Japan to wait a few years until you grew up. Sports don't work that way. Your dad was what, thirty, thirty-one at the time? You had to know he couldn't play for long in Japan. Not at that age. I know it's not what you wanted, but you could have postponed your plans for two years. You could be coaching together now. You didn't have to cut him out of your life forever."

"I didn't!"

"But you said—"

"I wanted to go with him, Garrett." I cut him off—my words sharp as knives, but I'm the one who's sliced open, the memories spilling like blood. "I wouldn't have let him go anywhere without me. He was my hero. My best friend. So while he and my mom were talking divorce, I ran to pack my suitcase. I didn't want him to have to wait. That's all I was thinking about. Grab what I needed and Mom could send the rest later. I rushed out to the living room with my suitcase and my coat and said I was ready."

I'm suddenly back in that house. Standing on gray tile. The ceiling fan clacking overhead because Dad hadn't tightened the bolts. The air smelling of burned beans Mom had forgotten on the stove. It's all twisted with the memory like a song that pulls you back to a moment of time.

My breath shudders out. "I didn't even think twice about leaving Mom. That's how much I loved him. And he kept staring from my suitcase to my mom. She kept saying his name. 'Clay. Clay.' She was pleading with him. I thought for herself, but it wasn't."

Garrett reaches for my hand, but I shake him off. I need to finish this. "He said he'd get settled first, and then he'd send a ticket. He said that way I could finish school. So I rolled my suitcase to the landing by the front door and I left it there. Three months," I choke out. "That's how long it sat there."

"God, Josie."

"I checked the mail every day, but there was never a ticket. He started texting less and less. There were no phone calls because of the time difference, he said. Still, I didn't get it. I was pretty dense until, finally, I saw it all spelled out in an article." I gather a shaky breath. "You know why he wanted to coach Little League? He'd found out one of the parents was a Japanese businessman with contacts in the Nippon league. It wasn't an accident. He used me as an excuse to coach and meet the guy. All of it was a lie because he would do anything to play the game again." I draw in a breath and lock gazes with Garrett. "The same way you would."

"I wouldn't lie to you, Josie."

"You might. My own father did." I blink back tears. "I kept that suitcase in my closet, packed and ready, for another six months because I still couldn't believe he'd abandoned me that way. That haunts me. How trusting I was. How stupid." Tears spill over, and I flick them away hurriedly.

A quiet settles over us, but it's a restless silence. My words fill the space around us, creating space between us.

Garrett finally says, "That's why you don't trust me. Us," he adds. "I guess your mom thinks I'll turn out to be like your dad, too?"

"You're so much alike. She met my dad in high school. And he was sweet to my mom and charming and he made her laugh and he made her heart beat like crazy." I wonder if he realizes he does that to me. "The things she felt are the things I'm starting to feel."

"The things I already feel." His chin rises with determination. "How do I prove I'm not like your dad?"

"I don't know. Time, I guess. Can we take it slow?"

"I thought we were."

"Slower, then."

He sighs, leaning forward so that our foreheads touch. I want to pull him close even as I'm trying to push him away. "If that's what you need, we'll try slow. But there's another thing that might help."

"What?" I ask.

"Let me meet her."

• • •

When I get home, Mom is out. A date with James. I'm glad. I need time to think.

I set my pack on the kitchen table—it feels so much heavier with the ASU folder inside. Restless, I wander through the house we've turned into the first real home I've had. Even as I tell myself I'm not heading anywhere special, I end up in Mom's room, my heart suddenly racing.

The past, like all good monsters, is hiding under the bed. Flipping up the burgundy quilt, I kneel down and pull out the plastic white tub. The lid is layered in gray dust that catches in my throat when I pop it off. Lying on top is the baseball glove my dad bought me when I turned twelve. Black leather with red laces and "Joe" stamped into the palm.

How do you deal with the fact that your dad doesn't want you? That maybe, most likely, he never did?

I'd just turned thirteen when Mom told me there would never be an airplane ticket in the mail. Even then, even though the texts and emails had slowed to a trickle, I didn't believe her. I thought she was trying to turn me against him because by then the divorce had turned ugly. But the article came out soon after. Two months later, a Google alert told me my father was in California for a visit. He never tried to see me. He never even called. I finally understood that when Dad said it would be easier for me without him, he meant it would be easier for him without me.

After that, I didn't know how to be me. I was confident and strong, and then I wasn't. The day I started to feel better was the day Mom drove me to the dump and I took my Yankees-blue suitcase, still packed with all the things I couldn't look at again, and sent it flying down to lie buried with everything else no one wanted.

He didn't want me? Well, I didn't want him. I didn't want baseball.

I didn't want dreams.

The only thing spared during the purge was this glove. Mom said she wanted to keep it, without explaining why. I know now she saved it for me. I press it to my cheek, breathing in deeply. The glove smells of old leather and disappointment. But it also feels like a piece of me.

Where do I go from here? Do I stick with my plan? Or do I consider the future Garrett is dangling before my eyes? It scares me. To pack my heart and my future in a new suitcase and follow a whole new path.

Can I do it?

My inner voice says no. It says don't take the risk.

Of course it does. It's the voice of my thirteen-year-old self.

Chapter Thirty-Six

The following week is a whirl of activity as Garrett and I finish the feature, editing together the questions and answers along with commentary on recent changes to the game. We're both impressed with how it turns out. We also call two more games—both of them Cholla wins that clinch our spot in the playoffs. The guys are all swagger and bluster and I take great joy in playing the role of snarky non-believer while secretly I'm starting to think they actually might win State.

On Tuesday, Mai officially ended things with Anthony. She did it in true Mai fashion. Bluntly.

"I told him he was becoming a distraction from what really mattered."

"Mai!" I winced when she told me that night.

"I know. It sounded as bad then as it does now."

"Are you okay?"

She shrugged, but I couldn't remember seeing her look so sad. "I'll be fine."

We were quiet for a long moment. "What happens when you see him?" I asked. "How did you leave it?"

"I fixed it. I think."

It turned out better than I expected. After a weird couple of days, Anthony seemed his usual chill self. They settled into being friends...friendly...though he didn't eat lunch with us again.

I was planning to bring Garrett over and tell Mom about our broadcasting experiment, but she came back from her date with James with puffy eyes. She brushed off my offer of pralines and cream, which is the only known antidote for sadness.

"I'm fine," she said. "It was my decision. It wasn't going to work. Better to end it now."

But she started the week in a funk and never came out of it. I found her pouring out the special James fragrance yesterday, with a vacant look on her face that was worse than tears. No way could I bring up the broadcast plan with all that on her mind. And I wanted her to be in a good mood the first time she met Garrett.

So instead, Mom and I focused more on the business, since that's the only thing that seemed to help. We had a party on Thursday and did a test run of the new website, helping everyone to place orders online. The ladies loved the look of the site and there was only one minor glitch—a link to product videos that didn't work. The folder for ASU's broadcasting program stayed unopened in my pack while Mom sent me Pinterest ideas for a new desk to go in the office. *My* desk. On top of all of that, there was schoolwork and graduation announcements and my birthday plans and a boy who was trying to move slowly while I figure out where I'm headed.

How could I have been so sure of my future for so long and now, with graduation a month away, I don't know what to do? Garrett's been patient, but I know it bothers him that a week has passed since our talk and nothing has changed. I'm still keeping him at a distance, still putting off a decision about ASU, and I still haven't introduced him to Mom. But he's also still training with Kyle Masters. When I get to the booth on the following Tuesday, I wonder if maybe his patience has run out.

There's a flower on my stool.

I take a quick glance around and see Garrett's stuff and all the equipment.

But no Garrett.

The rose is pink, the petals still in a tight bud, the stem stripped of thorns. I close my eyes and inhale the perfume. Much better than anything that comes in an AromaTher bottle.

I open my eyes and take in the view through the window. The dirt infield that's been smoothed out with brooms, the clean white of new chalk and the kaleidoscope of colors that dances on the edge of my vision from the bleachers. There's a hint of tobacco mixed in with the scents of dirt and grass and something sharp that I think is pine tar.

That crackle of energy is in the air again, punctuated by the *thwack* of balls hitting gloves, and the chatter that filters in from the dugout below as the players warm up. Memories resurface, but the sting is gone, and it feels safe to go back in my mind. I used to love warm-ups when I was playing the game. The way my throwing arm would stretch and loosen. The joy of releasing a ball and watching it fly...feeling like you could fly yourself.

Starting a game on the mound with the chance that this might be the day when you pitch so well, you're still standing on the mound at the very end. It occurs to me that I'm looking at a baseball field and *not* seeing my dad.

I'm seeing it the way I used to see it. The way Garrett sees it.

There's a loud rattle as footsteps pound up the metal ramp to the bleachers and the booth. I know it's him before the door opens. His presence is overwhelming in this small space. My skin warms, my heart skips—every part of me chiming in to say I'm happy to see him.

He plants a quick kiss on my cheek before walking past to his stool. He's got a cable in his hand that he connects to the mixing board. "You're late."

"I am not." I hold out the flower. "And what is this? A flower at a baseball game?"

"I thought the sport could survive one rose." He leans out the window to adjust the mic.

"You know pink means purity and innocence?"

"What?" He yanks the flower from my fingers. "We don't want any of that." He tosses it over his shoulder.

I laugh and push him aside as I retrieve the flower.

He settles on his stool, looping his headset around his neck.

"Thank you," I tell him.

He leans in to give me a quick kiss, which turns into a second, slightly longer kiss. "I thought the rose smelled like you," he says, "but I was wrong. You smell better."

There's a bang on the wall of the booth. "Yo, G. Quit making out with your girlfriend."

"I'm not his girlfriend," I call back, but I'm blushing. The booth is completely open to the field and I can't be sure I didn't just moan a little. *Oh God.*

I busy myself with the job at hand. Garrett checks the feed and the audio levels and I'm kind of impressed now that I'm taking a second to watch him. "You had to learn all of this yourself, didn't you?"

"What? The equipment?"

"All of it. How to handle the feed and upload the broadcasts."

"It was the only way I could think of to stay close to the game." He looks out the window, and I know all he's seeing is the distance from here to the pitching mound.

"It's still not close enough, is it?" I ask.

He shrugs and shifts his gaze back to me. "It's turned out to have some positives. I never kissed any of the guys before a game." He clicks open the screen to check video and sound feeds. "Did you look through the course catalog?"

I take a sip from my water bottle. "Not yet."

"You're going to get a dent in your ass."

"What?"

"From sitting on the fence so long."

"Ha. We don't even know if we'll win the contest."

"That's why we fill out the application. We get in the old-fashioned way. Like everyone else."

"But if we're not good enough to win a local high school broadcast contest?" I let the rest of my question hang in the air.

"We have to get better. But look at how much we've improved in the past month."

He adjusts a black knob and then a red one. Absently, I wonder if I'll have to learn what all the knobs mean. I like calling the games with Garrett, but the rest of it, I'm not so sure. "Scottie told me we're drawing traffic to the recordings. He thinks more locals are going online to listen even after the game is over."

"Because we're good." His mouth hitches up on one side and I want to grab him and kiss him.

"You're cute sometimes."

"And sexy all the time?"

"Forget I said anything."

He laughs as he turns back to the field. "It's a perfect day, isn't it?"

"Yes." But I'm not thinking about the weather.

"That's another thing I love about the game. Number eighty-six on the list of top one hundred: the field always looks so pretty this time of day. The way the sun skims off the mowed grass."

"And the chalk lines around the batter's box." A bittersweet memory fills my head. Chalking the batter's box was one of my jobs the season I coached with my dad. "I love how clean and perfect they are right now. The calm before the storm to come."

"Number seventy-two," he says. "And the scoreboard. The way it's all zeros at the start. That's number forty-two."

"You don't actually have these written down, do you?"

"It's all in here." I think he's going to point to his head but he doesn't. He points to his heart.

For a second, for his sake, I wish he wasn't sitting beside me. I wish he were down on the field where he wants to be. Then he lets out a tiny sigh, one I don't think I'm meant to hear, and he flips on his mic. He announces the national anthem and off we go.

We call the game with our knees touching and the rose on the counter between us where I can keep glancing at it. Finally, between the fifth and sixth innings, he turns to me. "So when are you going to say yes?"

"To what?"

"To being my girlfriend."

"Is that why you brought me a rose? Because that romantic stuff doesn't work with me."

"Yeah, it does."

He grins, and oh hell, he's right. It does work with me.

Before he turns the mic back on, he says, "Don't panic, Walters. You can say yes later. We've got a game to call."

· · ·

It isn't until much later...until after the game is over and I've eaten dinner with Mom and finished my homework.

And after we've watched an episode of *The Great British Baking Show* and are starting on the second.

And after Garrett texts and says, "Walk outside. I left you a surprise."

And I walk outside and the surprise is Garrett, who ran over, which is why I didn't hear a car.

And he's in a tank top and running shorts and he's all smooth skin and sweaty muscles and I don't care when he tugs me around the corner, away from the porch light and the moths fluttering uselessly against the glow. I'm like a moth, helpless and blind to everything but this guy who makes me want to believe in things like dreams and happy endings and even the beauty of baseball.

And his hands slide around my waist and mine slide up his bare arms and his mouth is on mine. And I bite his bottom lip the way he does, and he groans into my mouth.

And after, when we're both shaking and our pulses are racing and our foreheads are pressed together. I reclaim my breath and find my feet still on the ground but my heart untethered.

That's when I find my voice and I say, "Yes."

Chapter Thirty-Seven

"Josie," Mom says. "I can't get this link to work. How do I fix it?"

"Hang on." I'm standing beside her at the kitchen counter, adding samples of face serum to the party bags.

"Josie!"

The last one hits the bottom of the bag, joining the peppermint toothpaste, the orange essential oil, and the hibiscus lozenge. "How is it possible for you to turn my name into a dirty word?"

"Would you please help me?" She runs a hand through her hair, and passion-berry mist drifts my way. She's been in a rotten mood since she stopped seeing James, and if this is the result of no secret sex, then I'm sorry I ever had an issue with it. "If we're not out of here in fifteen minutes, we're going to be late."

"Fine," I say. Tonight's party is for a book club that just read about holistic healing and decided an essential oil demonstration would add to the discussion. Targeting book clubs is such a good idea, I told Mom we should advertise that on our website. Which reminded her about the link that still isn't working.

I lean over so I can see her laptop screen. "You can't fix it from the website. I told you. You have to go to the admin page."

"I don't see it in the menu."

"You have to log in on a different site. Remember?" I gesture to the screen. "Pull up a new tab."

Instead, she shoves the laptop toward me, moving my phone out of the way. "Can you do it for me?"

"You're the one who told me not to help, that you wanted to learn it all yourself."

"I've changed my mind. When you're out of town, fixes will have to wait."

"Why would I be out of town?" I pull up the admin page, giving her a quick glance. I don't expect to see flushed cheeks and lips pressed tightly together. She does that when she's said something she didn't mean to.

"Mom, what?"

"Not now." She points at the screen. "We're going to be late."

I pull my hands off the keyboard and fold them over my chest. "What?"

"Josie!" But I know she's frustrated with herself. "It's supposed to be a surprise."

"Tell me or we'll be here all night."

"I'm sending you to New York this year for the annual trade show."

"Me?" I sit back, startled.

"More than that." She smiles and it's the first real happiness I've seen from her in a week. My unease blooms into near panic. "It's in Manhattan and I've already looked into hotels near Times Square and"—she pauses for effect— "I've spoken to Mai about joining you there for the weekend.

I'll buy her plane ticket, too. So it's business plus a girls' trip."

"Mom." My throat fills, along with my eyes.

"Happy early birthday." She watches me expectantly.

I know I'm supposed to scream with joy like those people on the radio who win concert tickets. But all I can think of is that next September I could be at ASU. In the broadcasting program.

"It's too much, Mom. It's too expensive. And you love the trade show."

Her smile fades. "I thought you'd be excited."

"I am. It's just…" *Oh shit.* While I've been making plans, so has she. "I have to tell you something. I really, really don't know how."

Her eyes fill with panic. "Are you sick? Are you pregnant?"

"No! God, it's nothing like that." I take a breath. "It's just that I'm not sure anymore."

"Sure of what?"

I stare at the computer screen. At the dashboard for the website of Melissa and Josie Walters, AromaTher Proprietors.

The laptop closes with a *snick*. Mom's fingers press into the metallic cover. "Not sure about the business?"

"I've been thinking I might want to try something different. You know. Before I go right into it."

"Something different?" Each syllable is painfully enunciated. "We have a meeting with the lawyer in ten days. When were you going to tell me this?"

"It's not for sure. It's something we've been talking about."

"We?" Her eyes widen. "Oh my God. This is about Garrett, isn't it? The baseball player."

"He's not a player. He wants to go into broadcasting."

"What does that have to do with you?"

I swallow, knowing there's no good way to say this. "I

might want to go into broadcasting, too."

Her mouth falls open. "You're going to follow him? After six weeks in a high school booth? Without knowing anything about the profession? Without any research? You just suddenly think you might like it? Do you hear how crazy that sounds? And you of all people."

"What does that mean?"

"It means you know the danger of following. Blindly." Her words sting. "More than that, you make reasoned decisions. You're practical. Grounded. You don't take crazy risks."

"Or any risk," I mutter.

Lines deepen across her forehead. "Suddenly risk is good? Is that what you learned from your baseball player? After everything you went through with your father, that's who you're going to listen to?"

"Should I listen to you? You're more afraid than I am. You broke up with a great guy because you were afraid to take a chance, and now you're miserable."

"Because I let it get too far. In the long run, I made the right choice. Can you say the same thing?" She slaps her hand on the counter. "You're going to change your life for a boy who will never do anything but disappoint you."

"You don't know that!"

"I know he's no good for you. You've been dating for a month and already he's turned you into a liar."

"I haven't been lying!" My voice shakes, but I won't back down. "I knew you would react like this, so I just didn't tell you yet. And also, I was giving it time, seeing if it's something I might really want to do. You always said if there was something else I wanted—"

"Yes! Something *you* wanted. Not something you want to do to hold on to a boy."

"Never mind," I snap. "It doesn't matter what I say. You were never going to like him."

She grabs her laptop and shoves it into her shoulder bag. "How would we know? I've never even met him. If he's such a good guy, why have I never met him?"

A knot the size of a baseball lodges in my throat. "Because I knew you'd be like this."

"Concerned?" she says. "Worried? Scared out of my mind? Yeah, Josie. I am."

"You should be happy for me. Because I have a chance to do something that maybe I'll love. I don't have to be trapped in this business with you."

"Trapped?"

Even as she repeats the word, I want to take it back.

"You feel trapped?" Her eyes glimmer with hurt.

"I didn't mean that."

She stares at me, the word still echoing between us.

"Mom!"

With sharp, jerky motions, she pulls her pack over her shoulder and grabs the box with the neatly packed sample bags. When I move to take it from her, she shakes her head. "No. I'll handle this one on my own. You stay here. You think about what you want." She stops at the door and turns back. "We'll cancel our plans until you're sure. A partnership requires two people who are committed. You think about that, too."

I listen to the sounds of her leaving. The door slamming. The truck door. The whirl of the garage door and the final *thud* when it closes behind her.

What am I doing? What am I risking? And for what? I think about what Mom said—about requiring two people who are committed. And she's right.

Chapter Thirty-Eight

It takes me eighteen minutes to walk to Garrett's house.

I'm relieved when it's Garrett who opens the door. Emotions flicker across his face. Surprise. Happiness. As he gets a closer look at my face, worry.

"What are we doing?" I blurt before he can say anything.

He opens the door wider, and I can see him looking over my shoulder. Probably for the truck. "Did something happen? I thought you had a demonstration party?" He reaches for my hand and pulls me inside.

"What are we doing, Garrett?" I repeat.

"Let's go to the TV room."

I suddenly think of his mom. "Is your mom here?"

"At the store."

I nod, glad I won't have to make small talk, and follow him to the room with the big TV and soft leather couch.

"What happened?"

He sits on the couch, but I can't. I start pacing. "I told my mom."

"And?"

"We had a fight. She's putting our partnership on hold. I'm risking everything I've planned for, and you're still working on your pitching. Your heart is still going in a different direction."

"Josie." He reaches for my hand and stops me. "I feel like I'm watching a tennis match. Will you sit down? Please."

"Tell me."

"I'm playing it out. That's all. The lessons have been paid for—you know that."

"Until when exactly?"

"Two more Saturdays. Last lesson is May fourth."

My birthday. "And you'll be able to let it go?"

"Yes." He reaches for my hands, and I let him wrap his fingers through mine.

"What if you start throwing well?"

"I won't."

"You're trying, though. I'm thinking about changing everything, and if you could play, you'd be gone in a heartbeat."

"No, I wouldn't." He tugs me forward until we're both sitting, our knees touching.

"You would. You love it too much."

"Yeah, but it's not the only thing I love."

My heart stutters in my chest. I'm suddenly hot. Dizzy. I tug my hands free, but he won't let me.

"I love you, Josie."

"You do not." My heart has started again, banging hard against my ribs, echoing in my ears.

His smile is unbearably sweet. "That's not exactly the response I expected when I told a girl that for the first time."

My gaze flies to his. Deep blue rimming pupils so wide I want to fall into them.

His voice is rough. "I don't know how else to explain the way I feel when I'm not with you. I've been happy with girls before. But I've never been miserable without them."

I squeeze his fingers. "That's an awful way of saying that."

"Thank you for critiquing my pronouncement of love."

I smile into his smile.

"Don't be so afraid," he says softly.

"I can't help it. I feel like something bad is going to happen."

"You're waiting for something bad to happen. It's not the same thing."

Is he right? Am I? "The last time I felt this happy, I was coaching with my dad and he was planning to leave me."

"I know that. And I know what we're talking about is a big change for us both. But when someone throws a wild pitch, you don't question your good fortune. You run for the bases."

I slowly unwind my grip on his fingers and slide my hands up his wrists to his forearms. Warm muscle moves under the brush of my fingers. "She's canceling all the plans. She says I can do whatever I want."

"Then do broadcasting. We'll submit our applications whether we win or not. We'll take the classes we need, get the internships we can, and come out of ASU with a degree in broadcast communications."

"That easy, huh?"

"I'm not going anywhere, Josie."

My heart vaults into my throat and every nerve in my body sparks to life as he shifts closer, eliminating the space between us. He tilts his head so that our lips are almost touching. "I know how you grew up. I know you never want to move again."

"Well," I say, "maybe just an inch." I lean in and we're kissing.

Chapter Thirty-Nine

It's overcast when I wake up on my birthday. I'm not sure what woke me and then I check my phone and find a text from Garrett.

GARRETT: Woke up thinking of you. Happy birthday, Walters. See you soon.

I sigh as I sink back into my pillow, my phone pressed to my heart. If only it was just Garrett and me. But it isn't.

My stomach quickly rearranges itself into knots and my brain is a fog of images from the past week.

True to her word, Mom hasn't pressed me. She quietly canceled all the plans for today—even the cake she ordered. I've offered to continue helping with the business, but she said a break would be good for us both. She said it might give me clarity. That's such a homeopathic-naturopathic-everything-pathic word that I found myself getting mad all over again. My emotions are riding a teeter-totter, and I can't get off.

I'm starting to think clarity is a bunch of bullshit. You just have to decide. *I* have to decide. If only we'd heard back from ASU about the finalists for the contest. Cholla's final regular-season game was on Tuesday, and we submitted the entire packet the following day. They promised to announce the top three finalists online within a week and the winners soon after. They want to give the winning team time to plan and prepare for the Diamondbacks game in June. If Garrett and I are top three, that would be a sign.

"Can I have a sign, please?" I say to the ceiling, hoping someone up there is listening.

My phone beeps, shocking me. I glance at the screen, but it's not God texting. It's Mai.

MAI: Happy birthday. Can we get drunk on Cheetos later?

ME: You're so wild.

MAI: What are you doing this morning?

ME: Waiting for a sign.

MAI: I can make you one. What do you want it to say?

I laugh to myself, but my best friend has made a very good point.

ME: I'm going to go surprise my boyfriend.

MAI: Does that mean you're not wearing underwear?

Still laughing, I climb out of bed. Mai is exactly right. Instead of waiting for a sign, I'm making my own and it's going to say:

Fill out the effing application and go show your boyfriend.

If there's extra room on the sign, it will also say:

And bring him home to meet your mom.
You big weenie.

Mom has gone to the farmers market this morning—she decided she might as well after we canceled our meeting with the lawyer. I'd already taken the day off at Page & Prose. Lianne seemed happy about it—she's been hinting she can handle it on her own. Even if she can, no way am I quitting early. The best part of my week is reading those kids a story and making all of us laugh. I still get to sit on a throne one more time next Saturday, and no one is cheating me out of that.

Part of me would like to take over this morning, but what I need to do is important and now that I've decided, it feels like it can't wait.

I take a quick shower, and though I'm impatient to go, it's also my birthday and I want to look special. I take time for makeup and a few minutes with the blow dryer and a round brush. A tank top, capris, and my ugly sandals complete the ensemble because even my footwear makes me think of Garrett.

Makes me smile.

I pick out a schedule of classes for the fall semester, filling in the sheet with my choices. It's more of a symbol than anything because I'll have to do it all online. When I write the date at the top, it makes me pause. I'm eighteen. An adult. I wonder if it's why I feel different, or if I feel different because I'm about to change my future.

He'll disappoint you.

Mom's words hover in the back of my head. That's fear talking. *Her* fear. Okay, and maybe mine. But today is special for more than just my birthday. Today is also Garrett's last lesson with Kyle Masters. I can stop worrying about him miraculously getting his arm back.

A moment comes to me from a few nights ago. A moment I know I'll replay a million times. We were at Garrett's. We were sitting so close I could only see pieces of his face. The soft skin beneath his eye. The bumpy curve along the inner part of his ear. The stray hairs at the end of his eyebrow.

We'd been kissing. Soft, light kisses that had no end and no beginning. Kisses like breaths...like breathing...like heartbeats. When he pulled back for air, there was a long minute when we just looked at each other. Everything I felt swelled inside of me—so many feelings I didn't know what to do with them.

"I love you, Josie."

I closed my eyes, still not comfortable hearing the words.

"Hey," he said, his thumb brushing across my lips. "I'm not going away just because you close your eyes."

Maybe that was the moment I started to believe that he really wasn't going anywhere.

I haven't said the words to him, but I almost did then. I'm not sure what stopped me—maybe I'm as superstitious as a ballplayer. If I said the words, what if it jinxed us? Which makes as much sense as thinking a blue Gatorade will help you hit home runs. So today is the day.

Today is the day for a lot of things.

The clouds have burned off and it's sunny when I start the walk to school. It seems like a million flowers have bloomed overnight, or maybe I never bothered to really look. Today the world feels different. I've got the schedule in my hand and I want to show it to Garrett first thing. Then we'll hug and he'll kiss me and there will be a rainbow overhead and a choir of unicorns will sing *Hallelujah*. I laugh to myself. Ciera and the other kids wouldn't doubt it for a second.

Garrett has never told me what kind of exercises Masters has him doing, but I'm guessing quick-hand and bucket drills. So I'm surprised when I reach school property and hear the crack of a ball hitting a bat. Is Garrett throwing live pitches to a hitter? Has he progressed more than I thought? More than

I let myself think?

My heart in my throat, I cross the parking lot. It's empty except for Garrett's black Hyundai and a white sedan I'm guessing belongs to Masters. They're on the far practice field, and I have to walk past the main field to reach them. Fences are in my way. Then the dugout. But I can hear the bat.

He promised to tell me if he was making progress. He promised.

I round the last corner, and the field is in clear view. I stop, my mouth falling open in shock.

Kyle Masters is standing on the mound. He's feeding balls into a pitching machine set up beside him. The guy in the batter's box, the guy in gray baseball pants and a black tee, wearing batting gloves and a helmet, the guy grinding his foot in and sinking into his stance, is Garrett Reeves.

My boyfriend.

He isn't trying to make it back as a pitcher. He's trying to make it back as a hitter.

Chapter Forty

I watch, frozen, as a ball shoots out of the machine and curves over the middle of the plate. Garrett swings—and misses.

Automatically, I scan the field. My baseball brain is still working while the rest of me is stunned. I note the balls scattered across the field. Most of them were either hit shallow or lie in foul territory. The largest number of balls is piled up along the backstop, meaning Garrett never made contact. My eyes narrow as I watch him prepare for another ball. Wide stance. Weight loaded onto the back leg.

Another swing and another miss.

Good! I'm sickened by how glad I am. The other emotion gaining strength by the second is anger. He lied to me. Let me think he was trying to pitch again. Let me worry about the damage he was doing to his arm. And all that time he's been working on his hitting? My pulse beats hard and fast, staccato punches of fear matched by a pounding in my head. The chances he could make it back as a pitcher were never good.

But as a hitter?

It's an easier path to the game for him. Most pitchers start out as hitters, but once you get to high school, coaches take the bat out of your hand and you focus only on throwing. Pitchers only, they're called. Like Garrett. That doesn't mean he didn't know how to hit. Or he couldn't hit.

He whiffs a third ball. Barely gets a piece of a fourth.

He's missing. He can't hit the curve.

My breath calms as I study him more closely. My father might be a self-centered ass, but he was also a damn good hitter. And now, he's a damn good hitting coach for a minor league team. In one way or another, his skill with a bat is what brought in a paycheck for over two decades. In those early years when I followed him everywhere, I was a sponge. There are things I know now without remembering when I learned them. As I watch Garrett, it's all there in my head. Stance. Load. Swing plane. Rhythm. Finish.

My stomach churns like a washing machine on tilt.

"I can't see it," Garrett calls, his frustration obvious.

No, he can't. But even with tears welling in my eyes, I see what he doesn't.

He looks up then—spots me. I see the instant when he realizes who it is. The bat drops from his hand. A ball spirals into the fence, forgotten.

"What's going on?" I hear Masters ask.

"Josie!" Garrett shouts. Masters turns, and when he sees me, the whirr of the pitching machine goes off.

"Give me a few," Garrett shouts over his shoulder. He's already jogging my way.

I'm rooted in place and spinning at the same time.

Then he's in front of me, breathing hard, his eyes shaded behind the brim of his cap, his hands still encased in batting gloves. I didn't even know he had batting gloves. Or a bat. Or a shin guard.

"Hey, birthday girl. What are you doing here? Everything

okay?" He reaches out a hand and I shudder, pulling my shoulder back before he can touch me. He frowns, his gaze stalling at my hand, and I realize I'm still holding the folded schedule. The middle is crushed where I unknowingly wadded it in my fist. I fold it quickly and shove it into my back pocket.

"How long has this been going on?" I ask.

"The hitting?" He glances back to the field. His hands rise to his hips. He looks good in uniform. Looks more comfortable than most guys look in their own skin. "Couple—three weeks. It's just something I was trying."

"Just something you were trying?"

"Are you mad?" He seems surprised. "I've never lied about what I was doing."

"You let me think you were pitching."

"I let me think I was doing anything and everything to get back in the game. And that's the truth."

"It's not the same." My anger spikes because he's actually right.

"You knew that I had to try right up until the end, Josie. If you want me to apologize for having a dream and fighting for it, then you're out of luck." Now he's angry, too, his eyes sparking blue heat.

"That's not what I want."

"You sure about that?"

"Of course I'm sure." The words are emphatic, but I look away because the truth is I might be lying.

"I also told you that if there was a chance I could play again, I'd tell you. But you can't trust me, can you?"

So many emotions swirl around us, thick and palpable. Anger. Fear. Desperation. Betrayal. Which belong to him and which to me? "I have reason to be wary."

"None that I've given you." He rips off one glove and then the other, stuffing them in a back pocket. "You had to have seen me hit on your way out here. I've been working for weeks and I don't see the curveball. I'm like Evan Harris, who you like to make fun of every damn time he comes up to the plate."

I blanch. I remember how tense Garrett would get every time Evan came up. Every time he struck out. "You don't have to hit the curveball, Garrett. Not if you're good enough hitting the fastball."

"That isn't true. Not if I want to play at the highest level."

"You can still play college."

"I've already told you. I don't want to hang on and watch other guys move up knowing I never will. Even if I did, I don't have that option and you know it. I've got a deal with my dad. One last spring to work on my game and one last tryout."

The final two words shock me into a startled, "What? You have a tryout?"

His hands fist at his hips, but there's no apology in his eyes. "I didn't tell you about it, because I didn't see it happening. And it won't."

My voice is like sandpaper. "What tryout?"

"A junior college coach in Florida knows me from summer leagues. He'll be watching some guys in Phoenix next weekend. Said if I wanted to come by, he'd take a look. But there's nothing for him to see. It's done. I'm…done."

His voice cracks and he looks away. I look away. My heart feels like it's just cracked, too. I want to hold on to my anger, but there's a crushing weight on my chest. I look back at the field, at all the missed balls. He wants this so badly. He wants this as much as I want him.

"What about broadcasting?" I ask.

"It's the only thing that's kept me from losing my mind." He pulls off his cap, runs his arm across his forehead. When I raise my gaze to his, it's like I can see his heart.

The heart that will only be mine once baseball is in the

past.

All I have to do is walk away. Forget what I've seen. He'll take all that love for the game and he'll channel it into broadcasting. Into us. Into me.

"Let me finish up here," he says. "I'll see you later the way we planned. All right?"

Tears spring to my eyes. "All right."

I turn to leave, my heart screaming, *Coward!* I start jogging. I'm suddenly desperate to put distance between Garrett and me. Between me and everything I just saw.

Because it isn't hopeless. Because Garrett isn't the same as Evan Harris. Because I've seen hitters like Garrett struggle before, and there might be a way I could help him.

If I do, baseball wins.

And I lose.

Chapter Forty-One

Mai is waiting at her front door when I get there. I sent a pathetic, needy text, and I can tell she's doing an inventory of me as I walk up. Puffy eyes that have produced enough tears to water a baseball field. My rumpled tank streaked with wet sticky splotches where I wiped my cheeks and nose.

Without a word, we make our way to her room. I kick off my sandals, dusty from the baseball field. I'm going to have to throw them away, I realize as I crawl onto her bed. They'll remind me too much of Garrett. Both of us curl toward the other, except this time with a box of Kleenex between us. She doesn't say anything, just waits while I pull a tissue and mop up my face one more time.

"It hasn't been the best birthday so far," I say.

She cracks a tiny smile. "I always thought adulthood might be a scam."

I try smiling, but that only makes my eyes leak again. I'm going to miss Mai so much. She just told me the other day about a summer program in California she plans on attending. She'll be gone three weeks after graduation. How do I survive that on top of everything else? The thought does nothing to help the tear situation. I take a deep breath and blink a few dozen times.

"I made myself a sign. It said fill out the ASU schedule and go tell Garrett that you want to be a team."

"And?"

"I surprised him at the school field. And then he surprised me."

"Uh-oh." She bites her bottom lip, and that reminds me of Garrett, too.

"He isn't trying to pitch again, Mai. He's hitting."

I know she's running through everything she knows about baseball—which takes about two seconds. "So?"

"So he was never going to make it back as a pitcher. But he *could* make it back as a position player as long as he can hit well enough."

"And can he? Hit well enough?"

"No."

"That's good." Her eyes brighten.

"But he could." I swallow thickly.

"Yeah, except today is his last day, right? So it's over."

"That's the point. If he knew, it wouldn't be."

"If he knew what?"

"That there's a chance."

She shakes her head. "You're not making sense. There's always a chance, right? That's why guys hang on too long."

"This is different. You know my dad is a hitting coach—he's in charge of all the minor league players for a major league organization for a reason. He knows his shit. I saw him work with guys like Garrett. I saw him fix them."

"You can fix a player?"

"Sometimes." The tight ball in my stomach unravels with the truth I don't want to face. The decision I don't want to make. "I think I can help Garrett."

"But." She shakes her head. "He's got a coach, Josie. Don't you think if it was that easy, Masters would have done it already?"

"It's not a technique thing. It has to do with how he sees the ball. My dad struggled with the same thing."

"And you think if you showed him, then he would be able to hit the ball, and he'd go back to playing baseball?"

I nod because that's exactly what I think. What I know. "Broadcasting, teaming up with me—I'm the consolation prize. The team he really wants is a bunch of guys wearing pinstripes and spitting seeds."

"Can't he have two teams?"

A sob rises from low in my chest. "Baseball isn't just a job. It's a life. I'd be forever competing for his time and attention. Always wondering when I'd be left alone with my packed suitcase."

Her frown deepens. "But he said he loves you."

"He loves baseball more." I press wads of tissue to my eyes. "Is there something wrong with wanting to be first, Mai? With wanting to be most important?"

She squeezes my shoulder. "Of course there isn't."

I cry harder. I cry the way I did when I realized my dad didn't want me. And I know that whatever it takes, I'm not going to give Garrett the chance to not want me, too. It takes a few awful minutes, but finally I get control over my emotions. "Sorry," I mumble.

Mai answers by shoving two more tissues into my hand. "Don't be sorry. You just broke up."

"Not officially." I blow my nose. "I have to tell him."

A long pause follows as various expressions chase themselves across Mai's face. Confusion. Surprise. Calculation. "You didn't tell him you could help him?"

"I couldn't." I roll to my back. The familiar stain is there, but it gives me no comfort. "I'd just filled out my schedule of classes. All of it was in my head, you know? The future. Us. I couldn't do it."

"And do you…have to?"

My breath catches. "I can't lie."

"You're not lying. You're not even sure you can help him. As far as he knows, he's given it his best shot and it didn't work out."

My heart grasps onto her words. A lifeline. A way forward to the future with him I want so much it hurts. And really, there's no guarantee he makes it no matter what I show him. So many guys don't. Who's to say he doesn't go play college ball and get a career-ending injury? It already happened to him once. And by then, the broadcasting opportunity would have passed him by. It might be the best thing if I don't say a word.

The stain on the ceiling shifts like a Rorschach image, and I'm suddenly seeing Garrett leaning out over the window of the booth, his need to be on the field so strong I can feel it myself. Is it right for me to keep what I know from him? If I won't follow him, is it fair to make sure he follows me?

"Should or must," I murmur. But I know what I have to do. I haven't told him I love him, but I do. Too much to lose him.

And too much to keep him.

I sit up.

Mai does, too. "What are you doing?"

"I'm going to tell him." I pull my phone from my back pocket. I've turned it to mute and see now that there are four texts from Garrett. "I'll always feel like I trapped him if I don't."

"You going to be okay?"

"Eventually." The heart is a muscle—it can get injured like any other muscle. But it'll heal in time. Just takes lots of ice.

I start texting.

ME: Get your baseball stuff. Meet me at the field in half an hour.

GARRETT: Why?

ME: I've got something for you.

GARRETT: What?

ME: Your dream.

"You want me to come?" Mai asks.

"I'll be okay."

"Call me when you're done. We'll eat pralines and cream and watch *Pride and Prejudice*."

"The Colin Firth version?"

"All nineteen hours of it."

"It's six hours," I say. "You think it's longer because you hate it. We can watch something else."

"Nope. We're watching it. And you know that when I fall asleep, I'm still there for you."

I give her a watery smile. "In that case, we'll watch the extra features, too."

We hug for a long time, and on the short walk home, I gather my emotions and tuck them away. If I'm going to help Garrett, I have to think clearly.

More than that, I have to think back.

For so long, I avoided everything to do with baseball. The sport stole my dad and taught me that it was worse to dream and fail than it was to not dream at all. But the game didn't betray me, and it's taken Garrett to remind me of how much I love it. With my memories, my experiences, I have an advantage his other coaches don't. I have a father who suffered from the same issue standing in Garrett's way. And I still have the link to my father's online training log.

Chapter Forty-Two

Garrett is waiting for me at the field. He's sitting on the bleachers, his feet stretched out and crossed at the ankles. In a button-down black shirt and khaki shorts, he looks like anything but a player. And he looks so good, I want to forget this stupid plan and hold on to him anyway I can.

I shove away the thought and remind myself I'm here as a coach. "You're going to hit in those shoes?" I ask. At home, I packed a workout bag and changed my own clothes.

He glances at the black boat shoes I've never seen him wear before. "I'm not hitting."

"Yeah, you are."

"Nope. It's your birthday." He pushes to his feet and works his way down to the bottom step. "You had something in your hand earlier. I didn't ask what it was, but I think I know."

"Garrett." I silence him with a glare. "Where's your baseball bag?"

He slides his hands in his pockets. "I'm done, Josie."

"You're not." I look back at the batting cage and see the

pitching machine set up in there, but the balls all picked up. "You have the key to the equipment closet?" I hold out my hand.

"Why?"

"We need a bucket of baseballs."

"Quit it, Josie."

"I wish I could." He has no idea how much. I wiggle my fingers. "Keys."

He's getting angry again, which is good. It's easier for me to deal with an angry Garrett than a sweet one. He separates a silver key from his ring and hands it to me. A line from the movie *A League of Their Own* comes to mind. *There's no crying in baseball.* I know Garrett would know the line, too, and the movie and the year it came out. He probably has it rated somewhere on his top one hundred list.

"One of the things I love about baseball," I say, "is that there's a ridiculous level of analysis on every aspect of the game. Including how the ball spins off the hand of a pitcher and how the eye sees that spin." I take the key and head toward the equipment shed. Over my shoulder I call, "Get your baseball bag."

"Josie—"

"Do it, Garrett."

He's back with his bag by the time I wrestle open the padlock and lug a bucket of balls to the mound. His equipment bag must have been in the trunk of his car. He hasn't changed clothes or shoes, but it doesn't matter.

I unzip my workout bag and pull out my baseball glove. The dry leather complains when I push my fingers in. For a second, it fights me like some alien thing that doesn't belong on my hand. But then the leather loosens up and muscle memory kicks in, my fingers working deeper into the rough inner material while my other hand punches lovingly into the palm of it the way I did a million times before.

"Another great thing about baseball," I say, my throat thick. "The feel of a broken-in glove."

His expression is unreadable. "Number two on my list. I think you're up to about twenty things by now, Walters. You better watch it or you're going to have to admit you love the game after all."

"I can't love a sport that steals everything I want."

He steps toward me. "Josie. It never could. It never will."

"Don't," I say, before he can reach out to me. "I can barely do this as it is."

"Then don't. I'm not even sure what you're trying to prove."

"That you can hit, Garrett. That's what I'm trying to prove."

"Then this is stupid. I've been working with Masters. I've had lessons with two other hitting coaches. I can't hit the curve."

"You don't have to."

"What are you talking about?" But he's listening now, his fingers restlessly working in and out of a fist.

"I'll tell you while we warm up my arm."

A faint smile crosses his face. "You're going to pitch?"

"I still remember how to bean a player, so be careful what you say."

His smile widens but he says nothing, just unzips his baseball bag and reaches in for his glove.

We start by playing catch. My shoulder is stiff, but it only takes a few minutes to start feeling the movement again.

The pace increases. The heat of the throws.

"Not bad," he says.

"Good enough."

We throw back and forth, and I slowly increase the space between us, each step back feeling like its own form of goodbye.

"So what did you mean?" he asks. "About not having to

hit the curveball?"

His throw hits my glove with a satisfying sting. "The thing is, almost no one can hit a good curveball. But most pitchers can't throw a good curveball either. At least, not consistently. The problem is guys like Evan Harris chase the outside balls and strike out. If you lay off the curveball, let it go, eventually you'll get a fastball. And that's the ball you hit."

He shakes his head. "If it was that easy—"

I throw the ball back to him. "It's not easy. Because you still have to see the curveball. You have to recognize it in order to lay off."

"That's the problem. I don't see it."

"I have a theory about that, too."

"Yeah?" The word is skeptical, but he returns the ball, and I can tell he's waiting for more.

"You've been practicing with a pitching machine, right?"

"So?"

"So that's the way it's usually done because it's hard to find a pitcher who can throw enough good curveballs to make it productive. Most hitters use a pitching machine. But here's the thing, Garrett. There are some guys who can't read spin off a pitching machine." I whip the ball to his glove. "My dad was one of those guys."

He pauses, his arm in mid-motion. Slowly, he drops his hand, holding the ball in his glove. Even from a distance, I can see a flare of hope in the way his mouth hangs open for a breathless second.

That's what I'll remember, I tell myself. When I'm missing him so much that it's hard to breathe, I'll remember this expression of hope, and that I gave that to him. The thought sends strength to my shaky arm. "You don't have to read spin off a machine," I add. "You're never going to face a machine in a game. What you need to learn—what you need to practice—is reading a ball the way it comes out of the hand." I hold up my glove, gesturing for him to throw me the ball. "Stand at the plate, as if you're going to hit."

He pulls his bat from his bag.

"You're not going to swing," I say. "I want you to watch my hand. You're studying hand movement. A curveball comes out with a hitch. Some people call it a hump."

I drag the bucket of balls to the mound. I can remember, so clearly, my dad running this drill with other players. Remember, so clearly, him telling them how he had the same problem. "These first ten balls are going to be fastballs. Ready?"

I'm out of practice and my arm is out of shape. A few bounce well in front of the plate and a few sail high. One nearly hits Garrett before he jumps out of the way. It doesn't matter. He's just watching my hand.

"All right," I say. "Here come ten curves."

He watches my hand as I release each ball, the thud of the balls hitting the back fence the only sound other than the occasional car driving by the school.

"You see it?" I ask.

He taps his bat on home plate. "I'm not sure I see spin. But I see speed."

"That's okay, too. My dad was like that. He swore he saw heat off the ball. Everyone's brain works differently. You need to watch live pitching. Start to recognize what's coming: a fastball or a breaking ball. I've got a list of drills that will help."

He drops his bat and jogs to me, a smile on his face that breaks my heart in half. "A list of drills? I can't believe you remembered so much."

"I didn't." I reach behind me to pick up a few loose balls, dropping them back in the bucket. Sadness wells behind my eyes; heat gathers in my throat. "I went online and found my dad's training logs. Password was still 'home run.'"

He stops me with a hand on my arm, slowly pulling me to face him. "Josie."

I raise my arms between us before he can pull me any closer. I'm still staring at the second button of his shirt. I can barely keep myself together. If he holds me, I'll crumble. "We're breaking up, Garrett. This is it."

"What? We are not."

I wipe at my cheeks, because damn it all to hell, I'm crying again. "I told you. I can't follow where you're going."

"We don't know that I'm going anywhere."

"You will be."

"That doesn't change us."

"Garrett." My voice breaks in spite of myself, but I finally look in his eyes. "It changes everything." I shove my glove back in my pack and toss the key at him.

Reflexively, his hand flies up and he catches it.

"We're not breaking up," he says, all steely-eyed and certain.

And wrong.

"You have work to do. You've got to find someone who can throw a good curveball. You said that Florida coach will be in town next week. That's not a lot of time."

A slight frown forms, and I know he's thinking it all through. Wondering if he can be ready. Wondering if it's really possible.

Hello, dream. Goodbye, Josie.

He's standing, frozen, balls spread across the dirt around him. He's torn. Fighting with himself over whether to leave it all or not. Whether to go after baseball or me.

His hesitation is proof that I'm right. I don't want a guy who has to think about it. I want a guy who wants me. More than anything.

I stride to the truck, focusing on each step, on holding back the tears.

I still have my pride. Right now, it feels like that's all I've got.

Chapter Forty-Three

When Mom comes home, we're on the third episode of *Pride and Prejudice*, and Mai has been asleep for half an hour.

"Hi." Mom sets a bag of groceries on the counter. She pauses as she takes in the scene. Mai and me. Mr. Darcy on the TV and an empty half-gallon carton of ice cream on the coffee table. Her smile fades. "What happened?"

"I broke up with Garrett."

I'm expecting relief or even happiness, but instead her face pales as if it's her heart that's broken. "Josie, honey. Are you okay?"

There's too big of a lump in my throat to do more than nod. After everything I've put her through...the things I've said.

Mai stirs with a tiny snort and then comes awake. She sits up, a little disoriented, then looks at the TV. "Is it over yet?"

I shake my head, stopping the show. "My mom's home."

Mai turns. "Oh. Hi, Ms. Walters."

Mom looks from Mai back to me, and I'm sure she's wishing there was an essential oil for this. "What can I do?

More ice cream?"

"No, it's fine. I'm fine."

"I bought stuff to make cupcakes. For your birthday. And lasagna."

"Homemade biscuits?" Mai asks hopefully.

Mom smiles. "Of course. Join us?"

"You don't happen to have Cheetos in that bag, do you?" When my mom tilts her head, confused, Mai says, "Never mind. I'm in."

"How come you bought all this stuff?" I ask. I'd told her Garrett was taking me out for dinner.

She pulls a box of noodles from the bag, but I don't miss the blush on her cheeks. "I knew you were going out, but I always cook for your birthday. I thought I'd at least make cupcakes. The lasagna could be for tomorrow." She pulls a small pack from the bag. "I even got candles that don't blow out."

"You're not supposed to tell people that in advance."

"I'm terrible at surprises."

I think about my birthday surprise—the trip I told her I wouldn't be taking because I'd be studying broadcasting. With Garrett.

As if she's thinking the same thing, Mom's eyes meet mine. "It'll be okay. Even though I know it doesn't feel like that now."

Mai, who hates mushy stuff, quickly stands. "Can we help, Ms. Walters?"

"I've got it. You girls go back to the show."

Mai groans so loudly that we all laugh.

We end up making my birthday dinner together. Mom does the lasagna and Mai and I make the cupcakes. We frost them, piling on every container of sprinkles and candies we find in the pantry.

For small moments in time, I even forget that it's the

worst night of my life.

It's nine when Mai hugs me at the front door. "Come spend the night tonight if you want," she whispers. "Text whenever. I'll keep my phone on in case."

Just like that, I want to cry again. What am I going to do when Mai leaves me, too?

Mom is sitting on the couch, hovering almost, and I know she's waiting to see what I need. It hits me that something else has changed. Is changing. Maybe it's because of the fight or maybe it's the way it happens. I've always been her daughter, but now I'm also my own person. She's giving me space. I wish I knew how to tell her I understand, and it means a lot to me. But right now, I just want to crawl in her lap.

Then I start crying, and it turns out she still knows exactly what I want. She's up in the next breath, her arms around me, gently leading me back to the couch. I'm eighteen and I want to be a kid again. I want the kind of problems that my mom can fix.

She lets me cry until I've finally gotten it all out. Once and for all, I hope.

"Tell me what happened?"

"He wants the game more than he wants me."

"Then he doesn't deserve you."

"I know. But I still love him."

"I'm so sorry, honey."

"You never liked him," I mumble.

"I never met him," she corrects. She runs a hand through my hair. "Why didn't you ever bring him home?"

I curl my feet under and lean my shoulder against the back cushion. "I was afraid you'd look at him and see Dad. And then I would, too. But he isn't, Mom. He's not the same." I'm not sure why it seems so important for her to know. "He never lied to me. It wasn't like that."

"Then why did you break up with him?"

"He was trying to come back as a hitter, not a pitcher. I saw him today. Taking BP off a pitching machine. He couldn't see the curve."

Our gazes meet, and in my eyes she sees the answer to her question. "Like your dad."

I nod. "So I showed him. Got my glove out from under your bed and went through the sequence the way Dad would have done it. I went online and looked through his training logs. Found a list of all the drills he did."

Her eyebrows shoot up. "That must have brought a lot back."

"I thought it would be worse than it was."

"That's one good thing, then." Her smile says she knows it isn't much. "So you think Garrett has a chance and that's why you broke up with him?"

"Pretty much. Baseball is his dream. How do you compete with a dream?"

She nods. She knows better than anyone. "You're hurting right now, Josie, and I know you have a lot of feelings to work through. But I also want you to know that our partnership is still there if you want it."

I let my head sink against the couch cushion. I've never been so tired. I just want to stop feeling like this. Things can go back to being what they were. What I planned. What I wanted before I knew I wanted Garrett. My mom. The business. Or if I want to pursue broadcasting, I can still do that. Without him. A few months ago, there was no Garrett and I was okay.

I can be okay again.

Chapter Forty-Four

On Monday morning, I dig out a plain tee—every quote shirt I own will make me think of Garrett. I've just brushed my hair when Mom appears in the door of the bathroom. "How about I do your makeup?"

"I wasn't going to bother."

"It might help you feel more together if you look the part."

So I follow her to her bathroom where she's got all the products. I sit on the counter and let her hide signs of my misery under moisturizer, anti-puffing eye gel, and skin-tightening serum.

"You'll get over him, honey. It just takes a little time."

"Are you over James?"

She pauses with the mascara wand in her hand. "Getting there. But it's like a bug bite compared to what I went through with your dad. What you would have gone through with Garrett if you'd let it go on longer." She applies the mascara and then seals the tube. "It's waterproof, by the way."

"I'm not going to cry at school. I'm done with that."

Then I find myself thinking about Garrett's text last

night. He let me know we'd made the finals. Top three. Then he'd added:

GARRETT: I love you.

I give Mom a watery smile. "Waterproof is good."

. . .

As the days pass, I'm proud of myself. I'm handling our breakup like a mature eighteen-year-old.

The baseball guys have been cool about it all, saying hello in the halls but not pressing me about what happened. The team is in the playoffs, and Garrett is running the broadcasts on his own, or so Cooper told me when they stopped by our lunch table yesterday. Mai has been crazy busy with AP exams, so I haven't seen a lot of her, but even that's for the best. She'll be gone for her summer program, and I'm going to have to get used to doing without her. She's finished the valedictorian speech but said I'll have to wait to hear it with everyone else.

My job at the bookstore is also coming to an end. Even though I'm sad, I know there's no one better for the job than Lianne. Saturday is my farewell party, and I'll be ready to go after that.

Everything, in fact, is going great.

Except for Garrett.

At first, when he started turning up everywhere at school, I thought I was imagining it. Seeing him because I was thinking of him. But then I realized that no, he was purposefully putting himself in my way. Around every corner was a glimpse of blond hair or the sound of his laugh. And when I walked by, he stopped to call out, "Hey, Walters."

Wednesday was the worst. He caught me on the way to English. He gave me one of his sexy half smiles combined with a little head tilt. The chemistry between us flared as hot as the bleachers in August.

"Don't," I said.

"Don't what?"

What could I say? *Stop looking so good? Stop making me want you?* "How's the hitting going?" I asked instead.

"You can't avoid me forever."

"Won't be hard once you're on that college team." I knew he was making progress. I had Mai ask Jason who asked Evan. They said he'd been working with the pitching machine every morning before school and hitting live after school. "When's the tryout? This Saturday?"

"Yep." He stepped in closer. "You were right. I'm starting to see the ball better. I'm also missing you like hell." His voice lowered. "I love you, Josie."

I met his gaze, held his eyes for a long second. "My dad said he loved me, too. But he loved baseball more."

"Nothing I say is going to change what you think, is it?"

"Nothing," I tell him. "Move on, Garrett. I have."

"Okay then. That's how it's going to be."

He walked off.

Okay?

I don't know how long I stood there until I remembered I was standing in the middle of the hall. I snapped my jaw shut.

Idiot. You got what you wanted. Be happy.

Chapter Forty-Five

Garrett has finally given up.

It's official.

I was pretty sure yesterday when I only saw him twice and he didn't try to talk to me either time. But this morning, there are no texts from Garrett. As Mai and I walk to school, there's no honk, no window rolled down, no dark-blond head leaning our way calling, "Need a ride, beautiful?" He's nowhere in the halls before first bell or between class. It's literally been seven days. Seven! And he's over it.

I check my phone for the hundredth time. Nothing.

"You're going to get an arm cramp lifting that thing over and over," Mai says.

"He finally got the message."

"You're supposed to sound happy about that."

It's lunch and we make our way to our usual table, brown bags in hand. Avi and Jasmine are already there.

"Did you guys pick up your caps and gowns?" Avi asks. "They're made of Saran Wrap."

Jasmine nods. "We're going to drown out the band

walking in them."

From gowns, the conversation moves to the caps. We're discussing possible slogans for the top when my neck prickles, telling me someone is standing behind me. I recognize Cooper's body spray a second before he sets a tray on the table between Mai and me. "Hey, guys."

Tucker and Anthony are suddenly at the other side of the table. I hear Mai's sharp intake of breath but then everyone is shuffling around. Avi and Jasmine are forced to slide over, though Jasmine looks happy when Tucker sits beside her.

I roll my eyes. "Do you not ask before shoving your way in?"

"Ask what?" Cooper wedges himself in. His tray is loaded with pepperoni pizza and an energy drink. "Isn't this cozy?"

"Did you guys catch our first playoff game?" Tucker asks.

I shake my head. "Congrats on the win."

"Adams hit a two-run bomb," Cooper announces, eyes shifting to Mai.

"Not surprised," she says. "He's got good hands."

There's a flare of something in Anthony's eyes—but it's gone so fast, I can't read it. I'm not even sure if I saw it. His smile is friendly, relaxed. "Way to use a baseball term correctly."

"Thank you."

But her smile is still sad, and I feel shitty for giving Mai such a hard time about him. I was worried that she'd get in over her head, but I should have known she wouldn't do anything reckless.

"It was a comeback win," Cooper says. "Those are the best." He wipes his fingers on a napkin, leaving orange streaks of pizza grease. "It was like the New England Patriots. Super Bowl 2017. You all remember."

We give him blank stares.

"The Patriots were down twenty-five points to the

Falcons. Twenty-five!"

Warning bells begin ringing in my head.

"Not even Tom Brady could come back from that. Stick a fork in them, everyone said. Until Tom Brady brought them back and they went on to win. Surprise." Cooper grins and gives me a meaningful wink. "Everyone was so sure they knew how it would play out."

"Garrett sent you." I smack his arm.

"Hey, don't hurt the messenger."

"Then the messenger better be able to run fast."

He laughs and picks up a slice of pizza. "Just saying, Josie. You never know. In sports. In life. That's why you gotta play it out."

Tucker points with a French fry. "You know, that reminds me of this other story. The US hockey team. The Olympics. 1980."

"Mai has her protractor," I snap. "A sharp one." My voice is stern but my heart is bouncing all over my chest.

"Just saying."

I glare at Anthony, because I can't take any more or I might do something stupid like burst into tears. "Don't you say a word."

He gives a crooked grin, and in unison the three of them get up, taking their half-eaten lunches with them.

Jasmine watches them go. "What was that about?"

Mai crunches on a veggie stick. "I'd say someone hasn't given up at all."

"Then he's wasting his time." But my heart has stopped turning somersaults, and now it's doing a happy dance across my ribs.

"Garrett should know better," Mai says. "As if a sports story is going to convince you of anything. Who cares about a stupid game?" She takes a pretzel from my baggie. "It's not like Marie Curie. I mean, when you consider the discrimination she faced when her husband died and she took over his research in radioactivity? No one would have thought a woman could succeed in that field, but she shocked them all when she got a Nobel Prize in 1911."

I gasp. "You too?"

She helps herself to another pretzel. "He stalked me for two days." She smiles, but there's no apology in it. "He happens to be right. You can't predict outcomes. You gotta play it out."

"He gave you a script?" I shift on the seat so I can glare at her directly. "Did he give you the line about Anthony having good hands, too?"

"No!" She scoffs. "I came up with that on my own, thank you very much."

"Well, it doesn't matter. There are a lot of stories with happy endings. But many more without." I loudly wad up the rest of my lunch.

But deep down, a small flame warms me through and through.

Chapter Forty-Six

There's a record turnout at the bookstore on Saturday. Every familiar face adds to the lump in the back of my throat. Lianne has outdone herself in the cake department. There are two—one chocolate and one vanilla. I told her it was too much, but then more kids kept arriving, and now I'm glad.

Brandi brought me a gold crown and paper hats for the kids. Javier is worried that the rubber bands on the hats will be a choking hazard, but I put him in charge of keeping an eye on everyone's safety, and he's good with that.

I read the final story—a funny book about a dinosaur cookie. It keeps everyone laughing—and keeps me from crying.

What is it with me and tears these days?

After story time, we parade through the bookstore with me leading the way. When we get to the activity room, the cakes are sliced and ready to go. The hour flies by so fast that when I see the parents returning, I want to tell them to go away and come back later. Like in ten years.

Tears are pressing behind my eyes when the regulars

approach. I say goodbye to Kate and Fiona, Julia, Javier, and Bryson. Finally, it's Ciera's turn, and she attaches herself to my neck and hangs there like a monkey.

"Ciera," her mom chides.

But I use it as my chance to give her a huge hug. "It's all right. I love monkeys."

"I love you," Ciera says. "I'll always think about you when I read a story."

"And there's one special story, isn't there, Ciera?" her mom asks.

"I almost forgot!" Ciera nods and claps her hands with excitement. "It's a good story, Josie. It's about a rabbit only he's a really big rabbit so he's called a hare. And there's a turtle only he's really big so he's called a tortoise. And the hare is fast and the tortoise is slow. And they have a race."

I crouch in front of her so she knows I'm listening, but I also shoot her mom a puzzled look. *Why is Ciera telling me the story of the Tortoise and the Hare?*

"Anyway," Ciera says, "everyone knows the hare is going to win and the whole time it looks like he will. But he wants to goat with everyone there, so he sits down to wait."

My knees wobble as I suddenly understand. "You mean gloat."

"Right," she says. "But the hare falls asleep and the tortoise wins. And that's why you've got to play it out."

I look up at Ciera's mom. Her smile says it all.

"He got to you. How did he get to you? When?"

"This morning."

My knees give out, and I hit the carpet. Today is his tryout. What's he doing coming to the bookstore? I look at Ciera, my heart roaring in my ears. "Is he...here?"

"No." She pouts. "The cookie man is gone. Everyone is leaving."

"I'm going to miss you, Ciera. More than you know. But

I promise I'll be back to visit."

After they leave, it's time to say goodbye to the staff. I make it quick, which means I pretend to go to the bathroom and instead grab my stuff and head out the back door. I'll email Brandi later. I can't handle another goodbye.

In my truck with the door closed, I pause and rest my head against the steering wheel. I'm weakening. I can feel my determination hanging on by one tiny, ragged thread. I need someone to talk some sense into me. Now. Before I do something stupid.

Chapter Forty-Seven

The AromaTher booth is next to Fresh Bounty, a husband and wife team who sell bread. My mouth is watering by the time I get to our table, draped with gold cloth and a sign that reads THE BEAUTY OF ESSENTIAL OILS.

The farmers market is winding down, and there are only a few people wandering the stalls. Mom is working a crossword puzzle when she sees me. "Josie! You're early." I don't usually pick her up for another half hour.

"Is that our garlic or his?" I point to the bread stand.

"His garlic and his rosemary. I couldn't compete." She smiles so I know she's done okay sales-wise.

"Maybe we should join forces. Aromatherapy bread."

"Not a bad idea." There isn't an extra chair, but she turns over a plastic crate she uses to carry things and pads it with her cushioned laptop cover. "Five more minutes and I'll start packing up."

"I can help. If we're going to be partners, I need to do more of these."

She closes her book of crosswords and sets it on the table.

"And are we?"

More freaking tears fill my eyes, and I'm mad at myself. Mad at *him*.

"Did something happen?" she asks.

"He's been getting people to tell me stories about comebacks or people doing impossible things. Why is he doing this?"

Mom smiles in that knowing way of hers. "You know what he's doing. He's fighting for you."

"He's also trying out for a coach today. He's going to end up playing in Florida, and I'll be the pathetic girl waiting with her suitcase."

"Josie, there are a lot of stories that start the same way. That doesn't mean they end the same."

"But when do you find that out? Five years down the road? Ten? Fifteen?"

"You don't find it out," she says. "You're not waiting to see what happens in your life. You're living it. You're making choices."

"But…" I'm struggling to make sense of her words. This isn't what I was expecting her to say. "What about Dad?"

She grabs my hands and squeezes. "The first man you loved abandoned you. I know it changed you, because it changed me, too. You were right, Josie. I broke up with James rather than risk my heart. And though I want to protect your heart as if it's my own, safety comes with risks, too. Risk of regret. Of opportunities missed. Of love lost." Her thumbs smooth over the back of my hands, warm and comforting. "And I haven't been fair to Garrett. He deserves the chance to be judged for himself. I was wrong to paint him with the same brush as your father."

I blink back tears. "You think I should give him a chance?"

"I don't know." She releases a long sigh. "But it does make

me think about Elizabeth Arden. How she wanted to start a makeup company at a time when makeup was associated with prostitutes. It was impossible to think that she could succeed in changing so many minds."

I cover my mouth with a hand, but it doesn't stop a loud gasp. "You too?"

There's a hint of embarrassment in her shrug. "Me too."

"You...you met him?"

"This morning. He was here as I was setting up. I knew it had to be him even before he introduced himself. All that nice hair and boyish charm. He has a finger gun. Did you know that?"

I laugh in spite of myself. "It's awful."

"Truly." Her expression softens. "He came to tell me that he deserves a chance like Elizabeth Arden. That people can change your mind if you keep it a tiny bit open. He proceeded to tell me stories about Estee Lauder, Coco Chanel, and a chemist named Balanda Atis who started up the Women of Color Lab. He ended the whole thing with—" She pauses, and I make the air quotes with her because I know what's coming next.

"You gotta play it out."

My breath is coming so fast, I'm a little dizzy. It's so much to absorb. Mom's *smile* is almost more than I can handle. "So did you... I mean, do you... Could you like him?"

"He's very charming. I told him so, in fact, and he said he has a way with mothers. That's when he pulled the finger gun." She laughs, and the sound is better than a gallon of pralines and cream. "He was actually very sweet. And yes, Josie, I think I could like him very much. The real question is, how do you feel?"

Chapter Forty-Eight

Mai texts Jason who texts Cooper who texts the location of Garrett's tryout.

It's a high school about ten miles west. My heart is sprinting while I sit in the parking lot wondering what I'm going to do.

I'm not positive, but I think that maybe I'm playing it out.

Gathering my courage, I head for the baseball field, a diamond of grass beyond the school. With each step, the blurry figures come into focus, the colors sharpening, the smells of dirt and damp grass growing stronger. There are guys in various uniforms in the dugout. A couple of players warming up on the field and four men standing behind the fence. Two are wearing jerseys from the college in Florida, and I'm guessing the one with gray hair is the head coach.

A man with a clipboard says something, his voice carrying my way but not clearly enough for me to hear what he says. The guys in the bullpen react, and one carries his bat to the plate. Not Garrett. But he's there, standing in the dugout, and though I can't see his expression, I can imagine it. Determined. Focused.

He's going to get his chance.

A lump forms at the base of my throat. He's fighting for what he wants. A life in baseball.

But he's also been fighting for me.

I've reached a berm, too far from the field for Garrett to see me but close enough that I can watch. I sink down on the crabgrass, crossing my feet in front of me and feeling cold even with the sun beating on my shoulders and the back of my neck.

What am I fighting for?

As the first player takes his cuts, my mind travels back. After Dad left, I'd had enough of dreams. I became a planner. A practical thinker. College. A good job. A guy down the road who wanted a house with a wall where we measured our kids' height. I didn't think about whether that sounded fun or exciting or challenging.

A new hitter is up; the first one wasn't bad but wasn't great, either. This one seems to be more of the same. I listen to the soft slaps of balls being fouled off or hit weakly to the infield. My thoughts drift again.

Plans not passion. It's always my line, but is it also an excuse? Is it really easier to put cream on people's necks than it is to figure out what I like? What I might love?

Am I willing to love anything?

I see now how careful I was to protect my heart. AromaTher wasn't a passion and I liked that. Even when I shifted to broadcasting, was it something I loved? Or did I love that Garrett was my partner? Would I love it if it were only me?

Another batter comes to the plate, and I hold my breath, but it's not Garrett. There's a sharp crack of the bat and I watch a ball fly deep. This guy has some power. My gaze follows the next few crisp, well-struck balls and try to remember what it felt like to play myself. To stand behind the fence and watch my dad play. My gaze shifts to the man holding the clipboard. To coach the kids' teams.

I'm waiting for my heart to answer, but it's my stomach that pipes up with an unpleasant rumble. I realize I've been feeling sick ever since I left the bookstore this morning. The only two jobs I've ever loved were coaching Little League and running story time.

Why did I quit that job?

Before the question can circle my head a second time, I answer myself: because it wasn't a real job.

But could it be?

My breath stills as I watch Garrett climb out of the dugout. Something flashes in his hand—something metallic—and I bite my lip when I realize what it is. The key chain. The M.

The reminder to keep fighting.

I'm up on my feet as he rubs his back foot over the chalk line in the batter's box and then settles in his stance. God, he looks good. Shielding my eyes from the sun, I watch as he hits three balls deep, working the ball to right and left field—not something every hitter can do. He takes the same dozen swings as the others, and I see the coach gesture to the pitcher. *He wants to see more.* My heart surges in my chest, pride for Garrett, for how much he's improved. *Sometimes, the universe gets it right*, I think. *Persistence pays off.* Garrett has worked for this. He's fought for it.

Maybe it's time I started fighting, too.

Each crack of his bat is one more swing at the obstacles standing in front of him. I'm not sure where his path will take him, but he's brave enough to go after what he wants.

Even if that includes a girl too afraid to listen to her own heart.

It's time I focused on where I'm going. I can't stay stuck in place for fear of getting lost. I have to find my own way.

And I have to stop planning for the worst and open my heart to risk.

Even if that includes a stubborn baseball player.

I square my shoulders, commentary running through my head as if I'm in the broadcast booth. *Walters, you're up to bat. What are you going to do with your chance at the plate?*

Chapter Forty-Nine

Garrett told me that Coach Richards starts every week going over the baseball accounts, so I know where to find him on Monday morning. He's in an office in the basement of the gym that's a lot of gray cement and cheap metal furniture.

The door is open, but I knock anyway. He looks up from his computer screen, and for a second I'm not sure if he remembers who I am. Then he smiles. "Josie Walters. We missed you last week at our first playoff game."

A blush prickles up my neck. "Sorry about that. Nice win, though."

"It was." He rocks back in his chair. He looks older without the baseball cap on, the gray more obvious in his hair. "So what brings you to the dungeon?"

It is a little dungeon-esque, right down to the colder temperature. Unless that's my nerves. "Garrett told me some things about you. Including that you run summer baseball programs."

His smile grows warmer. "Garrett told me some things about you, too. Why don't you have a seat and tell me what's on your mind."

And so I do.

. . .

Cholla's second playoff game is scheduled to start right after school. It's a home game, the last one of the season, because if the team wins, they move on to the quarterfinals and neutral territory. I skipped the first playoff game, but I'm not going to miss this one.

I use the excuse of "girl issues," which is embarrassing because it lacks originality, but I don't have time to be clever. Mr. Evans actually rolls his eyes, but he releases me fifteen minutes early. I've never missed a minute of class, so I don't feel too bad about it. Besides, I'm a girl and I have an issue, so it's not even a lie. I've got to run to my locker, grab what I need, and reach the broadcast booth before Garrett does.

When I get to the field, the visiting team is loosening up in the outfield while pitchers are warming up in the bullpens. There are the usual noises from the dugout below—players organizing their equipment and Coach Richards barking advice. I give Scottie a quick wave; he's raking the dirt infield like an artist—creating swirls in the freshly watered earth. Someone mowed earlier, working the angle of the blade so the grass looks like it's striped in deepening shades of green. The sun is a bright golden ball streaming over the top of the bleachers like a spotlight from the heavens. It seems like a holy place. For Garrett, I know it is.

Today, it is for me, too.

The booth is cooler, protected from the direct sun, but with the front completely open to the field, the slight breeze has kept the air fresh. I move quickly to get everything set up. I've only barely finished when the door flies open.

Garrett pulls up short when he sees his stool. I've moved

it to the center of the floor so it's hard to miss. He sets the equipment on the counter, and then his gaze finds me where I'm standing against the wall.

He cut his hair and his tan looks deeper and his eyes seem bluer and I'm so happy to see him, it hurts. My heart is going crazy and I want to launch myself at him. I want to grab him by the ears and kiss his face off. A sense of relief sinks all the way to my bones. This is who I want to be with, no matter what.

Does he still want to be with me?

My nerves choose that moment to make an appearance. I watch as he walks to the stool and picks up a rose. The petals have begun to open, the color as vibrant as the scent is sweet.

He raises his eyebrows. "Yellow?"

"Apology."

He picks up a second rose. "White?"

"Forgiveness."

He adds the third rose to his small bouquet, his teeth working a dent in his bottom lip. "Red?"

"It's actually orange. Just looks red in this light. It means enthusiasm."

"Liar." He steps closer. The hope in his eyes makes my knees wobble. "Does this mean you finally came to your senses?"

"I saw your tryout on Saturday."

"You did?" He breathes in the roses. "Then you saw it went okay."

"Better than okay."

"You're a good coach."

"You're a fast learner." I glance out the window. Our team has taken over the field now. Not much time before warm-ups will be over. "You're going to Florida?"

He nods. "If I want to."

"And you do?"

He leans back against the counter and crosses his legs at the ankle. "I do. I just have to figure out how to convince this stubborn girl not to break up with me."

"Stubborn, huh?"

"And not very bright, honestly, because if she had a bit of sense, she'd see that she's got me so messed up that even baseball doesn't feel right without her."

"Not very bright?"

"Did you hear any of the rest of that?"

I step closer. "Maybe you should say it again."

"I'll say whatever you need to hear."

"Five minutes!" The voice booms loud enough to drown out the growing noise of the crowd. It's getting close to game time, but I don't move and neither does Garrett. "The day when I threw you those pitches...when I left...you didn't come after me. You stayed. To practice."

He nods. He knows what I'm talking about. "A lot had just happened. You know? And part of me was trying to make sense of it and part of me was mad."

"Why mad?"

"Because you gave me back my dream. You don't do that for someone unless you love them. And then you walked away." Hurt flares in his eyes. "You don't want to follow me, but I'm supposed to chase you."

The words strike deep, the way hard truths usually do. "That's what the white rose is for."

He looks at the bud and then glances out the window. The umpires are meeting with the coaches in the center of the field. "I want to keep playing baseball," he says. "And I want to keep seeing you. Even if we have to see each other on a screen for a while." He worries at his bottom lip again. "I know I promised I wasn't going anywhere, and Florida is across the country. I haven't figured that out yet, but I'm going to work on it. In the meantime, I want to support you, too, Josie. I'll get the whole team using essential oils if you want. We'll be one big ocean breeze or whatever you want us to smell like."

I smile at the thought, at the sincerity in Garrett's voice. He would do it, too. "I'm not going to be selling AromaTher. At least, not full time."

"You're not?"

"I'm switching my major from business to education. I'm going to be a teacher."

His eyes brighten. "That feels right."

"And I spoke to Coach Richards. I'm going to help coach his summer leagues."

His cocky grin has never been so wide. "Told you I'd get you to love the game."

"Really?" I say drily. "Because someone recently told me that you can't predict outcomes. You have to play it out."

"I hope more than one person told you that, or I'm taking back the chocolate bribes I passed out."

I laugh. "I can't believe you got to my mom, too."

"It wasn't how I wanted to meet her, but I'm glad I finally did." His smile fades. "You know I've got a top one hundred list, and that's always been number one. Other sports, there's a clock. You can hold on to the ball and wait. You can stop trying, give up or hold out. In baseball, there's no clock. You have to play the game to the very last out. It's the only way to know."

I join him at the counter, seeing what he sees. Seeing a future I would never have imagined a few months ago. A future so bright, I'm filled with its light. "My number one favorite thing about baseball is you."

"Well, that goes without saying." He throws an arm over my shoulder.

I tip my head into his neck. "I'm going to regret telling you that, aren't I?"

"Oh yeah." He pulls me closer until we're touching in too many places to count. His hands are warm around me, so solid. Like Garrett. "All the time my uncle Max was teaching me about the game, he was really teaching me about life. You never quit on the people who count on you, and you never quit on yourself. That was the lesson of baseball. If it matters, if it's important, then it's worth everything you've got. You, Josie Walters, matter. You're more important than I can say."

My eyes feel full. My throat is so thick with emotion that I have to swallow twice before I whisper, "I kind of love you, Blondie."

He pulls back until our eyes meet, and everything I'm feeling is reflected in the shiny blue of his gaze. "Yeah?" His smile breaks my heart.

"Way too much."

He brushes his lips over mine.

I brush my lips over his.

Soft, patient kisses. The kind you give when you know there are going to be more. A lot more.

"Garrett!" There's a pounding on the door. "You're putting on a nice show, but people are here to watch baseball. You ready with the national anthem?"

He curses under his breath as I flush and pull back. "One second."

Cheers come from the crowd as he takes out the soundboard and I turn on his laptop. It only takes a minute for him to cue up the recording. As it begins, we stand side by side, hands over our hearts.

Mine finally has everything it wants.

Chapter Fifty

It's dark—after midnight—and there's no one here but the stars and us.

"I can't believe it," I whisper. "I'm starting my life as a high school graduate by breaking the law."

"It's only a crime if you get caught." Garrett says this as he's perched on the outside of the broadcast booth, his feet balanced on the metal rungs of the bleacher support, one hand gripping the side of the wall and the other trying to shove in the Plexiglas covering the window. Turns out that's how they protect the booth during the five days it rains in Phoenix. With a sheet of Plexiglas that must be screwed in from the inside.

"Enough, Blondie," I say. "You're going to break your other arm, and then how are you going to play?"

Just then, the Plexiglas caves, clattering as loudly as a bag of metal bats. I wince and search the baseball field expecting to find a security guard. But all I see in the weak moonlight are discarded maroon caps, strips of gold confetti, and empty beer bottles. It's hard to believe that a few hours ago, we were marching across the football field accepting our diplomas.

The door of the booth opens, and Garrett grins, a streak of dirt across his chin. "No problem for a finely toned athlete like me."

"I think the actual phrase is finely honed."

"That too." He gestures to the counter and I follow his lead, sitting on the linoleum and then swinging my legs so they dangle out the window.

"What a night, huh?" Garrett says.

"It was pretty perfect."

The strains of "Pomp and Circumstance" are still floating through my head. The feel of the plasticky gown and the indent that might still be on my forehead from the elastic around the cap. Walters is a terrible last name for a processional, and all I could see were the backs of everyone's head. Once I got to my seat, I first searched the stands to find Mom. James was sitting beside her, trying to capture it all on his video camera. Mom has been so happy since they got back together. She's even concocted a new fragrance for him that includes clary sage—an essential oil for optimism.

From there, I searched the rows for all my friends. I was like Javier at the bookstore—I wanted to be sure everyone was in their place. Cooper, Tucker, Anthony—proud members of Cholla's State Champion baseball team. Avi and Jasmine. And of course Garrett, who draws my attention no matter where he is.

I didn't have to search for Mai because she was up on the stage.

"You're not sorry to miss Lock In?" Garrett asks, bringing me back to the present.

Seniors had the option of spending the night at Alleys, an indoor theme park, where chaperones would monitor the grads and once the doors were closed no one would be allowed in or out. Mai and I had talked about going, but

Jason decided to have a party at his house. We'd all gone, including Jasmine and Avi, and when we got there it turned out to be an even bigger group than I expected. There were band kids and some of the football guys and Scottie was there along with a few friends of his I knew from math lab. I loved seeing the groups mix in a way they rarely had in the halls of Cholla. If this was how the real world worked, I was going to like it a lot more.

Just before midnight, Garrett had led me from the party and to his car. I wasn't surprised when we ended up here.

Where it all began.

"And to think it all happened because of a game of pool chicken."

Garrett smiles. He's heard the story of spring break and the pool where Anthony and Mai met.

"She gave a great speech," he says. "I knew she was smart. I didn't know she was so wise."

"Wise? She told everyone she didn't have the answers."

Garrett reaches for my hand. "I liked the Henry David Thoreau part. It was simple but genius."

I nod. Mai started with a quote most of us had heard: "Go confidently in the direction of your dreams." Then she called it bullcrap. She said few of us were confident, few of us had real direction, and not everyone had the luxury of following a dream. But she finished by saying that Thoreau got one word right: "Go." That's the trick. Forward movement. You can't take a next step until you take the first one.

"I'm going to miss her so much," I say.

A moment of quiet passes, and I know we're both thinking that Garrett is leaving, too. I squeeze his fingers. He couldn't quite honor his promise not to go anywhere, but he got pretty close. He arranged another tryout—this one in Tucson. The coach said yes, and he'll be leaving in August, but only going a hundred miles south.

We both tip our heads back, and for a second I see us from a distance, poised on the edge of this booth, a tiny moment of calm before we're pitched into a future we can't predict.

I know he's thinking the same thing when he says, "If you hadn't helped me, we'd be going to ASU together in the fall."

I shake my head because I'm done looking back. "We're still going to get our chance to be broadcasters."

His fingers tighten over mine, and he kisses the back of my hand.

The day they posted the contest winner, Garrett and I were at my house, playing our own game of chicken. The computer was on the counter and one click of the refresh button would show us the results.

"You do it," I said.

"No, you."

"You should. It was your idea."

"You made it happen."

"Oh for heaven's sake," Mom said, and she stabbed at the return button.

We were still laughing when the results flashed and there were our names. Garrett Reeves and Josie Walters.

We both froze, a little in shock.

"Congratulations!" Mom cheered and squeezed both of our shoulders and then headed back to the office to give us some privacy.

We both had to hit the refresh button two more times before it finally sank in.

"Are you disappointed?" he asked me then. "Not to be pursuing broadcasting?"

"Not really," I said, and I meant it. "I'm glad we did it, though. You took a place full of bad memories and turned it into something good."

"And I wanted to be close to the team, but I also wanted to matter. You gave that to me."

"We're incredible, aren't we?" I said.

We enjoyed annoying everyone with our victory for the next few days, and during the school's final assembly, we stood at the podium and accepted a check for five thousand dollars to the baseball program. My own check for one thousand dollars is still sitting on the kitchen counter. I'll be adding it to the car fund. I'm going to need my own transportation in order to be at all of Garrett's games. On June twenty-sixth, we'll be calling an inning of an Arizona Diamondbacks game. I got my revenge, and found that I don't really need it, or want it.

"You sure you're okay with me going?" Garrett asks me now. "I don't know how long I'll be in Tucson. Maybe one year, maybe two. Or maybe I'll wash out."

"Garrett."

"Maybe if I did, it would be the best thing."

"Why would you say that? You're hitting with power, you're locating the ball, you're making contact with nearly every pitch."

"Because if I do well, it's all the crap you didn't want. Moving around. Small towns and bus rides and never knowing."

"I know what it is, Garrett."

He doesn't say anything, but I can feel that he's holding words back.

"What?" I ask.

Softly, he says, "If I do well, I'm worried that you'll leave me."

His words break my heart, but they also heal it. I know how much he loves baseball, but I also know how much he loves me. He tells me so every day. But more than that, I feel loved. I don't have to be anyone but myself. Maybe that's why the idea of moving doesn't scare me anymore. Wherever we are, I'll be at home with Garrett.

"I love you, and I won't leave because the life is hard," I say. "It doesn't scare me like it used to. I think it's because I'm figuring out what I want for me, too. So I'll have my life the way you'll have yours. Wherever we end up, it won't be about you or about me. It'll be about us."

"I love how you say the word *us*."

I smile. "I thought you loved how I say the word *we*."

"I love everything about you, Josie Walters."

"Even my sandals?"

"Almost everything about you."

He pulls me close. The baseball field is spread out in front of us. It's always been part of my past and now it'll be part of my future. A game where a bunch of guys spend their lives trying to get home. I press closer to Garrett and smile. It makes sense now that I've found mine.

Acknowledgments

I had a lot of help writing Josie and Garrett's story.

A huge thanks to Chris Cron who has been a part of professional baseball for over 30 years and answered questions about all aspects of the game. I also had help from my favorite ballplayer in the world—my son, Kyle—who pitched through college and helped me get the lingo right. Love you, Kyle! Thanks to Darren Zaslau who told me everything I needed to know about sports broadcasting. And to my husband, Jake, a fan of all things baseball, who provided ideas and inspiration. I love you more than I can say.

Thanks to Caryn Wiseman, my agent, who seems to wear a million hats, helping me through every stage of the process. I also want to thank my critique partners and friends who always keep me sane. Terry Lynn Johnson, Christina Mandelski, Marty Murphy, Erin Jade Lange, Amy Nichols, Tom Leveen, Gae Polisner and Nate Evans. And to Rachel, who loves reading romance as much as I do. Thanks for helping me brainstorm ideas. I love you, Daughter.

A special thanks to my editor, Stacy Abrams. Ten years

ago, in 2009, my first novel was edited by Stacy. I am beyond lucky to work with you again, Stacy. Your editorial genius has only grown over the years. More thanks goes to Judi Lauren. Your insightful comments helped make this story so much better. To the whole team at Entangled Publishing—thank you for bringing this book to life.

Finally, a heart-felt thanks to my readers. Your blogs, reviews, notes and support are appreciated more than you know.

About the Author

Amy Fellner Dominy is the award-winning author of books for teens, tweens, and toddlers. She started writing and submitting stories when she was a teen herself. Other young adult titles include *A Matter of Heart*, *The Fall of Grace* and *Die for You*. Amy lives in Phoenix, Arizona with her husband and a puppy who is training them. Visit Amy online at www.amydominy.com or follow her on Instagram at @amydominy.

Discover more of Entangled Teen Crush's books...

THE CRUSH COLLISION
a *Southern Charmed* novel by Danielle Ellison

Haley's had a crush on her brother's best friend, Jake Lexington, for as long as she can remember. To bad to him, she'll forever be off-limits. But with senior year comes new confidence. Haley's read to get Jake to notice her—whatever it takes. Jake's looking for an escape; Haley's looking for a chance. Together, they'll find exactly what they need...if only they're willing to cross that line and risk it all.

THE BOYFRIEND BID
a *Girlfriend Request* novel by Jodie Andrefski

Sarah Campbell's never bid in her high school's charity auction, and she's certainly not going to start now––when she's still hurting over a bad breakup. But when Sarah's friends bid on Chance DuPont on her behalf, she ends up with not one but *six* dates with Mr. Ego himself. Now a local blog is covering the story by following them on all their dates, too? Seems like everyone loves a good love story––except the two living it.

OFFSETTING PENALTIES
a *Brinson Renegades* novel by Ally Matthews

Isabelle Oster is devastated when the only male dancer backs out of the fall production. Without a partner, she has no hope of earning a spot with a prestigious ballet company. All-state tight end Garret Mitchell will do anything to get a college football scholarship. Even taking ballet, because he gets to be up close and personal with the gorgeous Goth girl Izzy. But she needs him to perform with her, and he draws the line at getting on stage. *Especially* wearing tights.

ALL LACED UP
a novel by Erin Fletcher

When hockey star Piece Miller and figure skater Lia Bailey are forced to teach a skating class together, Lia's not sure she'll survive the pressure of Nationals *and* Pierce's ego. But it turns out Pierce isn't arrogant at all. And they have a *lot* in common. Too bad he's falling for an anonymous girl online who gives him hockey tips…and he has no idea Lia and the girl are one in the same.

Made in the USA
Las Vegas, NV
29 April 2021